RINK

RINK

Chris Matravers

Elsewhen Press

Contents

For Anna. Thank you.

Chapter 1

Shoulders hunched, beanie pulled low against the wind and drizzle, Paul trudged through the gathering gloom. Fists balled in his pockets, his furious scowl parted the stream of evening commuters. Livid bruises beneath his torn jeans stiffened muscles that ached from the beating. His shirt caught where it stuck to the drying blood that oozed from skin ruptured where their boots and fists had thudded: when they'd tossed him from the club in the early hours. After sleeping rough and then a day spent in hiding, he was cold, miserable and out of choices. He had to risk going back to the flat. Then his day got worse. He flinched in terror as he sensed the first tentacles of my presence.

'What the …! What is this? Get the …!' Paul's psyche writhed and thrashed; panicky and confused as my thoughts and memories invaded and fought to overwhelm his, jostling for room in his overtaxed mind. His confusion and fear sought to overwhelm us both as Paul tried to resist me and I reluctantly shifted from the before to the now. The gut-wrenching twist as I fought the shift – resisting it with all that I had – was all too sickeningly familiar. I knew from the start that it was hopeless. As my selves and Paul's collided, I tried to hang on to … Something … Another place… Other … But then, agonisingly, they were gone; like dreams lost and unreachable. And I was there, in the now.

Shaking, out of control, we stumbled into the path of a young woman. Grimacing in annoyance she sidestepped around us with an uncaring glance. For long moments I rode incapacitating waves of emotion, his and mine, until I began to find my focus. Gradually I began to take control, my head ringing with the voices of my selves reacting to the new and the strange and Paul's hopeless attempt to repel me. Paul, my new now-self.

'What's happening?' As Paul weakened, his terror turned to anguish, then pleading. The body reacted. I staggered, unable, yet, to control the fear inspired surge of adrenalin that his body released. Overwhelmed, I slumped against some railings, loose limbed, momentarily helpless. Bustling pedestrians scurried past, heads down against the swirling sleet: their faces muffled by scarves. Except for one.

'Are you alright?' Her hand was light on my arm, her spare hand brushed her hair behind her ear as she crouched to look. 'You're very pale, you're shaking.' The skin around her large, brown eyes crinkled with concern. As I struggled to respond, I guess my vacant gaze must have seemed cold and distant. It scared her.

'Oh!' Flustered she pulled away. I flapped my arm weakly as I regained some semblance of control.

'Wait… Please, wait.' I managed a croak. She hesitated, on the verge of flight, before compassion won. She knelt beside me, apparently oblivious to the cold, wet pavement.

'What's the matter? Are you ill?'

It was a fair guess – wrong, but understandable. I straightened and turned to look around. The railings bordered a small park squeezed between terraced houses, shops and offices. It was a miserable excuse for a park. Muddied paths bisected moss-filled lawns and scruffy unkempt flowerbeds. Pigeons strutted then scattered, splattering fresh droppings. Behind me the street was choked by vehicles. I stared at the surroundings searching for more clues, read the street and shop signs, saw a few recognisable landmarks amongst unfamiliar architectures. Paul spoke in English… Is this London then? The thought rose, unbidden. I fought to pull myself together, whatever I'd tried last it obviously hadn't worked. I wasn't ill, I was healthy and alive but I'd shifted again when I wanted to be dead. I needed to accept it, to move on.

Giving her what I hoped was a more re-assuring look I struggled to stand. 'Thanks, sorry. I'll be fine. I just need a moment.' The first few times – long, long ago – I'd greeted each new awareness with wonder. I'd been energised and enthralled by the newness of it all. Then had come the cycles when, post shift, I'd become all but catatonic; when I'd been incapacitated for days, lost in the depths of depression. Now, I'd already begun to numb the despair and frustration that fought to overwhelm me. It was easier now, but that didn't make it easy. Despair was a self-indulgence I'd succumbed to in the past – I was only human – but I'd come to know it for what it was, a valueless emotion. Frustration was more useful. As long as I felt frustrated, I knew I'd keep trying, but it had to be kept in check. From initial awareness to the beginning of acceptance had taken mere minutes this time, after lifetimes of learning how. She grasped my arm as she watched my shaky recovery.

'Maybe you need to sit down.'

'I'm … I'm fine.' I managed eventually. 'Thank you, a dizzy spell, that's all.' This time she smiled. I guess I was looking more normal. Despite the aches, this now-self felt otherwise energised. A stark contrast to the bone-aching weariness of my final moments in the last there and then. That much I could recall.

'Are you sure?' She tried not to recoil as I breathed a deep sigh. It was clear I could use a bath and change of clothes. I managed another weak nod but she wasn't convinced. 'Look, there's a café down the street, perhaps you should rest there 'til whatever it is passes.' I looked blankly in the direction she was pointing.

'Could you show me?' I was still dazed but more than that I wanted, needed, company. Needed human contact to help ground me in this world I'd reluctantly rejoined.

'Just there.' She pointed to a green and white sign along the street. 'Starbucks.'

I pretended to look, to hide my confusion. It meant nothing to me, yet. She seemed to think it should. I tried again.

'Could I buy you a coffee, then, to say thank you?' I looked into her eyes, willing her to say yes. The hesitation was still there but eventually she nodded. 'Hmm, OK, c'mon then.' She held my arm as we walked the few yards. I smiled to myself, relieved. I was far from being in control but already I was able to exert some influence.

Chapter 2

Starbucks turned out to be the name of a café: one of a chain, I realised, as I began to access my now-knowledge. Sensing my hesitation, she took control.

'Look, you're still a bit wobbly, go and grab a table and I'll bring the coffees. What will you have?' I was about to argue but then thought better of it. My selves were still busy assimilating the now-knowledge and as yet I had few resources to spare to boost my physical capabilities.

'Um… Right, OK… I'll have a tall Americano please.' I wasn't sure what I'd ordered but the words seemed to make sense to her.

It was busy but there were plenty of spaces at the tables to the rear. I tossed my sodden hat onto a table against the wall, sank thankfully into a chair and sat facing into the coffee shop, watching the baristas – another word that came unbidden to my mind – serve the queue. I caught a glimpse of my reflection in a mirror on the opposite wall. A young man with piercing blue eyes and dirty, blond hair stared back at me, curiously comparing this image with the countless others I'd known. It looked a promising now-self, physically. Almost what I'd have picked had I had a choice, which I never did. I glanced around at my fellow customers: saw that apart from being dishevelled I was similarly dressed, not out of place. No-one took any notice of me. Most were staring at small devices they held in one hand, few talked to each other. This was new. I felt in my pockets, found a wallet and that I too had such a device. Hmm… Later. She was smiling as she came to the table.

'Here you are then.' She placed a cup in front of me. 'I brought you a pastry too.' She took off her coat and sat opposite me. She'd ordered a single espresso for herself – so that she could finish and then leave quickly if necessary? 'So, what do I call you?'

'Uh, Paul,' I said. 'Paul Mason'. But I'd hesitated, almost offering her my truename, Jay.

'OK, *uh Paul.*' She watched curiously as I sipped my coffee and took a bite of the pastry. 'Are you feeling a bit better now?'

'Yes, it's passing. You've been very kind, thank you. I skipped breakfast and lunch, I guess it caught up with me.' She seemed to accept it, made no comment about my appearance.

'So, where are you heading now?' She sipped her espresso, her lips pursed, her brown eyes watching me over the rim of the cup. I liked looking at her. Her concern for a stranger touched me, but it wasn't just that. I'd known many women but few had had her instant appeal.

'I'm just on my way home, like you I guess, I was heading for the tube.' The words flowed more freely as I accessed my now-self's knowledge and memories. I sipped my coffee and suppressed a grimace, hoping to God that I'd find better somewhere in this cycle.

'What do you do?' She asked with a small frown. She'd noticed how I favoured my aches and bruises. I smiled, helping her to ignore my torn, soiled clothes, my obvious lies. I was momentarily uncertain, then the thought came.

'I... I work with computers... I'm a network specialist...' As I spoke the words, the understanding became clear – hmm... Wow! Reluctantly I pushed aside my immediate need to know more. Later. 'What about you? Do you make a habit of ministering to those in need? Should I call you Florence?' As I said it, I knew I'd made a mistake: I'd been away too long, I was out of touch, outdated. She looked at me quizzically then smiled uncertainly.

'It's Margaret, Meg to my friends, Meg Jackson. That was a good guess though, I'm a nurse at Guy's, just around the corner. My shift just finished.'

'Ah.' It was my turn to be uncertain. 'But that's not exactly a nurse's uniform.' She was dressed like no nurse that I'd ever seen.

'Well, they frown on us wearing blood-stained scrubs on the way home from work.' Meg grinned then, self-conscious, she looked away; nervously twisting a silver necklace around the collar of her sweater. Before I could control it, I felt the now-self's leering reaction to her elegant jean-clad figure. Sometimes a now-self engenders immediate respect, even love at first contact. This wasn't one of those times. Disgusted, I slapped him down. I wasn't repulsed, had encountered worse, but at first sight Paul's self seemed to offer little of value. I began to corral what was good, preparing to discard the bad. It wasn't ruthlessness, just survival of the fittest. I'd survived many times before. I was fitter. I realised I was staring. She blushed as I ignored her joke, ran her fingers through her hair and looked down as she sipped her coffee. Strange, she seemed to like it. Disturbed by my lack of control – surprised by my own reaction to her – I steered the conversation towards safer ground.

'That's a tough job. You've had a long day and here I am adding to it. Sorry.'

'That's OK, but yes I am a bit tired.' She paused and looked around. 'I often stop here. I need to reconnect with the real world after a shift. I like to watch healthy, happy people coming and going about their business. It helps.' As she spoke a shock ran through me. '*I need to reconnect with the real world after a shift*'. It was exactly how I felt: same words, different meaning. It was my turn to be flustered. I fumbled in my pocket, reaching for Paul's wallet as she watched me; curious, aware that something had changed. She mistook my silence. 'I'm sorry, that was a bit heavy.' She blushed again and looked away. Annoyed by my clumsiness I felt my face redden.

'Look, sorry, I'm not myself yet. I didn't mean to be rude…' I was babbling. 'You've been very kind and now I'm embarrassed. Let me pay for these. Can I get you another coffee?' I knew I should end the contact but I didn't want to. She shook her head.

'No, really that's fine. I should go.' I read her

emotions. Curious or not she wasn't going to ask any more questions. I interested her but… 'But you stay and finish yours,' she said as she got to her feet. I rose too, an involuntary reaction from my more chivalrous, older selves. She started as I reached to move her chair. I felt myself blush again as I blurted,

'Well, if you're sure …' She hesitated, confused and then nodded.

'I am, um … Sure…' She gathered her coat and bag then softened the moment with a smile. 'But it was nice to meet you.' She turned and walked away before calling back over her shoulder. 'Goodbye Paul. Take care and don't forget to eat in future!' I watched her go, fighting the urge to call her back; disturbed by the attraction I felt and my need for human contact, especially hers.

Chapter 3

Paul was mostly quiescent during the tube-ride to his home. I remembered the tube from its earliest days. Judging from the maps it was much more extensive now, but I was surprised how little it had changed; how familiar the tired and worn stations and trains were. Feigning sleep, I studied my fellow travellers through half-closed eyes. I began to take more notice and was struck for the first time by the racial and ethnic variety and by the number of women, mostly young and unaccompanied. This was a London that differed wildly from the one I'd last known.

I watched them individually and wondered at their studied isolation. Most were absorbed in listening to whatever they were hearing through curious earpieces or watching and tapping on their tiny hand-held screens. Only a few held newspapers or books. They ignored each other, just as they'd ignored the billboards, flashing advertising screens and thrusting hands offering flyers on the way to the station. A dizzying clamour for attention that had assaulted my senses and threatened again to overwhelm me. They'd ignored, too, the news-stand headlines, the banks of TV screens in a store window that broadcast scenes of what I took to be a war and fleeing refugees. Screens and images that had transfixed me. According to my now-knowledge this wonder was commonplace. I alone had stood and watched, marvelling at the technology until I'd sickened of the scenes and moved on.

Still adjusting I felt isolated in the crowded carriage. There was no discussion between the travellers, no visible interest in each other or the world in which they lived. I struggled to come to terms with the bewildering onslaught of information that they'd so blithely disregarded. So far – Meg excepted – this seemed a lonely world. I pulled out Paul's device, another marvel, instant mobile communications! But its screen was smashed. So, I was alone too.

The weather was still bitter as I left the station. I trudged the streets, instinctively following the path my now-self had followed many times before. Paul's shabby, ground-floor flat in the middle of a terrace behind Southwark tube station looked far from appealing. There were other places I could have gone – other short-term havens whilst I completed the assimilation and transition – but it was close by and I figured it would give me a chance to learn more about 'Paul Mason'. I found his key, opened and closed the door and leant weakly against the wall. Glad at last to be away from the street bustle. The hall was musty and smelt of previous occupants, previous meals. After a few moments I kicked myself into action. I needed to eat, to restore the physical and mental energies drained by the transition.

The kitchen yielded ready meals and a microwave. Paul's memories provided the knowledge of what to do with them. What other conveniences would I discover in this new existence? I prowled the flat, thinking, absorbing. Compared to what I'd seen in the streets, and his clothes, Paul didn't seem to be wealthy by the cycle's standards. But he had many possessions – books, clothes, gadgets, tools. His cupboards and fridge were amply stocked. Was that usual in this cycle? That even the less well-off possessed so much?

Forcing myself to eat slowly from a still-too-hot bowl of chilli, I briefly contemplated the television, the computers and screens in the spare room, before reluctantly sinking onto the bed in the main bedroom. Tomorrow. There was much to learn about life in this new cycle. Paul's knowledge was, at best, sketchy but it had given me a start. I was already stunned by what I'd been able to absorb from him. During my time in the between world, in transition, I'd missed: a second world war; a cold war; the advent of antibiotics, contraception, a pandemic; global travel and instantaneous communications – an explosive growth in populations and technologies. The pace of development had been extraordinary. For the first time in countless cycles, I felt lost. But I felt, too, a stirring of anticipation as I began to sense the opportunities that Paul's skills and this world's extraordinary new technologies might provide. Perhaps this now-self wasn't as worthless as I thought. Perhaps this time I wouldn't fail. I was anxious to resume the work I'd been forced to leave behind in the last cycle but, right at that moment, shift-exhausted, I was too tired to resist. Sleep overcame me. I dreamt of Meg. And Lela.

Chapter 4

Street noises and weak sunlight through the thin curtains woke me to my new existence. For a moment, the crushing reality that I was once again in the world, that it hadn't been a dream, threatened to pull me down. Memories shifted and sorted. I was dizzied by the clamour of my selves demanding answers – why now? Why here? Why this youthful but loathsome now-self? I silenced them, pushed them aside. Untangling myself from the sheets, I swung my feet to the floor. I was in another cycle, another existence, another place. In time I'd find some answers but first I needed to get organised. By the time I'd showered and found fresh clothes I was making plans. I took stock of my situation as I wolfed down a plate of scrambled eggs.

I was in London, February 2026. I'd been ninety years in transition, a larger than average gap, almost the longest time I'd ever spent out of cycle. Why? Once again, I parked the question. Later. For now, I needed to focus on building my strength. On regaining my powers and accessing the resources I'd need. The shower had re-opened some of my wounds and the fresh clothes rubbed and chafed. The bruises, more livid now, ached with renewed vigour. Physically I was in poor shape and I paused to test my powers, to see if I could yet do anything to speed my recovery. I decided I could afford to apply a little will. The aches receded until I could ignore them. Good, progress. Mentally I was in better shape. My old and current memories and thoughts were now pretty well interlaced and interlocked in the complex mind-matrix I'd never fully understood. My accumulated and now personas were merging.

So, the good news was that though far from fit, it appeared I was young and healthy and living in a civilised city in a stable, developed country. A welcome contrast to some of the more malevolent existences and identities I'd shifted into. I could work with that. Instinctively 'he'; I was also relieved that this now-self was male. The cycles I'd spent as a female had been interesting but unnerving.

To my surprise Paul kept his life pretty well organised. A drawer contained a passport and other useful papers that I stuffed into a backpack. As I reviewed Paul's memories, I scanned the flat for other sources – photos, diaries – there were none. Emotional ties? It seemed not. His parents were still alive but retired, self-absorbed and barely engaged with the life of their only child. Aside from that he only had a few work colleagues and some casual friends. Hmm really? No girlfriend? No. Boyfriend? No. Seemingly there would be little if any thing to disentangle. Paul lived alone and there was no-one who would miss him, certainly not for the next few days. For once, an uncomplicated disappearance looked a possibility. That would simplify things. If I'd cared for him, I might have been sad.

Disappointed that Paul had only a superficial understanding of the world in which he lived I tried the television, tried watching the news. I watched scenes of poverty, hunger, suffering and despair being beamed into my safe and comfortable flat. A voyeur in cosy isolation; just like, I assumed, millions in other apartments and homes. I watched in amazement as the scenes were seamlessly replaced by sports news – as if this was of equal value – and then with adverts for the consumption of goods far, far beyond the reach of the impoverished and suffering. Were the senses of guilt, irony and embarrassment missing from this world? The gulf between the haves and have-nots appeared to be wider than ever, wider than I'd imagined it could be. After a while something called a reality show followed the news. I turned it off. It seemed that television was unlikely to be the source of the deeper understanding and knowledge I needed.

With my newly acquired skills I used Paul's computer

to go online. At first I was hesitant, using Paul's skills but my own instincts to find my way. The experience was mind-blowing. The ease of access to information – visual, textual, aural – and to research, opinion and analysis was breathtaking. I felt my heart surge at the possibilities this power would unleash. The potential it would give me to find what I'd been searching for so long. It was several hours before a deep numbing chill roused me from staring at the screen. I switched it off and stretched as I walked stiffly into the kitchen, rubbing my arms vigorously to restore my circulation. As the kettle boiled, I munched on toast and thought through what I'd learned.

It seemed that mankind had yet again failed to learn from previous conflicts or to be wary of the actions and intentions of social and political reformers. What a surprise, but it was unsettling too. The world I'd left before had been in search of peace after the great war but had succumbed to another. Now, after a few decades of relative peace the usual conflicts – over geography and natural assets, religion, politics, globalisation versus nationalism, individual freedom versus government control – were once again becoming more extreme. It seemed this world was neither as stable nor benign as I'd hoped.

Communism had weakened, as I would have predicted, but Democracy, corrupted by capitalism, was sickening too; threatening to leave a dangerously unfilled void. Europe had become more united – who'd have predicted that? – but was now in danger of falling apart again. The British Empire was a distant history and the United Kingdom was threatening to follow – as England, Scotland and Northern Ireland became fragmented by nationalism. America was an economic and military power house but becoming increasingly divided ideologically and politically. China and Russia had risen and fallen and were rising again in search of empires. The Middle East was once again a powder keg and, depressingly, the desire for religious faith was as strong as ever, thriving despite the development of science and understanding of the natural world.

The countries and continents long plundered for their human, geological and agricultural resources were still being plundered even as they sought their own independence. The haves were fiercely protecting their own whilst assuaging their consciences with charity, a smattering of foreign aid and platitudes. Meanwhile new crises were growing. The world was still recovering from a global pandemic – with fears of more to follow – and global warming and climate change were threatening to replace global war as mankind's greatest threat. I shrugged. Knowing about these things might be important if I was to succeed in this cycle, but otherwise the ways of the world meant little to me. They revealed that the essential nature of mankind was unchanged. What did I expect? That in only ninety years the mistakes of millennia would have been corrected?

I'd found no trace of Lela but I refused to allow my hopes to be crushed. I'd learned two things of importance: that our existence was still unknown, at least to the masses, and that my chances of success in this cycle were immeasurably greater than in any that had gone before. I was in London. So that meant a Phoenix Centre was close by. I sipped my coffee and searched my memory for the address, wondering if it was still there. It was time to get started, time to get re-acquainted with my own kind.

It didn't take me long to gather what I needed, just the tools and files I downloaded onto a memory stick that I slipped into my jeans. I stuffed a change of clothes into the backpack and took a last look around at the place that had been his home but meant nothing to me. There was nothing more that I needed from his life. Paul Mason was about to join the thousands of missing persons reported every year. That's what I was thinking about as I slammed the door and headed towards the tube. It was my first full day and I'd had a lot to take in, but that was no excuse. I should have been more alert. I started to turn as I heard the rush of footsteps, but I was slow, woefully slow.

'Mason! Mason, you slag! Where's our money!' The words registered as a baseball bat connected with the back of my knees. I fell forward, rolling onto my side, arms raised in defence. Again, too slow. Boots thudded and stamped on my thighs, back, chest, re-opening the wounds from the previous beating, deepening the bruises that peppered my body. I felt the crunch of cartilage as my nose ruptured under the impact of a balled fist then my collar tightened as a second hand grabbed my clothes and pulled me up against the low wall bordering the flats' gardens. There were no passers by, or if there were they chose discretion over Samaritan. The flats were dark, waiting for the commuters to return; the street lights barely lightened the gathering gloom of dusk.

'Fuck off.' Is what I meant to say: it came out as 'ffu o' as I spat blood in the face of the attacker. I knew who he was now, an enforcer working for the gang whose territory Paul had trespassed upon by dealing in a local club. As I worked it out, I didn't see the backhand that whipped across my face or the blow that smashed my head back against the bricks. The world dimmed as I greyed out.

'OK, stop now. I need him conscious.' I recognised the voice: the Estonian, the gang leader. I focussed blearily on his crouching figure. 'Why did you do it, Mason? Are you stupid? I told you. That you had to pay. Did you think you could hide from us?' His face loomed in and out of focus, I had a feeling his question was rhetorical. They'd given Paul a warning, a beating, taken his stash and demanded a further payment in compensation. Too consumed with dealing with the shift I hadn't given it any thought. I was paying for that now.

'No' stupi',' I managed through mashed lips. Ordinarily they'd have stood no chance against me but now, weakened and taken off guard, I was out of options. I began to prepare myself.

'You thought you could ignore me?' His voice was hard, uncompromising. Once again, I figured he wasn't expecting an answer. 'Well, you were wrong. Take his backpack, his wallet, his keys. Trash the flat.' I felt hands roughly searching my jacket pockets. 'Come and see me when you've recovered. We can talk about working off your debt.'

'Recovere–?' But the conversation, such as it was, was over. I felt the rush of air as the bat descended, plunging me into darkness.

Chapter 5

I hurt everywhere as consciousness returned. I could tell that time had passed, but not how much. I hadn't got my short-term memory back online yet.

I drifted off.

Came back.

Had I shifted again?

Slowly I was able to focus on her face. Light haloed around her hair as her head blocked the glare from the harsh strip lights. Slowly the memory of who she was returned. She reached to restrain me as I tried to lift a hand to investigate the source of the jackhammer throbbing in my head.

'Careful, you've got a drip in that arm, leave it for now.' Her voice was gentle but firm. I felt the sting of the needle in my arm as the tube pulled, looked around and began to register the stark white surroundings.

'Nur..gh…' I cleared my throat and tried again, 'Nurse Nightingale, good to see you again.' My voice was harsh, whispery, old man tired. She couldn't help herself. She smiled.

'Sshh now, you need to rest. I'll get you some ice chips for your throat.' I grabbed weakly at her.

'Where am I?'

'You're OK, you're in hospital, A&E at Guy's Hospital.'

'What day is it?'

'It's Wednesday, the evening.' Thought processes were returning. I worked it out. I'd only lost a few hours. I recognised her and she recognised me, so obviously not another shift; I was in the same cycle.

'What happened?'

'You tell us. You look as if you've been in another fight. You've had a bad blow to the temple. You've lost a lot of blood; they think you'd been there for a couple of hours before you were found.' I searched my memory, recalled nothing of value and then saw a flitter of concern cross her face as she felt my grip release and my arm fell back onto the bed. I heard her say, 'Stop talking; you need to rest,' as the jackhammering increased and a searing pain lanced between my eyes. Slipping back into unconsciousness I saw her fear as the alarms began to sound and nurses and doctors rushed around.

*   *   *

'Get out, get out, get out!' He'd fooled me. I'd thought we were assimilated, that his individuality had been absorbed, but I was wrong, or maybe my head injury caused some change, somehow released him. Whatever, Paul saw his chance, took it, pressed hard to regain control. I felt the surge of his will as he tried to force us out but he didn't know how. He never really had a chance but I couldn't blame him for trying.

'Give it up, Paul.' I wrestled with him, frustrated that it should be necessary; annoyed at myself for not taking greater care.

'Get out!' He pushed harder, a last desperate effort.

'For Christ's sake! Enough, you can't win!' I was weak but not that weak, I slapped him around a little. I'll give him credit, he kept trying.

'Get out, I will be Paul!' Like a child: as if saying it would make it happen. That seemed to be the limit of his repertoire. I began to get bored. The others joined in. Until then they'd waited, watching as he'd isolated himself, hunkering down. Now they gave him no choice. They forced him to open up.

'You're one of us now, relax, enjoy it!'

'Who are you all?' He could no longer hide from them or deny their existence.

'That doesn't matter, we're all Jay now.'

'But how? Who were you? Don't you care?'

'We are who we were and we're all Jay now. It's one and the same.' He was still in denial. It took some time.

They gave him no choice. They enveloped him, smothered him. Slowly he had to yield and in so doing he began to understand, to lose his individuality. I heard them introducing themselves, sensed his incredulity as he finally absorbed and shared.

''You were an American Indian... Really?' I felt Jacy's – Child of the Moon's – swell of pride. Together we relived a few fleeting moments of life on the open plains as she and Paul communed. The others clamoured to share, to help him understand. Time passed as experiences were offered, as thoughts floated, surfaced.

'So, four times you've been sailors?'

'Mariners!' I heard Jorge's riposte. I'd been a pompous, arrogant trader then.

'All those children? All those women!'

'And men...' I heard Jacintha giggling as Paul absorbed this and then shyly asked to know more. Later he asked, 'Is there anything we haven't done?' They went quiet as we considered this, then the ideas started to flow. Some of them surprised even me. It seemed we still had a lot of living to do. Finally I felt him accept it all, willingly this time. He let them/us all in, joined with them/us, relished the lives led and joined in eager anticipation for the lives to come.

'We're all, Jay, now.' Someone said ... We all said... And we drifted and communed in harmony until ... I was Jay again.

Chapter 6

Once again, I hurt everywhere as consciousness returned. It was getting repetitive. I coughed, as instructed, as they extracted the tube from my throat.

'It's OK.' The nurse eased me back onto the pillows. 'You'll be fine in a moment.' He reached behind the bed and flicked a switch. For the first time in days the hum from the ventilator, ever present as I'd swum in an out of consciousness, ceased.

'How long?' I croaked.

'How long have you been in ICU, or how long since your accident?' The doctor was watching carefully, checking with his own eyes what the monitors were telling him. The nurse was busy disconnecting and coiling tubes, satisfied now that I was breathing independently. I rolled my eyes, frustrated by the medic's seeming indifference.

'Both.' The doctor flicked through the chart at the end of the bed. 'Says here you were admitted through A&E just under a week ago.'

A week? It had been that long? 'Am I going to be OK?'

'Yes, but you've been lucky. Your head injury gave rise to an internal bleed which, fortunately, happened whilst you were being observed in A&E.'

'Lucky?' His dry delivery was annoying me now.

'If you hadn't been in hospital you'd have died, so yes, lucky. You were taken to surgery where my colleagues operated to remove a clot. We've kept you in an induced coma since then to allow the swelling on your brain to subside. We began to reduce the medication two days ago and you've slowly come around to the point when you began breathing normally.' A week, I'd been lying there helpless for a week. I was furious at myself for allowing it to happen.

'And how long will I take to recover?'

'We'll keep you in for a few days of observation, mostly to be sure there's no lasting damage. You were delusional and obviously hallucinating as you came out of the coma but we've no real reason to be worried. All your vital signs are normal. After that you'll just have to be patient. Your body took quite a beating.' He smiled brightly as he concluded his brisk summary – delivered with all the sensitivity of a weather forecast – before swooping on to his next patient.

'He's a cheery one.' I winced as I tried to raise myself to sip from the straw the nurse offered.

'Careful now.' The nurse guided my hand. 'Ah well, that's just his way, not much of a bedside manner but he's the one I'd want looking after me if I was in ICU.' He pulled a pillow into place to support me as I drank. 'I'm Tim, by the way. Now, do you want some pain relief?'

I got half comfortable, considered his offer. 'Thanks, Tim but I'll see if I can do without.' I wasn't being brave, my head felt like mush but I needed to sharpen up. I couldn't recall anything from my time in the coma, just some vague feelings of unease. I needed to regain control. I couldn't afford any more sedation.

'Well just push the button if you change your mind. Now, can you tell us a bit more about yourself. All we know is you're called Paul and you live in London. You had no identification on you, no wallet, nothing.' I looked at him quizzically. 'Nurse Jackson? Remember her? She recognised you in A&E. She gave us your name.'

I nodded. 'Paul Mason.' I managed a smile. 'And of course I remember her.'

Tim looked at me, his head cocked, seeming to weigh my response before finding it acceptable. 'That's good then, you called out your name when you were delusional but a load of other stuff too. We were beginning to wonder.'

'Can the rest wait? I'm not feeling so good.' I was exaggerating, needing time to think. After a moment he patted me on the shoulder.

'Sure, OK then but the police are keen to have a word about the attack. Also, Meg asked me to let her know when you were conscious. Is that OK?'

'Meg yes, police no,' I said weakly, unable to stop myself slipping back into a doze. I hadn't been exaggerating that much.

Tim chuckled. 'Aye well, that's how I'd have prioritised it too. OK, you take a rest now and I'll let Meg know.' But by then he was talking to himself.

*   *   *

This time waking up didn't hurt so much. I looked around. They'd moved me. A private room or a side ward I guessed. The knock that woke me sounded again. 'Come in.' My voice was almost back to normal. Meg's head appeared around the door.

'Hey you.' She smiled sweetly. 'I was coming to visit and they told me to wake you, that you needed checking.' I couldn't help my own broad smile. The reaction was instinctive, it was that good to see her.

'Hey yourself.' I said quietly. To my surprise I was shy with her. I beckoned her in. 'OK, check away.' I shifted my weight, pulling myself into a sitting position, dismayed at my lack of strength after days in bed. With brisk efficiency she checked my vitals before declaring herself satisfied. I couldn't help myself as I watched her work. Fresh faced, no make up and in A&E scrubs she was a knockout. I saw her faint blush as she became conscious of my stare.

'You gave us quite a scare you know.' She frowned as she tucked my arm back beneath the covers.

'I hear I have you to thank for saving me. You acted fast.' She blushed again, shook her head as if to shake off my words; picked up my chart to update the figures.

'I just did my job.'

'OK, well... Thanks.' It felt inadequate but I didn't want to embarrass her further, 'So, are you working the wards now then?' I asked.

'No, I told you, I came to visit and they asked me to help out.' She dropped my chart. 'They're a bit short staffed, this is just professional courtesy.'

'Ah, you came to visit me.' I couldn't help it; her answer had warmed me.

'I had to when I heard my mysterious Paul had regained consciousness.'

'Had to? So, I'm your "mysterious Paul" am I?' I couldn't help my smile.

'And now I can see you're better I can be on my way.' She said, ignoring my smug look as she tugged and straightened the bed covers. 'Maybe I'll look in again tomorrow.'

When she'd gone, I lay there savouring the memory of her soft hands on my wrist. As I rested, connections rebuilt themselves. I looked around for my clothes, saw them folded on a cupboard. I swung my legs gingerly to the floor. Things spun but I stayed conscious and with slow deliberation made my way across the room. With each movement my muscles began to ease. I breathed deeply, applied inner will and focussed some core energy on healing and recovery. I knew I'd pay for it later but for now I had no choice until I'd sorted things. I checked my trouser pockets relieved to find the memory stick. Good, I'd need it but those plans would have to wait. There was something else I had to do first.

*   *   *

Meg came back the next day, and the one after. Days that dragged as my body slowly mended and I chafed against the forced inactivity. Her visits were brief with little time to talk but I looked forward to each one. She asked about my life, family and so on – natural questions that I couldn't answer – so I distracted her by asking about hers. It was disconcerting to find how much we had in common. She was a loner. An only child she'd been orphaned by a car crash soon after birth and then brought up by an unmarried Aunt, now deceased. The concept of family meant as little to her as it did to me. I'd learned to minimise emotional encumbrances as a defence against the inevitable loss I felt every time I shifted, but I was sad for her. She brushed it off. 'It's all I've ever known.'

Despite my best intentions the attraction I'd felt for her when we'd first met only strengthened as I learned to admire her quick wit, her sense of independence, her intense compassion for those in her care. Try as I might to deny it, I was smitten. It was a complication I didn't need and couldn't afford but could do little about.

The police came and took my statement. I offered them only vague descriptions, gave no clue that I could identify my attackers and they went away clearly dissatisfied. I half expected them back but no-one came. The room became a cell, a sentence relieved only by Meg's visits. I worked on my fitness, sneaking out of bed when the nurses weren't looking to rebuild some flexibility and strength and to fight off the smothering claustrophobia. When I could exercise no more, I lay flat planning my next moves. Eventually the doctors told me I was recovering well enough to be discharged. During Meg's next visit I gave into temptation. Satisfied I was mending she'd perched on the edge of the bed to chat, but only for a few minutes.

'Wait, are you going back to A&E now?'

'No, my shift's finished. I just came to check on you before going home.' I reached out to grab her hand as she rose to leave. I couldn't help myself, I wanted more. She looked at my hand. I took it back, felt guilty, unaccountably shy.

'Sorry, but … Would you have a coffee with me before you leave?' I mumbled, blurted really. What was wrong with me?

She grinned, enjoying my all too obvious confusion. 'Are you up to it? Not too weak?'

I grinned back, re-assured. 'For you? Never.' She raised an eyebrow, weighing the pros and cons.

'If I do, will you tell me what's going on?'

'What do you mean?'

She sighed in exasperation. 'Twice we've met. Both times you'd obviously been in trouble, taken a beating. I can't just ignore that.' She had a point. I looked at her, shrugged.

'It won't happen again.'

'You're just unlucky then? What were they, unfortunate coincidences?'

I looked at her and told her the truth, for what it was. 'Coincidence? No. I'd done something stupid. People were angry.' She pulled away. I reached for her. 'But it's done now and I've learned.' I helped her a bit, not a lot, just enough so she'd accept it. And it helped that it was the truth. OK not all of it, but enough. I saw her struggle but I'd overcome her resistance and after a moment she sighed as if it was against her better judgement.

'OK, I'll go and change; wait here until I organise a wheelchair. I'm not going to be responsible for you having a relapse. Just for a quick coffee mind you and you're going to tell me more.' I nodded obediently and she looked at me doubtfully through narrowed eyes before deciding to trust me. With a shake of her head, she left. I needed to get fitter, had debts to settle and time to make up, but first I was going to allow myself a small pleasure.

Meg returned, pushing a chair. 'Shall we then?'

'I'm all yours.' I grinned.

'Hmm, don't get ahead of yourself.' Meg grinned back.

Chapter 7

In all my cycles, I'd spent little time really exploring London. I used the days after my discharge from hospital to change that. Armed with Paul's more recent knowledge I crisscrossed the city, learning, absorbing. I visited Highgate cemetery and accessed one of my emergency stashes. It would have to do until I contacted the Protectors. The gold I traded provided more than enough cash to pay for some new clothes and a cheap hotel.

I was sorely tempted to see more of Meg but I resisted, did the reverse. I broke off all contact with her. I'd seen enough of humanity to have few qualms about using people for my own ends but Meg was different. I didn't see myself as callous or uncaring – just practical – but I had my own 'ethics' – if that's what they were – for dealing with phems. Unlike others, I wouldn't demean them or cause them distress for my own pleasure. They were a resource to be used if it helped me reach my objective but I wouldn't abuse them unless they'd forfeited the right to be treated so. I told myself I was resisting out of respect for Meg and the care she'd shown me. But there was another truth. That Meg attracted me in ways that no one had since Lela. The truth was that I wasn't entirely sure I could control that attraction and I couldn't afford any distractions.

As I explored London, I grew more accustomed to the cycle, the changes in people, attitudes and behaviours. I wasn't yet fully acclimatised but I was getting there. More importantly I was getting in tune with myself. I exercised, meditated, rebuilt much of my mental and physical capabilities; enough for now at least, the rest could come later. I had a task to complete before I could move on.

*   *   *

In a way the Estonian and his thugs did me a favour. In a matter of weeks, I was fully assimilated after the shift. My body had healed fast since the beating and I'd recovered most of my powers, but I needed a way to test myself. It was close to midnight when I took a cab and had it drop me just south of the river. It was a cool and, for once, dry night. The air crisp and clear, I walked the last few miles to the club, to anticipate and savour the moment.

The doorman recognised me. He'd thrown me out during my last visit and now watched with disbelief as I sauntered towards him, past the queue of thinly dressed clubbers anxiously waiting to be granted entry. They watched resentfully as I skipped the line. I could feel them hoping to see me rejected, bounced back. The doorman straightened, flexed his shoulders, signalling to me. An archetype, a caricature – thick necked, bulging T shirt and dull eyes – I saw him smirk in anticipation as I approached. I gave him my most winning smile.

'Hi, I'm here to see Kardo.' I was being polite, as if I'd been invited – that the Estonian was my friend. It taxed his brain. I watched as he struggled to process the unexpected before reverting to type. He towered over me, glowering.

'Fuck off, toerag. And that's Mr. Rebane to you.' He was squared up, puffed and strutting, ready to enter the ring. The queuing clubbers watched with eager anticipation but they were going to be disappointed. I didn't want to give them a show. I wanted to test my other abilities. I stared him in the eye as I made small, subtle changes in my expression, posture and stance. I gave him more signals that at first befuddled and confused him and then made him vulnerable to persuasion. I focussed my will and compelled him.

'No. Stand aside.' It's important to use simple short commands. 'Open the door, please.' I watched as his expression changed from belligerence to submission and then acquiescence: watched as he stepped to one side not knowing why he made no attempt to stop me. As I strode past, he returned to glowering at the queue. I heard him snarl at the clubbers who sniggered at him and demanded they be admitted too. He reverted to type; forgot I'd ever been there. I'd passed the first test.

In the dim entry way, I checked the girl at reception with a look as she reached for the alarm button. She looked at me, glanced uncertainly towards the entrance, noted that the doorman had not tried to stop me. She withdrew her hand. So far so good. I took the stairs two at a time, up to the office above the pounding dance floor. It wasn't locked and three heads swivelled in surprise as I slipped through then closed the thick, soundproofed door and leant back against it. Hooded lamps cast pools of light on a broad mahogany desk that spanned almost the width of the end wall, and on the matching chesterfield armchairs and sofas that filled the rest of the room. I was smirking at some designer's idea of a mobster's den when they made their move. The enforcers who'd jumped me as I'd left the flat, now performing as guard dogs but not as well trained. I narrowed my focus, filled it with the two advancing bodies, working out the moves I'd make. I had the advantage of surprise. They were slowed by drink and the assumption that I was just Paul Mason, so it wasn't an altogether fair fight.

The first had barely left his seat when I crushed his larynx, an elbow strike, he went down for good. The other, the one who'd mashed my nose, made it to his feet but kept back; circling cautiously. He'd had some better training and already I could see he was re-evaluating the threat I posed. Nonetheless his lunge was too slow, easily avoided, and his eyes narrowed as I ducked his next swing and then stepped past and around him as if he wasn't there. He was struggling to release my choke hold as I twisted then snapped his neck. The crack was loud and crisp in the otherwise silent office. I dropped the body, allowed my focus to return to the room. I'd passed the second test.

Kardo Rebane sat motionless behind the desk. I was wrong, the office wasn't silent, a muted throb from the club below laid down a backbeat to the tension that rose between us. The gun in his hand gave him courage but he couldn't disguise his shock; it wavered as he pointed it at my head.

'Impressive. Not what I'd have expected from you, Paul. Quite a surprise.' The confused frown belied his attempt at nonchalance as he fought to assume control. 'What do you want? Do you really think you're going to get away with this?' He glanced at the guard dogs. 'I have plenty more to replace them.' I let long moments pass, watched as the pulse in his neck quickened.

'Want? There's nothing I want from you, Kardo.' I watched as the shake in his hand spread to his arm and increased. I'd added to his confusion. 'And Paul's long gone. It's not about him. This is about you.' I was calm, totally at one with my now-self's body. As in tune with all my selves and the skills they'd given me, as I'd ever been. He saw it in me and it heightened the tension. He was bewildered now, beyond confusion.

'What do you mean Paul's gone?' Finally, he was sensing that something was very wrong. That the situation was beyond any hope of control. I stared at him, capturing his gaze. For long moments we were locked together. The pulse in his neck was joined by another in his temple, synchronising with the base beat from below and the shaking in his arm. His features had turned ruddy and unhealthy in the lamp light. I could sense his panic growing as I nodded towards his gun.

'Is that making you feel safe?' His focus shifted from me to the gun. 'Hold tight to it.' My voice was low, compelling. 'Tight, don't move those fingers. Focus. Tight.' I saw beads of sweat begin to form on his forehead as I stepped to one side and he struggled to move his arm; to shift his aim, to fire.

I've heard it said, have read papers by learned psychiatrists and psychologists, that only sociopaths kill without remorse. I don't think I am a sociopath – or a psychopath come to that – but remorse was another of those emotions I'd long since lost much use for. When you've seen and done pretty much everything then the world becomes increasingly black and white. Somewhere, some time over the cycles, I'd pretty much lost the ability to compromise; to make allowances, to live and let live. I didn't see myself as judge or jury, the arbiter of good or bad. There was too little of the former and too much of the other to waste time sorting and judging. So now I just acted as I saw fit, without remorse. My sense of fitness was that the world would be better without the Estonian, his thugs and the drugs, misery and terror they inflicted on those around them. I knew that, maybe, in one or more of them there might have been a shred of goodness – maybe as fathers, sons, husbands – but I didn't care to weigh the balance.

Kardo Rebane died knowing none of this as I made him place the gun in his mouth and pull the trigger. He'd been a worthless person but another useful test. I felt satisfaction that I'd passed but nothing more, and I knew there'd be far stiffer tests to come.

I left the club without further incident. What had happened in the sound proofed office had gone unnoticed. The music still throbbed; the dance floor still pounded to the feet of the hyped-up clubbers. The doorman, still confused, had merely nodded as I left. When I returned to my hotel I slept without a care, rising at first light ready and impatient to access my resources. To establish a new base and to get started.

Chapter 8

I barely recognised Curzon Street. Once lined with Georgian terraces, the sweeping, elegant façades were now broken by modern inserts. The traffic and road signs were other stark reminders that more than a century had passed since my last visit.

There were other changes. I had no trouble locating the entrance to the Phoenix Centre but recalled that before there had been an elegant bell and a grille that opened to allow callers to be inspected. The painted and polished door was now plain. To one side there was a small screen and keypad. I pondered this for a moment before entering my identity code. The screen came to life and I found himself being scrutinised by an alert and curious Protector.

'Your name?'

'Samson.' My formal truename. The name I'd been known by since it all began. The name I'd been given at my first birth. The only name that was real to me.

'Verification?' I gave the codes. The screen went blank and there was barely a pause before the door clicked opened. The disembodied voice continued tinnily from the speaker. 'Welcome back, Jay. Come in. We'd been wondering when you'd show up again.'

I couldn't help but be impressed as I pushed through the door. There was always something new but this was a big change. In previous cycles it had taken days, weeks even, for the Protectors to satisfy themselves when I presented my credentials at first contact.

What had once been a classically styled entrance-hall was now a contemporary open plan office. Men and women of various ages – Protectors I assumed – who'd been working at desks, manning screens and phones, stopped what they were doing and regarded me openly and curiously. An attractive young Asian woman, expensively styled and dressed and about the same age as my now-self approached me uncertainly.

'Welcome to London, Mr. Samson, and to your new cycle.' I paused to consider the implications of her words.

'Is that an assumption, or do you know?'

She blushed. 'An assumption, but we've no other record of contact with you for many decades now.' She gestured at the computer screens around the room in explanation. I nodded in understanding, relieved but also disappointed that there wasn't some new technology that was allowing the Protectors to track Rinks automatically. I sighed, finding Lela wasn't going to be that easy then. 'As this is a new contact would you allow us to update our records?' I nodded again. 'We have some new procedures.' She continued. 'Please place your fingers and thumbs on this scanner and look directly into this lens.' It was well-delivered, polite words backed up by an unspoken command, but without confidence. Something was troubling her. As I hesitated a side door opened and the Protector I recognised from the entry screen joined us.

'We now record the finger and retinal prints and facial recognition parameters for all new contacts, Jay,' he said smoothly. 'It is just one more way of ensuring we can identify your now-self. For as long as you're with us this time, that is.'

For a moment I regarded him quizzically, studying the tall, elderly blond man who, for the second time, addressed me so familiarly by my Rink common name. He was severely dressed, a sharp suit, like a banker. I'd have felt shabby – in my jeans, sweatshirt, jacket and beanie – if I'd cared. North European I guessed, Nordic maybe. I shrugged, complied with the woman's request and placed my hands on the scanner.

'You speak as if we know each other.' I said. 'Have maybe known each other for some time. Who are you? What name have I known you by?' The Protector stepped closer; his eyes fixed on mine.

'Can you not tell, Jay? Look closely: some characteristic, some mannerism perhaps?' His voice was challenging, not teasing. It was a test. I looked more closely: allowing my recovering powers full rein as I read the other's body language and absorbed the signals that reveal the innermost nature of all individuals to those of us who are so adept. After a few moments I looked away, as if bored.

'Ah, so it is you then. Sora-san, or as I see you now, let me guess… Hmmm, Sorensen or some similar version would be more appropriate given your current appearance.'

The young woman gasped. 'I had heard you had this skill, but had scarcely believed it.'

I glanced at her and she looked away, embarrassed. I looked around the room, saw again the curious stares and began to understand the cause of her discomfort and uncertainty. 'It seems you know something about me but we've not met before, of that I am sure. May I know you now?' I phrased my request in the traditional, formal manner.

'I would be honoured. My true name is Ayeesha Rao, this is my third cycle.' She replied as she had been taught the conventions required.

'Ah…' I smiled. 'That explains it. When did the Protectors reveal themselves to you? During this cycle?' Ayeesha nodded, colouring.

'I'm sorry for my outburst, that was rude, but you're quite a legend.' With a glare Sora-san silenced the swell of muttered comments from the other Protectors who'd been watching and listening.

I grimaced. 'Don't believe everything you hear and don't be embarrassed, even I remember the confusion of those first few cycles. I am honoured to meet you Ayeesha Rao, and hope that we may know each other again.' I completed the formal exchange of greetings.

'Thank you.' Her composure now recovered she boldly returned my gaze. 'That would be my wish too.' As she busied herself updating the database, I turned to scan the others in the room.

'I greet you all too: I can see we've not known each

other before, perhaps we'll have an opportunity during this cycle.' I bowed my head respectfully. There was a moment's silence before they murmured and nodded in response. I turned my attention back to the elderly Protector. 'It's been a long time since we were in sync Sora-san.' I said evenly, revealing nothing of my true feelings.

'Too long, Jay.' Sora-san's reply was regretful. 'But I'm glad it's happened. We've never had a real opportunity to discuss.' He hesitated. 'What went before…'

'Is there anything to discuss then?' I kept my tone even as I read the anxiety in the other man. I made deliberate, subtle changes to my stance, my expression. He reacted as I knew he would. There was a distinct change in the relationship between us, Sora-san bowed his head in acknowledgement.

'Perhaps we'd be more comfortable upstairs.' He said, glancing around the room. 'Ayeesha and the others will begin preparing your papers immediately.' He waved his arm to indicate the side door through which he'd arrived. 'Shall we?'

*   *   *

The door closed on the bustle of activity in the open plan office. We were in a small hallway. Stairwells led up and down but Sora-san ushered me towards an elevator. I looked at him, registering again the age of his now-self and his physical infirmity.

'How long have you been in this cycle Sora-san?'

'Nearly eighty years. This now-self is over a hundred years old. Too long, I may end it soon.' He seemed unperturbed by the prospect.

'And how long in transition before then?'

He looked at me. A smile, almost a smirk flickered behind his eyes. 'How long have you been in cycle, Jay?' I shrugged.

'A couple of weeks.' I didn't count the time I'd spent in a coma. I saw him start as he absorbed this.

'Yet you are functioning so well already? Extraordinary.' He gathered himself. 'This time I was just ten years between cycles. Does that help you? Does it mean anything?'

'Just curious.' If it meant anything I wasn't about to share it with him. We entered the elevator and Sora-san turned to me; his face troubled.

'Whatever was in the past between us, Jay, I hope we can work together now.'

'Work together?' I knew there was no sign of the contempt I felt as I replied. 'I'm here for one reason only, I need your usual services, nothing more and then I shall be gone.' The elevator lurched and squeaked as it began the ascent.

'Even if I have news, information that may be of value?'

I looked at him coldly, grabbed his arm. 'What news? She is current?'

He blanched. 'No. No, I'm sorry, not that. According to our records there has been no contact.' He looked away, a poorly shielded emotion flickering across his face as he spoke. Was it shame or a lie? 'I'm sorry if I gave you hope.'

I waited until he relaxed again, tried to read him carefully but he was regaining control of his shields. I removed my hand, dismayed at my own lack of self control, my inability to manage the emotion that welled up within me. I paused to consider what I'd seen: the number of Protectors who were working downstairs, too many. Their need to identify me, their focus on tracking Rinks. This was new. Attention – interference almost – on a new scale. Something was out of kilter in this here and now. Why? With an effort I moderated my tone.

'What information then?'

'We think the Renegades have learned something new. They may be getting closer to their aims. Their actions are becoming more extreme.'

'In what way?'

'In the past they've ignored Rinks who chose not to join them. Now they treat us all as enemies.'

'All of us? Not just the Protectors?' Sora-san nodded and I considered his words as the elevator slowed and stopped. The Protectors had long since been dealing with the Renegades yet Sora-san was more agitated than I'd ever seen before. The doors opened into a well-appointed room. Large bay windows looked down on the street below. Heavy drapes, thick carpeting and dark leather furniture. A den rather than an office. I was more than just curious now. I was beginning to worry.

'You've quite a set up here, now. It's grown. There are a lot of Protectors downstairs. Why?'

'Progress, Jay. We're more centralised now. This isn't just a Phoenix Centre, it's the main headquarters for the Protectors.' Sora-san waved me towards one of the armchairs that flanked a low table. He took the other and continued. 'We've had to re-organise to control the threats in this here and now. It's not just the Renegades, there's more. The Seekers are increasing in power.'

I frowned at him. What was he trying to draw me into? 'You know I want nothing to do with any of this. The argument between the Protectors and the Renegades is your affair, not mine. Both sides know I have no allegiance to either. As for the Seekers, they or others like them have risen before and, as those that came before, these too will fail. Why are you wasting time and resources building defences against an empty threat?'

'This time it's different! You're still assimilating your now-knowledge. In time you'll understand the profound changes since you shifted from your last cycle. Changes that for the first time mean the Seekers have resources and capabilities that are a real threat to us. The Renegades too have access to knowledge and information like never before.'

'You speak as if the new technologies, the access to knowledge and information is of no value to you, to the Protectors. Surely if you too have access then the balance of power is unchanged?' Sora-san sighed.

'That should and would be true in the old order of things. But that too has changed.' He paused and stared at me until he was sure he had my full attention. 'The Seekers and some of the more extreme Renegades have joined forces.' He paused again, waiting for the import of his words to strike home. 'Now do you understand?' I stared at him. It had been the same for so long, every cycle.

Could things really have changed so much?

Chapter 9

The office was stuffy, the atmosphere redolent of ageing dust and times gone by. It was in need of a physical and spiritual spring clean. Sora-san and I talked for some time but he told me little more that was of any value. I listened to hear what he wasn't telling me, as much for what he was. Whatever else had changed in this here and now, Sora-san was still the man I'd mistrusted for more cycles than either of us liked to remember. Eventually I'd had enough: enough of Sora-san's secrecy and the Protectors' paranoia. I'd find out what he hadn't told me when and if it became important. Until then I'd focus on my own plans, there was so much to accomplish. I got to my feet.

'That's all very interesting, but as I said it's nothing to do with me. I'd like my papers now, please. I'm leaving.' I'd taken him by surprise. Sora-san half rose, flustered by my lack of concern.

'To go where? Will you return?'

I ignored his first question. 'Perhaps.'

'But the threat, the alliance between the Renegades and Seekers?'

'Is there one? When I know more, I'll decide.' My answer dismayed him further.

'If you'd work with us, we could help make sure they don't get in your way.' Sora-san was getting desperate. I looked at him coldly.

'It would be unhealthy for anyone to get in my way.'

'Suppose the Renegades thought you'd found what they've been looking for?'

The tension between us increased. I forced myself to be calm before replying but my tone slid from icy to arctic. 'Why would they think that? Who would tell them such a thing?'

'I...I...' Sora-san stuttered. Before he could answer, there was a knock at the door and Ayeesha entered with a sheaf of papers. She handed them to Sora-san who quickly passed them to me, thankful for the distraction. I scowled at him and checked them over.

'They seem to be in order. What about IDs? I'll need at least three.'

'I'll have them for you the day after tomorrow.' Ayeesha was eager to please. 'How should I contact you?'

'I'll let you know.' Still annoyed at Sora-san, my tone was abrupt. But it was instinct also: that I should give as little away as possible. Ayeesha flinched and I gave her a small smile to soften the impact of my words. I turned to leave but Sora-san stopped me again.

'I should warn you that your presence here will have been noted, you're likely to be followed as you leave.'

I raised an eyebrow. 'Seriously? Who by? Why do you allow this? Have the Protectors forgotten their purpose, their mission?'

It was Sora-san's turn to get icy. 'Don't presume to lecture us about our duty, Jay! We allow it because this way we learn as we watch them watching us. You know: "Keep your friends close and your enemies closer". I seem to recall you were around when that was first said. Sun Tzu, wasn't it?'

It took me by surprise, my control was still weak, too weak. I lost focus for a brief moment, as his words took me back and a previous-self's memories shimmered and surfaced. My vision narrowed and dimmed and I was once again a soldier in the Imperial Army... *A lowly infantry-man in training school. My back sore from marching. My throat dry and dusty as we sat in the scorching sun, watching the shadows creep ever closer as the sun moved behind the watchtower on the great wall and the Shuzhu, the garrison commander, droned on. How many times had he repeated the same text over and over again? The Art of War.*

In Sora-san's office I felt my longing for the cool shadow to move over me, or for the Shuzhu's lecture to end, as if it were yesterday. It had been one of my first cycles. I'd not yet encountered the Protectors, had still been finding my own way then, trying to come to terms with it all. Now, I pushed away the sights, sounds and smells of China, sixth century BC that had risen unbidden. Pulling myself back to the here and now, I blinked away the images – the circling condors riding the thermals on the ridge – and swallowed the taste of the dust; breathing deeply to flush the hot acrid smell of unwashed men and too close animals from my lungs. Sora-san was watching me closely. It had only been a split second but he'd seen my lapse in concentration.

'It was Wu Zixu actually. Sun Tzu stole it.' I answered calmly, as if nothing had happened. Back in control I focussed again on what he'd been saying. 'OK, so who are they, these watchers? What have you learned?' I saw Sora-san's eyes narrow but, unsure of what he'd seen, he chose to let it go.

'They're set up in an apartment across the road.' He gestured at the window. 'Employees of Connor Security, a global security firm. They've been there for the last year. They're working for a consortium of Seekers.'

'You're sure, not Renegades?' Sora-san shrugged.

'Renegades are Rinks, they know who we are. What would they expect to learn?'

'You must know more. Who exactly are these Seekers?'

Sora-san ran his finger along the desktop and paused before answering. 'My dear Jay, you're unwilling to work with us. Why would we share everything with you?'

I counted to ten, added five for good measure. 'You're showing your true colours Sora-san.' I smiled bitterly. 'You should do it more often. I'd respect you more.'

Sora-san coloured but refused to be baited further. 'We have other exits if you wish to escape their attention.' He murmured. A put down as much as an offer of help. And there was something more, he was urging me to leave. It was subtle but definitely there. Sora-san wanted me gone now, but why? I shook my head.

'I think I've had all the help I can take from the

Protectors today.' I turned to leave and was struck by a final thought. 'What about your own security? What about the database? I assume it contains details of all known Rinks – both those in cycle and those in transition – how secure is it?' For a moment I thought Sora-san wasn't going to deign to answer, but he couldn't resist.

'Don't teach us to suck eggs, Jay.' He said with a small sigh.

'God forbid,' I muttered, stifling the surge of excitement I felt as I absorbed the confirmation Sora-san had unwittingly just given me. 'I'll be in touch then. Bye Ayeesha.'

I took care not to slam the door on my way out. Someone had to show some class. I bypassed the lift and moved swiftly to the stairs, taking a few steps up to the next landing and waited, listening hard. Sure enough I heard Sora-san's curt dismissal of Ayeesha and the clack of her heels as she returned down the stairs to the office below. I retraced my own steps, moving silently on the balls of my feet, and through the still open door heard Sora-san on his phone.

'Samson is with us again,' he said simply, his voice faint but clear. I had no idea who he was calling but his tone was respectful. He was reporting to someone. There was a pause as he listened, then he continued. 'I mean he's returned, he's in cycle: he's not with us in that sense, he's not willing to co-operate.' Again, there was a pause as he listened. What he said next almost had me through the door, at his throat. 'I told him we'd had no contact with her but he doesn't know if I was lying. My shields were good enough to fool him. He'll carry on hoping we can lead him to her.' Sora-san's tone was flat as he relayed this, I focussed with everything I had but still I couldn't read him clearly. What was the truth. Did the Protectors know anything that would lead me to Lela? Something sour twisted in my stomach as I fought back the instinct to face him. To challenge him there and then but I swallowed hard and stayed still and silent. Listening.

'Is that wise?' There was doubt in Sora-san's voice. 'He's not someone you control–' His voice ended abruptly, whoever he was talking to had cut him off. When he spoke again he was surly. That much I could read clearly. He'd been put in his place. 'Fine. I'll do as you say.' I was wondering what he'd been told to do and by whom as I descended the stairs and walked unhurriedly through the open plan office and out of the front door. I'd had millennia of learning to be patient. I'd get the answers, but in my own good time.

Chapter 10

I was rusty, still getting in tune with the street vibrations of this here and now and at first, I missed them when I left the Phoenix Centre. I'd begun to wonder if Sora-san had been right when I finally identified the first tail. It was some time before I realised that they were working a box formation around me. Using both sides of the road with watchers and followers ahead, behind and to the left and right, switching positions every few minutes. They weren't just good they were very good and, now I'd identified them, I could see something else. They were fit, physically competent men and women. Each was what I instinctively identified as a 'soldier'.

I varied my gait and pace as I led them along a convoluted route from Curzon Street, heading first to Oxford Street where I window shopped: stopping and starting randomly to get my followers accustomed to a lack of rhythm, and myself in tune with the ebb and flow of the crowds of shoppers and tourists and the more urgent weaving and dodging of workers on their lunch break. When I was satisfied, I turned south and east, wending my way through the smaller backstreets of Soho and Chinatown. Stopping seemingly randomly to check out restaurant menus or the services offered by the bars and clubs. Their services seemed little changed since my last time in London – just more overt.

The first team was replaced after thirty minutes and then the original team returned at the turn of the hour wearing different jackets and headgear. I spotted the backup vehicles too, which was clumsy: they should have been kept well out of sight, perhaps they were getting complacent. All in all, it added up to a very costly set up, but for what? Was it a snatch team? I was on full alert but after a while it seemed clear they were content to watch and follow.

By now the streets were beginning to empty a little as the lunch hour ended and I'd had enough. It was time to turn the tables. I checked my whereabouts, wondering where would be best. It would need careful timing and I was still not in full possession of my powers. It was a professional team and I couldn't predict how they'd react if I messed up. It began to drizzle again and I made my mind up, I needed the streets to be busy if this was going to work. I stopped my meandering and headed for the spot I'd picked in my head.

At times I slowed so that the watcher in the lead, anticipating I was about to cross a road, moved too soon and got cut off and isolated from me by traffic, or so that those to either side got ahead of me and momentarily lost me from their peripheral vision. It wasn't long before I could sense I was right. They were getting bored and sloppy. I made my move at the busy junction on the corner of Leicester Square.

The lead watcher crossed too soon. Those on either side, anticipating I would cross at the next signal moved forwards and past me: the crowds pressing them towards the kerb, waiting for the lights. I hung back allowing the stream of pedestrians to flow around me and the follower to my rear to close up. As the lights changed and the crowd surged forward, I made a half step to my right then hesitated, as if I were about to turn back. Out of the corner of my eye I saw the rear follower instinctively turn away to avoid coming face to face with me and in that instant, and praying I wouldn't fumble the move, I whipped off my red jacket, turned it drab side out, pulled on my beanie and turned sharply back and to the left. Without hurrying I stepped out of the margins of the crowd that was waiting to cross and instead joined the flow moving into the tube station. From behind a pillar, I held my breath and watched as my follower paused and then turned back to face the crossing and, fooled by my body language, to search for me in front and to his right – for those were the directions his subconscious mind told him I'd taken – expecting to see my red jacket and blond hair. When he couldn't find me, I saw him urgently fingering his earpiece, muttering to the microphone concealed in his sleeve. Calling out to the others who'd crossed unaware I'd 'disappeared'.

Checking the movements of each of the watchers and followers, I kept myself concealed, using the cover of the crowds and moving my vantage point. I watched as the team frantically criss-crossed the busy junction trying to figure out where I'd gone. I watched until the leader arrived with the back-up team and support vehicles; watched as he pulled out his phone. Saw his body language change, his shoulders slumping then rising defensively as he reported in. Eventually he hung up and shoved his phone in his pocket, signalling to his men. The call obviously hadn't gone well. The chastened team, cowed by the leader's withering scorn, piled into the van. He took the other vehicle. I watched as they drove off. Now it was my turn. I hailed a cab. My driver, laconic as only London cabbies can be, sniffed.

''s double rates for special services… Followin' and wotnot.' He stared at me in his rear-view mirror. I met his gaze.

'How about treble rates for a silent service?' He nodded. We drove on for several minutes before he broke the rules.

'What now guv?' The two vehicles we'd been following, a white panel van and a nondescript blue Ford, were pulled up alongside each other at the junction ahead, each indicating the opposite direction.

'Follow the Ford,' I murmured.

'You're the boss.' He muttered as he pulled out to follow the blue car through the lights.

'Yes I am.' I murmured to myself. I was pretty sure I knew where the van was headed, back to their Curzon Street base opposite the Phoenix Centre. I was more interested in who the team leader was going to report to.

'Looks like we're heading for Knightsbridge,' I volunteered to the cabbie.

'Done the Knowledge then, have you?' He sneered. It

was my turn to obey the rules. I shut up. Sometime later we pulled up and the cabbie and I watched as the team leader parked and climbed the steps to a Georgian town-house in Ovington Place. The door was opened by a tall, willowy, blonde dressed severely in a dark business suit over a starched white blouse. She stepped aside, hurrying him to enter; closing the door without the merest glance at the street. The cabbie and I sat in companionable silence until he could bear it no more.

'Well then?'

I paid him off with a generous tip and set off on foot back towards Piccadilly. I had an appointment. It was a long walk but it gave me time to think. It seemed I was going to have to move faster than I'd expected.

*   *   *

At the ostentatiously up-market and up itself solicitor's office I was greeted by one of the junior partners. The solicitors had been instructed by the Protectors. It was a firm I'd not used before,

'Mr. Samson, is it? I'm Jeremy Curtis, delighted to meet you.' He offered me a well-manicured hand. His grasp was limp. I read his disdain at my casual dress. I'd met his type before. He was in his thirties but spoke as if he was from a previous generation. Physically he was young to be a partner but mentally and psychologically he was much older. He'd probably been primed and prepared from a young age for his position in life. I knew his type but curbed my inclination to puncture his smug superiority. An inclination I knew I should have long grown out of but one that somehow was intrinsic, integral to my core psyche, my persona. Oblivious to my thoughts, to the impact he'd had on me, he continued smoothly. 'Now, how can we be of service?' I passed him the continuity papers I'd been handed by Sora-san.

'I need these confirmed and executed as quickly as possible.' He took the papers, looked them over and then laid them on his desk, uncertain how to begin.

'Um, I…Um, look I'm sure you must know this is an unusual request?' I just stared at him, allowing his discomfort to grow. I wasn't his usual type of client. I could see his self assurance weaken. 'Not a problem of course.' He offered nervously, fingering his tie. 'We've handled similar before. I just wondered…' He hesitated again and then plunged on, 'I just wondered if you'd care to explain the circumstances…' His words tailed off as I remained immobile, implacable. I could see it dawning on him why the senior partner had instructed him to handle the meeting. I gave it a moment longer and then spoke.

'No, I wouldn't care.' I saw his shoulders drop. 'Now, will you continue or should I go elsewhere?' Defeated he didn't look at me as he quickly gathered the papers and left the office.

It took a while but once the lawyers had carefully checked its origin and authenticity, they accepted the "bearer letter of authority" contained in the continuity papers. It instructed the partners to accept and acknowledge the bearer as a new and majority stakeholder in a holding company: 'PP&F Assets'. A company I'd established long, long ago and named in a moment of whimsy – Past, Present and Future Assets. In effect a shell company at the head of a pyramid of investment funds. The other minority stakeholders were ghosts, paper identities. It was a process long established by the Protectors and managed down the centuries through successive cycles and with a succession of law firms. If questions were asked the fees paid provided more than adequate answers.

A now more humbled Jeremy Curtis requested the identity and details that would be added to all the necessary paperwork. I passed him the passport I'd retrieved from Kardo Rebane's office. As Paul Mason I assumed immediate and effective control of the corporation. I was now more than solvent. I had access to accounts and assets in countries and jurisdictions across the world. Accounts and assets whose total value I'd long since lost interest in measuring.

Chapter 11

The next day, the morning was bright and mild but when I got there, there were few others in the public gardens that run along Victoria Embankment. There was little to attract visitors. The bandstand was closed. The trees that in summer blanketed the sound of the traffic were bare of leaves and the lawns were scruffy with winter growth, the flowerbeds barren except for a few weeds. I'd called her the previous evening to arrange to meet her here. She'd arrived early, but I'd arrived first. I'd been watching her for some time. I could see that Ayeesha Rao was nervous but couldn't tell why. Nervous about performing the task with which she'd been entrusted or nervous about meeting me for the second time? She was nervous but not alert. She didn't sense my approach.

'Hello, Ayeesha. Thank you for meeting me here.'

She jumped as my voice came from behind her. She craned her neck awkwardly to look over her shoulder then, flustered, swung back the other way as I stepped around the end of the bench and sat beside her. I'd got there early to see if she'd been followed. Since my last contact with the Protectors, I'd kept a low profile but now I was re-establishing contact. That put me at risk of exposure to the Seekers or the Renegades, if what Sora-san had said was true. She calmed herself.

'Sorry, you made me jump.' She smiled weakly. 'I'm glad you called. We'd been wondering… We'd expected to hear from you before now. We wondered where you were, what you've been doing.'

'Ah, well, this and that. Adjusting after the shift, you know.' I watched her as she waited, hoping for more. 'So, do you have my documents?' She nodded and handed over a bulky package.

'Three sets, one from the US in the name of John Samson, another from Brazil, in those you're Joao

Samões and a third from Finland for a Joni Salminen. Passports, identity cards, driver's licences and so on, the usual; all genuine, straight from the issuing offices and backed up by the appropriate paper and computer records.' I grunted my thanks, once again stunned by the speed with which things could be accomplished in this existence. I stuffed the package into the pocket of my coat. They'd serve until I obtained my own versions. As I started to rise, she put her hand on my arm. 'The continuity papers, they were, OK?' It was a meaningless question, designed to forestall my departure. I scanned the environment. It was an automatic reaction, but I saw no cause for alarm. I turned back, read her tension and uncertainty. There was something else… A need.

'What do you want?' I waited, shifting my position on the bench and softening my expression: signalling to her subconscious, willing her to explain, making it easier for her to do so.

'I just thought I should check…' She was still flustered, uncertain how to proceed. 'But of course they were OK.' She blushed.

'Is there something else?' I asked gently. She looked down at her hands – her fingers entwined, moving restlessly in her lap – and then back up at me.

'I wondered… I mean…'

'Just say it, whatever it is.'

'I need someone to talk to.' She said abruptly. I studied her. Physically we were the same age. Mentally the gulf between us spanned more than just centuries and lifetimes of experience. I read her again, taking more care now. I saw fear, trust, respect, helplessness, hope… And deceit. Who could resist the plea in her voice? I could but, curious, I chose not to. I stood and sighed as if taken in.

'OK, come on then.'

'Where?'

'You'll see.'

*   *   *

The view, from the suite that ran the length of the building, from the Strand to the river, was spectacular. Not that I cared. It was just a temporary base, chosen for its central location, privacy and convenience.

'This is lovely.' She breathed, running her fingers over the polished table that stood centrally in the sitting room. The tall crystal vase brimming with fresh flowers provided a delicate scent that drifted in the breeze from the French windows that I'd opened on to the balcony. The chill that had greeted me when I shifted was gone; replaced, as it so often can be in England in February, with a temporary spell of unseasonal warmth. 'Do you own this?' She'd shed her coat to reveal an elegant, simple shift dress. She stood poised, almost posed, against the light from the windows that framed her figure, accentuated her curves. I smiled, seeing in her the eagerness, ambition, greed that I too had experienced when the prospect of my future existences had first become clear to me.

'The Savoy? No, there is no need. This suite, and others like it, is booked and paid for annually through a company I set up many years ago. Suites in hotels in every major city. Whenever and wherever I return there is always a suite available for me.' I made no mention of the properties I did own and that were unknown to the Protectors. My most private residences that, since Lela had left me, and so far never returned, only I ever visited.

'And it's the continuity papers that give you access to this and control of the company when you return?'

I nodded, wondering again why she was asking questions she knew the answers to.

Ayeesha was thoughtful. 'Why do the Protectors provide their services?'

I looked at her, had to remind myself that this was only her third cycle and that she was still learning. I shrugged. 'It's what they choose to do. Are you planning to work with them?'

'No, it's not what I want. This is just temporary, while I come to terms with all this.' Her eyes glittered as she rushed to explain. 'We have so many options! We can test, try, experiment. If what we choose first doesn't fit, we can change during the next cycle! Why settle for serving others?' I could see the prospect, still new to her, excited her in ways that no longer moved me.

'And when you've tried everything and are still looking? What then?' I shook my head. I doubted I could make her understand but I'd try. 'Sometimes it's not how you live your lives, Ayeesha, it's what you live for. For some, helping others fulfils a need. That at least is how and why the Protectors began to serve. Most have cycled twenty or more times. Can you imagine how that feels?' I was wasting my breath. I knew she couldn't. Yet. She was silent for a few moments but I could see she wasn't even trying to understand. My words had simply washed over her. I felt sorry for her. I knew it wouldn't be many cycles before she too would feel a sense of loss, rather than excitement, after each shift. Loss of relationships left in previous cycles and the anguish of each new awareness. The knowledge that once again she'd been wrenched from something unknown, her existence in the transition time. I guessed she was trying to work up to what she really wanted to talk about. She surprised me.

'Why 'Jay'?' she asked eventually. I chuckled.

'Hell, I took that as my common truename too long ago to remember why now.' But memories flared unbidden. Long forgotten voices calling my names: Joshua, Jared, Jasper, Jorge, Jao, Josephine, Jahangir, John, Jules, Jasmine, Jacob, Javier, Joe… I fought to subdue them. My control had improved but was still not perfect. Frowning, I continued. 'It's an affectation, probably foolish. I've always used a forename beginning with J for my now-selves. I've done it ever since my first conscious cycle.'

'Since you were born you mean?'

'Since I first became aware.' I corrected her.

'What do you mean?'

'My psyche, my soul – call it what you will – had existed, had reincarnated through many cycles before I became aware it was happening.'

Her eyes widened in disbelief. 'You're famous as the Rink who's cycled more times than any other but you're telling me you're even older?'

'How am I supposed to define age? I only have limited access to the memories and experiences from the selves before I became aware, no knowledge at all of the times in transition, between cycles.'

She looked worried. 'This is the third cycle that I've been aware. Is my soul three cycles old or were there more, before? If so, then why did I only recently become aware?'

'Does it matter?'

'It matters to the Seekers. Isn't that what drives them: a belief that the ability to reincarnate – to become a Rink – can somehow be turned on? They are seeking the secret of awareness. And the Renegades, they believe it's possible to control the gaps between each cycle, maybe even retain the memory of the time spent in transition. They're searching for that secret. Of course it matters.' I kept my face blank, wondering who was feeding her this. 'Wouldn't it be good if all Rinks could do that? Had the power to control how and when they reincarnate, rather than it be random?' She was genuinely curious, disturbed by my apparent lack of interest.

'Maybe. Tell me, what do you think about Phems: the ephemerals, who have no reincarnation experience. Would it be good for them?'

'The Seekers?'

'Not all Phems are Seekers. Very few know that we exist, that there are Rinks living amongst them. Just suppose someone did discover how to control reincarnation – as the Renegades and Seekers are trying to – who should be allowed that knowledge?'

'I… I don't know…' Her voice tailed of as she was forced to face the complexity of something she'd thought was so simple. I shrugged.

'I don't know either. I do know that because of the Renegades' fanatical search for this power the Protectors have begun to fear them. The Seekers too are becoming more of a threat.'

'So?'

'So, it's changing how the Protectors are behaving. The Protectors first formed to help newly aware Rinks become acclimatised and to keep our existence secret from the Phems. Now the Protectors feel a need to do more. They want to protect the status quo, to prevent the Seekers and the Renegades from achieving their aims. It's fear that is fuelling the Protectors now.'

'The Protectors say the Renegades will do anything, stop at nothing, as they search for this power.'

I shrugged again. 'Maybe, or maybe that's Protector paranoia. If I have learned one thing it is that fear is corrosive; it destroys, it consumes. I will not help fan its flames and if you want my advice stay away from them. You're just beginning, you're still learning. Live, enjoy, experience what it means to be a Rink.' She was roaming through the apartment as we spoke. I saw her glance into the master bedroom. She looked over her shoulder at me. She moved on, paused as she saw the laptop and other devices set out on a side table I'd been using as a desk.

'You haven't wasted much time becoming acquainted with the new technology.' I checked there was nothing of interest to her on either of the screens and shrugged casually.

'There's a lot I need to catch up on.' She circled back and took a seat on the couch beside me. She raised an eyebrow.

'So, what is *your* purpose in life then? And when did you know what it was, after how many cycles? How do I find my purpose?' Now she was asking the questions she really wanted answered. I could read it clearly in her face, the way she held her body.

'Ayeesha.' I was exasperated but kept my tone gentle, 'Don't expect to find the answers you seek so soon. You'll find your purpose in life but as to when, or what that may be, I can't say. Have patience, enjoy that testing, those trials and experiments and choices you talked about. You're right, we are blessed with a wondrous ability, but it can also be a curse and first you must learn how to deal with it.'

'You could help me learn. We could experiment together…' There was no misunderstanding her meaning or the offer she was making. I held her gaze.

'No, I can't. But thank you.' She just stared at me, ignoring the words she didn't want to hear; she hadn't given up.

'You didn't answer my question. What drives you? What's your purpose in life?'

I sighed, knowing that my answer would shock her. I debated with myself for a moment longer then gave her what she demanded, or at least an answer that was close to the truth. 'It's no secret. Sora-san and others know and they disapprove. I too want to learn how to control this endless cycle of death and re-birth and I want to learn what happens during the transition time between cycles. No Rink has ever had a clear memory of that, or if they have, they've kept it secret.'

She gasped. 'So, you're a Renegade!'

I grimaced. 'No, that's not it. They want control for other reasons. Reasons I could never share. I want to know for a very different purpose. When I know for sure what awaits us if we're no longer reborn, and if I've learned how, then I may choose my last cycle.'

'You'd turn your back on…' Once again, she was stuck for words. 'Well, on everything? You'd really end it all?' Disbelief dripped off every syllable as she protested my words.

'Yes, everything. I've devoted myself to that goal for many cycles now. Maybe this time I will learn the secret. I want to return to the transition and stay there. Never to return to occupy or absorb another now-self.' I watched as she struggled to process what she'd heard. Watched as she considered, filtered, rejected then chose how to respond.

'And what about Lela?' She breathed, hesitant, as if nervous to broach the subject. She'd surprised me again.

'What do you know about her?' I tried but failed to dampen the crack in my voice as I snapped the question. Ayeesha looked away.

'That she was the love of your life. That you synced with her during many cycles, finding each other and renewing your love during each new awareness, but that something happened. You've had no contact with her for many cycles now.'

'So, we're the subject of Rink gossip?' I snarled.

'No! You're both legends! They talk about you with awe and sorrow. They say that to have known you and Lela when you were together was to have witnessed the greatest love story. And no-one knows why it ended, that is the greatest mystery of all.'

'Mystery?' I grimaced bitterly. 'Yes, I suppose it must be, for I have never told anyone why and, unless they are lying to me, no Rink has had contact with Lela since we were last in cycle together.'

'When was that?'

'Seven cycles ago, during the seventeenth century.'

'And the Protectors really have had no record of her since?'

'So they say.'

'Is it possible she never returned from a transition?'

I looked at her wearily. 'Yes, it's possible but I have to believe she is still a Rink and that I may yet be reconciled with her.' I had to believe it. I had to believe that I could undo the wrong I'd done her.

'So, you are driven by your own needs, the Protectors are driven by fear and the Renegades are driven by the need for control – but for a purpose you haven't explained – and the Seekers by jealousy. Are there none who would use this gift we have for a better purpose?'

'Perhaps, but it will never happen.'

'Why not? Why could we never have a common aim?'

'Because, like Phems, we're human, each with our own needs and desires. Does humanity have a common aim, beyond survival?'

'So, if our existence, our survival, was threatened – say by the Seekers and the Renegades working together – might that create the conditions for a common aim, for us to work together?'

I said nothing. The silence between us grew as I stared at her. I'd had enough. Eventually I spoke. 'You say you want my help to understand but that's not why you're here. I wondered why they picked you to deliver the papers. You're not here for answers: you're here to persuade me to work with the Protectors, to join their crusade. Was it desperation that made you offer yourself to me? Did you think that would sway me?'

I wasn't angry, nor even contemptuous. Sighing, I crossed the room and opened the door. 'I think you'd better leave now. Tell Sora-san that it didn't work.' I held the door open. 'Go on, go.' She didn't move. Slowly the expression on her face changed as my words flowed over her.

'They told me this is how you might react; and they told me what to say if you did.' I waited in silence. She gulped. 'They said that if you broke contact ...' She hesitated. 'They said that if you break contact, they will be unable to help you to find Lela. That they know where she is.'

Now the anger flared and I fought it; my neck was rigid with tension as I controlled myself. 'Leave, just leave,' was all I could manage. It wasn't the reaction she'd expected.

'But...'

'They're lying Ayeesha. They're desperate and they're lying.' I couldn't look at her anymore. I went out onto the balcony and closed the French doors behind me. I breathed deeply; quelling my anger, confusion and – despite my best efforts – a surge of hope. I'd been disappointed too often. But what if they weren't lying? Could the Protectors be trusted? If they really knew something, would I have to force the information from them?

Below me the river moved sluggishly; flotsam rocked in the swell from a tug pulling a covered barge downstream. Above me contrails patterned the blue sky as aircraft circled and held for landing slots at Heathrow. I watched as the world went about its business and I waited for calm to return. Later I went back inside. Ayeesha had gone. I was back in control and I needed to get moving. The temptation to return to the Phoenix Centre, to force the truth about Lela from Sora-san would have to wait. I wanted desperately to turn my back on them all, to return to my search for the secret of death but I knew I had no choice. Despite what I'd told Ayeesha I knew I had to find out if the Seekers and Renegades really were a threat in this cycle. It was time to acquaint myself with the enemy.

Chapter 12

I spent the next morning reviewing the security system blueprints and the layout of the house in Ovington Place that I'd followed the Seekers to. Posing as a potential client I'd persuaded a local estate agent to provide the name of the architects who'd most recently refurbished the house. Paul's skills extended way beyond programming and the tools I'd downloaded from his computers proved more than up to the task of accessing the architects' computers.

Most security systems are designed to prevent entry. Few are designed to restrict movements once a perimeter has been breached. It's been that way since the days of moats and ramparts. I'd seen numerous changes in technology since then but the basic principle remained the same. I knew that the way to beat such systems was to find the weakest point of the perimeter. In the end the solution was pretty straight forward. I quickly discounted attempting an undetected breach of the main doors, ground floor or basement windows and focussed instead on the upper storeys and roof. I spent the afternoon shopping for the equipment I'd need, finding it all readily accessible in the specialist stores that line Tottenham Court Road. Someday soon this new cycle would cease to amaze me but for now, I continued to marvel both at the technology and peculiarities of a society which demanded such products.

That night I entered the communal gardens running behind Ovington Place. The gate lock was an easy pick and I crossed the lawn towards the back of the third house in the row. A house currently vacant. The electricity was turned off in the property and the floodlights stayed dark as I moved from shadow to shadow. The sturdy Victorian waste pipe provided footholds for a straightforward climb to the mansard roofs. A narrow ledge allowed me to make my way to the central skylight where they'd cut costs and failed to fit any alarms. I jimmied the lock and slipped cautiously into the attic space, listening hard. Keeping to the edges I crept down the narrow stairs that descended from what had once been servant's quarters under the eaves. Moving stealthily through a heavily carpeted and thick-walled house was child's play. I'd survived in forests where a cracking twig meant hunger to a hunter or discovery and death to the hunted. I'd been both many times. It took me less than an hour to set up the audio and video feeds.

The following day I picked up the rental van I'd booked and headed back to Knightsbridge. It was still early and the traffic was light. I found my first parking spot in a side street close to Ovington Place. I knew I'd have to move every few hours but with luck would be able to stay within range. Crouched in the van, I set up the laptop and tablet and tuned into the wireless feeds. The batteries powering the bugs I'd set were only good for two or three days and I hoped that would be all I'd need. Reception was good and I set the monitors so the live feeds ran to disk, so I could watch and listen and, if necessary, pause and think through what I was seeing and hearing.

For the next two days there was little of interest, just routine domestic activities. Every hour or so I opened the doors to ventilate the van, then took a short stroll before moving parking places. No-one appeared to take any notice of my presence. All was peaceful in the quiet, affluent back streets. Back in the van I'd fast forward through the recording to check what I'd missed and then continued watching and listening in real time. I heard the blonde, Selene, make a few calls but none of any importance. The other occupants were a housekeeper and chauffeur. Each night I returned to the Savoy as soon as I was sure the household was asleep, returning to my post soon after dawn. I was beginning to get bored and to worry about changing the batteries when, on day three, I got lucky. I struck gold and it got more interesting, a lot more.

On the screen I watched the image from the hallway as Selene opened the front door to admit two men. I could tell, from her body language and the timbre of her voice, that she was nervous and trying not to show it as she greeted them.

'Good afternoon, Mr Pietersen, Joe. Welcome to London'. The image jumped from camera to camera as she led them through and into the main drawing room. 'Can I get you both some coffee? A drink?' I paused the feed so that I could submit the images of the two men to memory, Pietersen seemed to be the boss. He waved her offer aside as I restarted the feed.

'Later, later.' Impatience was written all over him. 'You've brought us exciting news Selene, this is fantastic, well done! I want all the details.' The sound quality from the drawing room was almost perfect. The image from the webcam, mounted high in a corner and concealed amongst the elaborate ceiling mouldings, was crystal clear. I watched as the man she'd called Joe merely nodded brusquely as they took their seats. Selene sat, perched, on the edge of her chair; her elbows resting on her knees, hands clasped as she presented her case.

'OK, well, we're still working to validate the analysis but yes, this is exciting. It could give us the breakthrough your father has been searching for.' I watched carefully. Selene was trying to moderate Pietersen's expectations.

'We've read your report but tell us again. Tell us exactly what's happened.' Pietersen urged her.

Selene's delivery was crisp and businesslike. 'A few days ago, the watch team at the Curzon Street address identified a new and unknown contact. Their IT tech couldn't a get a match in the facial recognition database. They called me immediately and I went to review the recording. Selene was anxious as she made her report; momentarily chewing the edge of an immaculately manicured nail before realising her action and snatching her hand away. The two men did nothing to put her at ease. She continued. 'I agreed with them, he was a genuine contact. He didn't hesitate at the entrance and when he entered something on the keypad the door opened almost immediately.'

The man she'd called Joe interjected. 'They still can't read what's typed on that keypad?'

'No. The visual angle is wrong and it's electronically shielded, the sensors just pick up white noise they've been unable to filter out the individual key pulses.' She made no apology though he clearly expected one.

Annoyed by the interruption Pietersen signalled to her to continue. 'So, what happened next?'

'I checked that they knew the drill, that any new contact was to be placed under full surveillance until identity details and life history have been established and investigated. That they were to provide hourly updates and a detailed report within twenty-four hours. The back-up teams arrived and then we all waited. It was about an hour before the new contact left. I watched them set up around him and begin the follow then I returned here to wait for the watch leader to report.'

'What did he look like, the new contact? I've seen the photos, but what were your impressions!' Pietersen's eyes gleamed on the video. Selene shrugged.

'Like no-one special. Just a normal man, late twenties or early thirties: casually dressed. It looked natural, as if that was his usual attire – jeans, sweat shirt, jacket. You wouldn't look twice at him in the street.'

In the van I grinned to myself.

'So, what went wrong?' Joe interrupted again; this time Pietersen didn't rebuke him. I saw Selene steel herself.

'They lost him.'

'How?' Pietersen's voice purred, but there was no warmth in it. 'Did they at least tag him, plant a GPS bug on his clothing?'

'No, they didn't get close enough.' Shit! I'd been lucky. I hadn't even thought of that. I focussed again on the screen, listening hard.

'Jesus Christ!' Joe slapped the table in frustration. 'How much do we pay those guys? OK, so what's new now? Why have we flown thousands of miles to hear this?'

Pietersen raised his hand again. 'Give her a chance, Joe,' he murmured.

Selene was assertive, almost aggressive as she rounded on Joe. 'I called you over because now we know quite a bit more. We know he's definitely a new contact. We've no prior record of him and we've been able to ascertain that shortly after his arrival at the London Phoenix Centre an update was made to the Protectors' database. The record was encoded and encrypted using an algorithm we've not encountered before but we're working to break it.' She paused, I guessed she was gathering her thoughts. 'We also know he has some exceptional skills, as he demonstrated when he evaded the watch team.'

'How did he do that?'

'We watched it on CCTV footage that Connor security were able to get from the Met police. It was simple but extremely effective.' I tuned out as she explained to the two men how I'd done it. I was busy processing what I'd just heard. That despite Sora-san's reassurance it sounded as if the Protectors database security had been breached. Pietersen's growl brought me back.

'OK, let's cut to the chase. Why do you think it's him?' He was growing impatient, again. 'That's why we're here. That's the message you sent.' Though she was outwardly self-assured I could see Selene stiffening with increasing tension. The room was silent as they waited for her answer. Joe said nothing but moved in his chair, never taking his cold eyes from her. The audio was clear enough to pick up the rustle of the material of his suit. Like a snake shifting its coils.

'We're ninety percent sure it's Jay. He's overdue for return, either that or he's been back for some time and keeping his presence secret. We think that's unlikely.'

I stopped the feed and sat back stunned. So, I wasn't just some random Rink that had drawn the attention of the Seekers. I'd been targeted. They'd been waiting, searching for me. What did it mean? I had no idea. After a few moments I restarted the feed. Selene was still talking.

'Back in the thirties, when we believe he was last in cycle, your grandfather's research teams recorded an interview with another Rink who reported that Jay was getting close to the truth. If he is back, then he'll be eager to resume his work. He'd surely make contact with a Phoenix Centre as soon as possible, and not stay hidden.'

'That interview.' Pietersen interjected. 'That was "hands on"?' I saw Joe smirk as Pietersen fastidiously avoided referring to what I assumed must have been a forced interrogation. Selene confirmed it with a nod. 'Then how can we be certain the information was accurate?' Pietersen challenged her.

I saw and heard Joe snort.

'The researchers recorded their opinion that the information was reliable. They didn't always add such annotations to information they obtained in that way.'

Pietersen shuddered. 'OK, move on what else?'

'Whilst we can't read the truename they allocated to the database entry we have another clue as to what it might be.' In the van I leant forward in dismay as Selene continued. 'The Connor Security cyber techs have been monitoring communications between known Rinks. The evening that the new contact presented himself in London an email was sent to a Protector in New York. It requested identity papers to be prepared in the name of John Samson. Samson is, as of course you know, Jay's truename and we've been told he always selects a forename beginning with J for his identities. It could be coincidence, there are other Rinks who've used a version of the name Samson, but we think it is highly unlikely.' Pietersen and Joe were nodding now: as impressed by this piece of information as I was disturbed.

'So why is there any doubt that it is Jay?' There was more respect and less challenge in Pietersen's voice now. Selene shrugged.

'I think it must be Jay but one of our analysts warned that this could be a deliberate deception by the Protectors. We know they are increasingly worried by our contact with the Renegades and they know we're very interested in Jay. It's possible they are creating a red herring, to disrupt our activities and to keep us occupied.'

Joe snorted again. 'Speculation based on limited probabilities and no facts!'

'And that's why I think the analysis is wrong!' Selene snapped back at him. 'Unlike you, Mr. Trasker I am paid to think before I act.'

I made a note: typed "Joe Trasker" into Google on my tablet.

Pietersen ignored them both. 'If we assume it is him, what's next? How do we find him?'

Selene's shoulders slumped; I could read her frustration. Trasker was glowering at her as she struggled to answer. 'Sandor asked you how you intend to find him again?' I made another note: googled "Sandor Pietersen" on a new page.

'I'm working on it!' Selene eventually spluttered, unable to retain her composure. 'We've alerted all our contacts, every watch location. We know the Renegades are working on it too. I think they may have someone in the Protectors who is a sympathiser.' Trasker and Pietersen jerked forward as she shared this news. They were surprised. I wasn't.

'We have to find him before the Renegades do!' Trasker hissed. 'Or we lose any leverage we have with those bastards. And when we do, Sandor, what then? If you agree a "hands on" approach I can get it set up, in advance.'

'No! I disagree!' Selene rounded on Trasker. 'Keep your thugs away from him, please, Mr Pietersen. I have another plan, another way.' Something about the way Selene spoke made me take a closer look at her. There was something in her eyes, a dark, disturbing eagerness seemingly connected to more than just a desire to please Pietersen.

'So? How would you proceed?' Pietersen could see it too. I watched as Selene pulled herself together, focussing her attention on Pietersen, trying to blank out Trasker's brooding presence.

'If this really is Jay then he's seen everything,

experienced everything. So, how do we break him down?' She paused to let her words sink in. 'That's the real question. We're told that in past cycles he became a yoga adept, spent years in mystical and monastic retreats, conditioned his body and mind to the highest levels of self-control in his quest to uncover the secrets of re-incarnation. We're told that somehow these acquired skills get passed to each new now-self when he shifts. Would drugs work? I doubt it. He's used them all, explored their possibilities, knows their effects and their weaknesses. We know he's renowned for his ability to read expressions and body language and to interpret other's intentions and to anticipate their actions even before they are aware themselves. He uses those same skills to influence and manipulate those around him, again without their conscious knowledge. How then could we expect to fool him to tell us what he knows? I can think of only one way to proceed. We have to be open and honest. He has to want to join with us. We have to give him a reason for wanting to do so. He has to trust us. I want to work with him one on one. In a comfortable civilised setting. No cells, decent food, access to fresh air and exercise. He needs to know who we are, what we stand for and what we want.'

'You plan to tell him everything?' Sandor Pieterson's scepticism was growing.

'No, not everything.'

'But he'd know, if he's as good as you say he is. He won't trust you if he thinks you're holding something back.'

'He'll know I'm concealing something, but he won't know what. I have to give him enough so that he believes we want some of the same things and that he can trust us enough to work with us. The need to know what I am concealing will be an added driver. If I can convince him, that the only way he'll find out is to work with us, then that could be what finally opens him up.'

'And you think you're that good?' Joe Trasker's query was almost a sneer.

'You have your ways and I have mine.' Selene hissed. She stared knowingly at the two men, defying them to challenge her again. 'You both know I can make most men do what I want, and women, you've enjoyed watching in the past.' I saw the men stir as she licked her lips.' Trasker guffawed and clapped his thigh in appreciation of the naked expression that rippled across her face. Pietersen scowled in distaste then slapped the table. His eyes were burning as he focussed on Selene.

'Enough! Selene, we're close, I can feel it, so just find him! Find Jay then tell us, but take no direct action. It'll be Joe's job to make sure we don't lose him again.' He gave Trasker a meaningful look. 'But that's all, Joe, until I decide otherwise. Meanwhile keep me fully informed. I'm due to meet with the Renegades soon.' He paused and shuddered. 'It's necessary but not something I'm looking forward to.'

I paused the feed again. The surveillance had revealed far more than I'd expected. It confirmed that the Protectors were right to be worried. The Seekers and Renegades were working together. That I was being hunted was a surprise, but nothing more; I'd been hunted before but now they were chasing the same answers as me. How much did they already know? It was time to make a plan but first I needed to complete my mental and physical reconditioning and my re-education. The knowledge I'd acquired during previous cycles was now more than ninety years out of date. Whole concepts in science had been discarded; theories had been updated and replaced. I needed to master them and to adapt to the shifts in sociological and philosophical thinking that had led to new paradigms and behaviours: an overhaul of the acceptable and unacceptable norms. It was also time for Paul Mason to disappear. Already my presence, current identity and location in this cycle were known to too many. I needed new identities that neither the Protectors nor the Seekers would know about for now.

Chapter 13

I left London the next day and for a month or so I travelled the world. Not for the novelty of it, or for my amusement. My travels were not aimless.

In Bangkok – the 'forgery capital of the world' in this here and now – I acquired a selection of passports and identity papers in various names and nationalities. Most were genuine articles, stolen then flawlessly adapted to contain images and biometric data that matched those of my now-self. Using these I established new caches of papers, credit cards and cash in safety deposit boxes in major cities. A safety net should I ever need it.

Letters of introduction from the firm of solicitors in London smoothed the way with lawyers in those same cities. Lawyers, who for substantial fees, I engaged to perform services on my behalf. Through them I gave instructions to private investigators to prepare reports on Connor Securities and to trace the ownership of the house in Ovington Place, London. I also used them to instruct a specialist transport and security firm to be on stand by.

Google had provided more information about Sandor Pietersen. He was the Chief Executive of Pietersen Industries, a multinational conglomerate founded and chaired by his father, Viktor. Joe Trasker held the title 'Director of Special Projects' and there were hints and implications in various online articles of dubious business activities. I sent investigators to find out more about them too. But my real focus was elsewhere. I searched for Lela. For any indication or trace that she might have left since we'd last been in cycle together. I'd searched before, of course, but with nothing like the tools I now had at my disposal. In my spare time I prepared myself.

When I'd taken on the Estonians, I'd been getting stronger. Now I studied, meditated and used focussed will and exercise every day to bring my brain and body back to a peak of fitness. I also built on and honed what had turned out to be some exceptional hacking skills that I'd acquired from Paul. I used them now to travel the main paths and the more remote and hidden backwaters of the world wide web. Pausing to note and sometimes to access and browse through servers whose databases stunned me with their depth and variety of content. If Paul had been able to leave the drugs alone, he might have pursued a much more lucrative and safer criminal profession. Amongst other things, I found disguised Rink websites and wondered what would become of the collaboration and communication between communities of Rinks in this cycle that was on a scale and of a kind that had never occurred before. For now, I avoided direct contact with them, preferring to monitor to watch and to learn.

Neither I nor any agents I employed found any trace of Lela. No record of any of the aliases I'd known her to use. No mention of her in any emails or online discussions – other than the occasional toe-curling reference to the 'legend of Lela and Jay'. I searched the land registry records for properties I'd known her to own and I tried to track changes of ownership or the trail of money from sales in the hope it would yield some clues. Nothing. I did the same with bank accounts. Nothing. I checked countless solicitor's records and systems looking for evidence of shell corporations and peculiar or unorthodox transfers of ownership. I found a number, used by fellow Rinks, but none of them were Lela. It was like looking for a needle in a haystack.

I looked in the obvious place, of course, the Protectors' database. As I learned from the Seekers, it was far from secure, despite Sora-san's claims. I suspected complacency rather than incompetence and without too much trouble, I found what I'd hoped for, what Sora-san had unwittingly confirmed was there – a complete record of Rink cycles over the ages. I plundered their data and I made note of some Rinks I might want to contact in person but, once again, I found no trace of her. If Sora-san had been telling the truth then any information they had was hidden elsewhere, but on balance I didn't believe him. I added another layer to the pile of scores I'd settle with him one day. For now, I left him untouched. The Protectors were seeking to manipulate me, well I could play that game too. Meanwhile I wasn't giving up. I kept looking.

As I travelled, I used my time in the different cities and cultures to further understand what was happening in the world. I experienced at first hand the novelty of travelling thousands of miles across continents, borders and oceans in a matter of hours rather than days and weeks. I used the opportunity to access and renew the language skills I'd accumulated over countless cycles. Some, obtained from now-selves in communities and nations long assimilated by others, were no longer of any practical use. Others were in sore need of an update as grammar, idioms and pronunciations had changed.

I watched the behaviour of my fellow travellers with quiet amazement and amusement. The holidaymakers for whom, on their outward journey, everything was fine no matter the delays or crowding. Holidaymakers who, for the most part, seemed so much more jaded, tired and intolerant by the time of their return journey that I wondered why they had bothered.

The hierarchy that had been so common place on the trains when I'd last been in cycle had now been transferred to air travel: First and Upper, Business and Club, Premium and Economy classes to differentiate the rich and privileged from the moderately well off and the poor. I learned how valued and important "points and miles" were to the frequent flyers who wielded their wheeled bags with ruthless efficiency as they manoeuvred deftly and sneeringly through the dawdling masses of holidaymakers who dared to impede their paths. Passengers who were proud of the status afforded by priority boarding, better seating and superior meals, but endured the same jetlag, fusty atmosphere and bone aching weariness of long-haul flights. I wondered how and when the miracle of universally accessible, rapid global travel, had become such a tawdry, tiresome, under-valued and under-appreciated experience.

As I searched for Lela I trawled too for evidence of the Renegades and Seekers. There was plenty of it. Since arriving in this cycle, I'd been struck by the inequalities I'd seen. The gap between the haves and the have-nots. It had always been thus of course – in every cycle, in every civilization and community that I'd inhabited – but this time there was a difference. Where before the gaps had mostly been between the ruling/controlling elite and the proletariat within communities and countries, there were increasing gaps, now, between whole nations of haves and have-nots. And behind too much of it I detected the malign influence of the Renegades.

The Renegades were, every man and women of them, sociopaths of the first order. There was no other way to describe them. They were Rinks who'd given into the unlimited and unrestricted freedoms our existence allowed. For them, the here and now was nothing more than a playground in which they could indulge their every whim and fantasy. Relishing in ever increasing extremes of behaviour until each cycle ended. Resetting and renewing their hungers and thirsts after each new shift. Above all, they loved interfering in the ways of the Phems: finding ways of escalating the exploitation and suffering of mere individuals to whole societies and mass populations. They were less evident in the developed world. Their activities blunted and neutralized by more stable regimes, democracies, law and order, though their impact on crime and prostitution was clear. I recognized at least two serial killers as Renegades I'd come across before, and I suspected several others. Elsewhere they ran wild. In the Middle East and in Africa. Internal revolutions that had grown and spilled across borders were being fuelled by jealousy and religious fundamentalism stoked and inflamed by Renegades who sated themselves amidst the chaos. I looked for signs that their influence was somehow being recognised but saw only actions being taken to increase the haves' security and isolation. I tried to tell myself it was none of my business. I'd never concerned myself with the world of the Phems before, so why should I now?

I saw several Rinks in the papers and on TV, on-line, some in movies: Rinks who occupied positions of power or prestige in the Phem world. I didn't recognise their physical now-selves, of course, it was the subtle markers that identify all reincarnated souls that gave them away. I made no attempt to contact these, leaving each to his or her own devices. We all had our own reasons for choosing the way we lived during a cycle in the here and now. I saw few fellow Rinks in the flesh, which didn't surprise me. Collectively we made up a miniscule proportion of the world's population at any one time. I chose not to make contact with most of those I did encounter and they, following the accepted protocol, respected my privacy as we went our separate ways. None of them were Renegades and I'm not sure what I would have done had I met one. None of them were Lela either.

There were two I did spend time with. Rinks I sought out. Rinks like me who'd had centuries of experience in the here and now, through cycles almost as numerous as my own. I found both living in relative seclusion. Each had long since satisfied their appetites for material possessions and physical pleasures and now spent their time, before returning to the transition, satisfying other needs. One had retreated to monastic life and a contemplation of the unknown, the other had taken a similar but more active path as a professor of theoretical physics in a major university. From each I sought their views on the changes I could see in this here and now. Both agreed that the changes were occurring on a scale and with a rapidity that they'd never seen before but each was detached, distant. For them it was just another Phem phenomenon. One of countless others they'd observed, endured and, in time, would file and remember with interest. There was always another cycle, why be concerned?

They did add one thing that was new. 'Was I aware that Rink cycles appeared to be getting shorter? That there were reports of Rinks whose cycles seemed to end abruptly?' Reports of mysterious accidents, unexpected deaths from "illnesses" and straight forward disappearances. I asked for details, confirmation. They'd shrugged. 'Check with the Protectors', they said, before signalling they'd had enough of the conversation. Their indifference troubled me. Was I alone in being concerned? Had I changed, or had they? Had I been like them, had something about this cycle changed me? I knew there was no point in contacting the Protectors. I'd known Sora-san was hiding something, maybe this was it, but I also knew he'd never answer a direct question. I'd have to find another way, and it looked as if I'd have to do it alone.

Chapter 14

On two occasions I revisited London, once following a dead-end lead in the search for Lela. On neither occasion did I seek out Meg. I thought about her often, too often, but I controlled the temptation. On the second visit I was hopeful of a very different and more fruitful outcome.

I had no concerns that Paul Mason might be wanted in connection with the killing of the drug dealers. I hadn't radically changed my appearance but no-one would confuse the sleek, suited businessman that I'd become with the dissolute drug dealer he'd been, and my new credentials and papers were impeccable. I used my newly honed skills to check the police systems and sure enough found that Paul was among the quarter of a million missing persons reported each year in the UK but I found no evidence that there was any active search to locate him. I was surprised, therefore, to detect a tail as I left the London City airport. There were two of them and they took the next carriage as I boarded the Docklands Light Railway. I'd intended travelling all the way into the city but instead I got off at West India Quay and headed north, leading them away from the busy walkways and towering buildings of Canary Wharf and into the quieter, narrow side streets that thread their way amongst the terraces of low-cost housing and light industrial units. I figured that by now they would have called for back-up and that I needed to act quickly. After a few minutes I led them into a cul-de-sac, bordered on three sides by high fencing that screened us from view. I turned to face them. I wanted to question them, to find out how they'd identified me and been able to track me but they didn't give me a chance. They tried herding me into a corner.

'Mr. Samson, we don't have to do this, our client only wants a word. She's coming now. Can we do this the easy way?'

She? Selene? They were speaking to distract me, not expecting I'd comply. I stood my ground, watching to see which of the two would come at me first. It's usually the smaller man – the one with the most to prove – who is more aggressive. But it was the shorter of the two who began to hang back. So, I focussed on the taller man, waited until he was close enough and signalling his intentions. A vicious looking baton whipped and extended as he snapped his wrist.

The trouble with weapons is that they become the focus of the attacker. The tall man was so intent on landing a blow he forgot everything else. I swayed and avoided his swing, let my weight settle on my hind leg and then powered forward extending my leading leg, transferring my weight as my foot crunched through his knee joint. He collapsed with a tortured scream. One down. I turned my attention to the short man. I'd been wrong; he was smarter, not weaker. That's why he'd hung back. He was good, very fast and I'd not shown him enough respect. I swayed to avoid the thrust and his knife ripped through my jacket. I felt the sting as it slashed skin and muscle. Until that moment I'd been prepared to let them go with a warning. Damaged, yes, but otherwise I'd have let them both live to fight another day. Shorty changed that. It was my turn to retreat as I tested how much he'd hurt me. Without taking my eyes from him I fingered the wound, felt blood flowing but not pulsing uncontrollably. The gash was deep but hadn't penetrated the abdominal wall. I was good to go but I signalled otherwise, luring him in as I winced and curled protectively. He stabbed viciously but, overconfident, he'd made his move too early. I grabbed his knife hand and felt the soft tissues in his wrist tear as I grasped the hilt of the knife, reversed it and pounded it deep into his chest. His eyes rolled back and the whites greyed and dulled as I eased his lifeless body to the ground. Two down.

As I turned back to him the tall man watched in silent agony, his teeth gritted against the pain as he lay curled, clutching his ruined knee. He'd seen what I'd done to

Shorty and as I leant over him, I showed him how little it meant to me. He shuddered and I knew I could ask him anything and be sure of his answers. There was more than fear in his eyes.

'You're from Connor Security, yes?' He nodded. 'How did you find me?' He swallowed hard, controlling the pain so he could speak.

'Border security, facial recognition...' He forced the words out.

I thought about it. It made sense. It also told me I still hadn't grasped the power of this cycle's technology. I hadn't considered this. I should have thought about the increased risk of using the London City airport, so much smaller than Heathrow or Gatwick – London's major airports – so, fewer passengers and an increased risk that I might be identified. I needed to do better. I looked him in the eye, saw him cringe as he read just how pissed I was. I knew he was only a low-level operative, unlikely to know more. It was decision time.

'Tell your client. No more warnings. No-one else gets a second chance. You're the last.' His face, white from shock and the pain in his knee, flushed red with relief as the realisation that he was to be spared coursed through him. He was nodding vigorously, beyond words, as I checked the entrance to the cul-de-sac. It was all clear. We'd not attracted any attention. I left him to explain the body. I didn't care how.

As I'd thought, the wound was not as bad as I'd feared. Blood seeped now, rather than flowed. As I walked, I was able to staunch it with a handkerchief and hide it beneath my jacket. I bought a basic first aid kit from a pharmacist and superglue from a hardware store and in my hotel room that night I washed and cleaned the wound before using glue and tape to seal the edges. With some focussed healing I knew I'd be fully recovered within a matter of days. I'd been lucky. I'd show more respect next time.

*   *   *

The following morning, I was a little stiff but otherwise unhindered by the injury. I rose early, shopped for supplies and filled my daypack before a cab dropped me close to Trafalgar Square. I prepared myself for what I knew might be a fruitless wait. Cockspur Court, running behind Admiralty Arch and in front of the British Council building is one of the few streets in London not visible on Google Street View. There is little of interest in the dead-end street but the guarded emails I'd intercepted between Sandor Pietersen and Selene, combined with the conversation I'd overheard, were enough to lead me to believe there'd be a meeting with the Renegades there sometime that day. From my vantage point I could see all lines of approach.

I was replacing my water bottle in my daypack, wondering if I had enough to last the day when I saw the man shouldering his way through the crowds gathered around Nelson's Column. It was just after midday. Office workers lunched on the steps and benches, grateful for a few minutes in the Spring sunshine. The tour buses had just discharged their cargoes to fight for position for group photos in front of the famous lions. Head down, Iril Karzan bulled his way between them and I could tell he was hating the crowds. That, as much as anything, is what had caught my attention. I'd prepared myself for it, but this was not good. Amongst the Renegades, Karzan was close to the top of my list of the most bestial and brutal of them all. His aura was unmistakeable. I'd encountered him before and I knew how he hated cities. I could almost read his mind as he inhaled the stale, re-breathed air, the melange of manufactured smells – fast food, exhaust fumes. I knew that the dismissive contempt he felt for the crowds was automatic, inbred. It had never left him: a legacy of his first cycle, of life on the Steppes when he'd ridden in the great Khan's wake. I was in no doubt that his first-cycle experience had imprinted personality characteristics indelibly on his psyche. I was also in no doubt that if he was here, others would follow. I watched as he impatiently brushed aside an elderly

Japanese lady. A tour guide looked angrily at him as she helped the old woman regain her balance and opened her mouth to remonstrate but he was gone, his broad back and shoulders impervious to her glare. She didn't know how lucky she was that Karzan had other things on his mind that day.

Not long after that I watched Sandor Pietersen follow Karzan past the archway to Cockspur Court. I waited patiently. Karzan was a serious player but I feared there would be another attending. An hour later my patience paid off. This one I knew even better than Iril Karzan. We'd had more than just encounters in the past. And I wished it could have been anyone other than him that I saw arriving now. His presence in cycles throughout the ages was well chronicled in the history of human misery. Caligula, Torquemada, Jack the Ripper were the most well-known of the now-selves he'd used to satisfy his lust, his need to dehumanise his victims. Protectors had orders to kill him on sight, to keep him in transition and out of cycle for as long as possible. His presence in this here and now had been kept so secret I'd had to come here today to confirm it. I watched until Dandy Tom, the most immoral and dangerous soul who'd ever lived, entered the dark doorway at number 13. For a moment I considered following him, thought about a confrontation but I had what I'd come for. I knew, now, who I was dealing with. I picked up my daypack and searched for another cab. I wouldn't need to worry about finding Pietersen or the Renegades again. I already had plans for that. When I confronted them, it would be on my terms, and it wouldn't be long now. That night I headed for Switzerland.

Chapter 15

I'd experienced so many bizarre coincidences over the centuries that it was almost tempting to believe that they weren't random. But I'd also seen the ruinous effect of beliefs in "higher powers" and in spurious religions. As a result, the temptation was at best weak. Still, as coincidences go, this was a doozy.

When I'd chosen Geneva as the discreet, secure location for an institute researching the secrets of reincarnation, there'd been no sign that, in time, the city would also become globally renowned as the location for mankind's greatest endeavour – to discover the secrets of the physical universe.

I'd founded the International Institute for Philosophical Studies, based in a grand old house on the shores of the lake, at a time when the facilities at CERN – the Conseil Européen pour la Recherche Nucléaire – had occupied only a simple shed-like laboratory on the outskirts of the city. The scientists employed there had been focussed on studying the little understood atomic nucleus. There had been no sign, then, that within three generations the focus would have expanded to all of high energy and particle physics and that the Large Hadron Collider would have been built in a vast ring of underground tunnels running for twenty-seven kilometres, crisscrossing the Swiss and French borders.

Sora-san had been right. The pace of change during my absence was as nothing I'd ever experienced before. So much had happened that it was no wonder that I had trouble absorbing it all. Now, as I entered the premises of the IIPS, I smiled to myself. During the previous weeks I'd immersed myself in a review of the scientific, social and political developments but whilst news articles and the academic literature were full of reports about CERN there had been no significant coverage of the IIPS. That the work of the IIPS was, in my expectation, at least as likely to impact the future of mankind as the work at CERN was not something the world needed or would be allowed to know.

The Director's office was on the ground floor, not on one of the upper floors with views looking out over the lake as one might have expected. It was a necessity. Access for Director Lindt's wheelchair was facilitated by the ramp that marred the symmetry of the building's façade. The planners had been unable to prohibit it but the building was old and its protected status precluded the installation of a lift. I presented myself to the receptionist who, after a brief phone call, buzzed me through to an inner office where I was greeted by Lindt's personal assistant.

'Joni Salminen?' The tall effete young man looked me up and down as if trying to gauge my worth and status. His gaze was haughty, almost imperious. Another of life's individuals so insecure and unsure of their own worth that they feel impelled to constantly assert themselves. I should have been the bigger man. After all my cycles of experience why did I still react to bullying popinjays – an ancient term, but one that has never been bettered. I guess it's just part of my make up. So, I bullied back. I waited a beat before replying.

'You are?' I said simply, pointedly ignoring his question.

'Ulrich Fanderl,' came the crisp reply. 'Personal Assistant to Director Lindt.' Fanderl held himself stiffly alert as if still waiting for me to acknowledge his importance and to justify my presence. I allowed another beat or two to pass.

'Then, Ulrich' – using his first name as a deliberate put down – 'you know who I am as the receptionist has already told you, and now you are delaying my appointment with the Director. An appointment you surely know about… As her Personal Assistant.' I made the title sound trivial, unimportant.

'Mr Salminen–' Fanderl began but was cut off as I interjected firmly but quietly,

'Dr. Salminen.'

Fanderl was flustered. 'My apologies, Dr. Salminen, yes of course I was aware of your appointment. May I ask what it concerns?'

I paused, as if considering the request, 'No.' I continued waiting, enjoying his increasing discomfort. Fanderl coloured, unused to being rebuffed and dismissed so effectively, then capitulated as gracefully as his annoyance would allow.

'In that case, please follow me, I shall not delay you further.' He led the way down a corridor to a pair of ceiling high double oak doors, knocked and then opened both standing aside to allow me to enter as he announced, 'Dr Salminen from Finland to see you, Director.'

'Thank you, Ulrich,' I murmured.

'Director, may I remind you your next meeting is in thirty minutes?' Fanderl said pointedly. 'Shall I sit in on this meeting to take notes?' He posed it as a question but made to close the doors and to pull up a chair for himself. Alexandra Lindt had wheeled herself from behind her desk to shake my hand. Irritated by Fanderl's tone she swivelled to face him.

'No, that will be all, Ulrich, thank you. You may leave us.' She turned back then added, 'Oh, and please tell the Director of Finance that this meeting may overrun, I'll call him when I am free.' Fanderl scowled as he gave a stiff bow, exited and closed the doors. Alone, we gazed at each other for long moments.

'Is it really you?' she said finally. 'After all these years?'

'Yes, Sindri,' I answered quietly. 'It's me.'

'Sindri?'

'Sindri Lundsdottir, do you really doubt me?' At my use of her truename she sagged in her chair. I waited calmly until I saw acceptance and recognition sweep away the confusion from her eyes.

'It's been so long. I'd begun to fear we'd not sync again during this cycle.' She reached out and I grasped her frail hand, her skin, leathery and wrinkled against my soft, taut palm. The reverse of when we'd last touched, so many years before. I leant forward and kissed her gently.

'It's so good to see you again my old friend.' She rested her head against mine and for a moment we allowed our memories to re-establish the bond between us.

We'd first come into contact one or two cycles after I'd lost Lela. I couldn't be exactly sure when, that period was lost to me in a haze of depression and drugs that Sindri had helped me escape. Since then, we'd synced and found each other twice: during one cycle both enjoying youthful contemporary now-selves. I doubted we'd ever be lovers again, should the opportunity even arise. That was done between us. It had been fun, as all true passion should be, but was not the basis for our bond. When I'd seen her last, she'd vowed to continue my quest as I'd prepared to end that cycle. As her now-self matured she'd built the IIPS into what it had become today. She pulled back and raised her hands to hold my face, looking deep into my eyes.

'I don't have it, Jay.' Her lips trembled, I saw sorrow in her face, heard defeat in her words.

'I didn't expect you to have.' I brushed the back of my fingers lightly down her cheek. 'Be at peace; don't be so hard on yourself. Tell me what you do have and then I have news for you. Trust me. We're close, as close as we've ever been.' I watched as relief and hope sparked new life in her eyes.

'Then let's begin. It's so good to see you but I'm tired of this cycle, this body. I must end it soon but first give me reason to believe our goal is within our grasp.'

Because I wanted to, not because she needed me, I manoeuvred her wheelchair into position by her desk and made her comfortable. I pulled up a chair. We had a lot to cover, would need days, a week or so to assimilate it all. I could tell I'd arrived just in time, that she was reaching her limit. I didn't tell her that I too was under a time pressure. I knew it would take them a while to organise but now that I'd come out into the open it wouldn't be long before they acted. I wondered who would come for me first, the Seekers or the Renegades; maybe both, together.

Chapter 16

Sindri and her team had done an amazing job. Before I'd ended my cycle and returned to the transition, we'd known a great deal about the concepts of reincarnation, and not just from our own experiences. We'd known that a belief in rebirth or reincarnation was common to many cultures. It was to be found the world over. In developed, complex literate cultures as well as in simple, tribal non-literate cultures. In fact, it was so commonplace that some academics were arguing that the belief arose contemporaneously with the origins of human culture – though none went as far as to argue that it was a real phenomenon, or proposed any explanation as to why or how the phenomenon, if that's what it was, had first occurred.

In the decades since I'd last seen Sindri her researchers had scoured the world for any and every scrap of information, myth, belief, legend and report that related to re-incarnation. They'd catalogued and cross-referenced examples in the classical philosophies, religions and mythologies of India, Greece, Africa and Egypt, in aboriginal lore in Australia, the pacific islands and South America and in just about every philosophy and religion, whether mainstream, such as Christianity, Islam, Hindu and Buddhism, or cult, like Scientology or Rosicrucianism.

They'd investigated and cross-examined every Phem who'd declared an experience of reincarnation and they'd interviewed every Rink who was willing to participate in the research. As the age of the internet dawned, their access to information had undergone a step change and the content of the Institute's databases grew exponentially. Finally, I was able to see and truly understand the advantages of social media, which had so bewitched the people of this cycle. Without it Sindri and her team would never have been able to build and maintain the network of contacts that they had. They compared the results of those interviews with religious and other teachings and philosophies, searching for a common thread, a common understanding or rationale for reincarnation. They didn't find one. The purpose or process of reincarnation was variously held to be: to allow an individual to progress through levels of attainment, to "ascend" to a euphoric state of being; or that it was to allow an individual to make amends for a previous life – a cruel man might be reborn as a pious saint (positive reincarnation); or that it was to punish an individual – a greedy man might return as a hog (negative reincarnation). There were endless variations on similar themes. All of which revealed more about the psychology of mankind than it did about any definitive purpose for reincarnation, let alone the processes that governed it. They hadn't found the secret but it was nonetheless valuable work. It revealed what we didn't know.

They'd done all of this through agencies and proxies, using research grants dispersed to universities and colleges and investigators hired through third parties and cut-outs. Everything that had been learned had been returned to and processed by the small team at the Institute, the purpose and existence of which had otherwise remained discreetly in the background. The Protectors were aware that something was going on but so far, our security seemed to have held. We didn't need their help and didn't want their interference. We had, however, wanted their knowledge and I'd known they'd never have willingly shared it with us. That didn't matter now, I'd been given the tools to bypass their consent and I'd used them.

'This is incredible, Jay!' Sindri's eyes had sparkled with excitement when I revealed the contents of the Protectors' database. Records of every known Rink cycle. For each individual a record of how long they had been in transition between cycles. The age at which they'd left a cycle and the age and sex of the now-self they'd shifted into at the next. Data stretching back millennia. Data that had long been collected on paper, distributed around the world but protected and preserved. Data now consolidated, digitised… and no longer secure. Data I'd raided from the Protectors' database. 'But it's also terrible! If you have this the Seekers may also! And the Renegades!'

I shrugged. 'Maybe, but I'm not so sure. Most of the detail behind the primary records was very well shielded and encrypted. I had to develop new skills and tools to penetrate the defences. And when I'd seen and taken what I needed I rebuilt the defences and sent instructions to Sora-san and the Protector leadership telling them what I'd done and urging them to take greater precautions. Maybe it was too late, that's another thing I have to find out, but let's hope not.' Sindri looked at me quizzically.

'Find out? How?'

I smiled. 'Don't worry about that. Now, to work!' And work we did. For days we worked on developing pattern-matching algorithms: looking for correlations between the age of a Rink before and after each shift; the length of time in transition; geographical movements – Rinks who left cycle in one continent and shifted back into another; changes in sex or sexual orientation. We looked for anything that might yield some clue as to what governed or influenced the mechanism of reincarnation. Any clues that we could contrast and compare with the few leads that had been thrown up by the rest of the Institute's work.

We also knew, from the Institute's extensive research, that in nearly all cases the religious or spiritual belief in reincarnation was accompanied by a belief in a between times existence. Plato had described it most poetically, claiming that "souls travel to the plains of forgetfulness to take up residence on the banks of the river of indifference", then later, leaving "like so many shooting stars" to be reborn. The most consistent theme was that souls or psyches were sent from the between world, from the transition, to make amends for past transgressions and to improve the world of the living but we had so many questions. Was what we Rinks experienced in fact reincarnation, as described in religious beliefs? Or something else – transference? For millennia we'd referred to ourselves as Rinks but very few of us shifted into new-born bodies. Mostly we became aware in adult bodies of varying ages and merged with their personas, acquiring their knowledge. For Sindri this was a fundamental question. For myself I didn't see that it mattered much. Whatever the philosophical differences between reincarnation or transference the fact was that in both cases the soul or psyche went somewhere during the transition. Where was that and why couldn't we retain any memory of it?

I didn't tell Sindri but this felt like my last chance to find the answers. In previous cycles I'd tried exploring every mystical, spiritual and philosophical avenue to unlock the secrets of reincarnation without success. So now I was applying the religion of this era – science – to try and find the answers. We'd try applying logic, reason and analysis where introspection, contemplation and imagination had failed. In all honesty, did I expect to succeed? No, I didn't. But I'd committed to myself that I'd live trying.

We worked long hours.

Each day I monitored the environment around the Institute but detected no immediate threat. When I was sure the analysis was safely underway, managed and co-ordinated by a re-energised Sindri I decided to leave them to it and to risk a short trip. I had another itch I needed to scratch.

Chapter 17

I'd tried but couldn't get it out of my mind that the Phems were at a greater risk from the Renegades than ever before. I'd tried telling myself it was none of my concern; that I should focus on my own objectives, but it was no good. I couldn't say why, but for some reason I felt compelled to try and do something. I wasn't sure what was driving me, why it seemed so important. If I was honest, I had another reason for seeking a distraction. I'd put aside the disappointment that thus far I'd failed to find Lela. I told myself there was time yet, but now another hope was threatening to consume me. The hope that this time we might, just might finally find the answers I'd sought for so long – the secrets of reincarnation. I tried to control it; I wasn't sure how I'd handle another disappointment. So, by way of displacement therapy, I was on my way to see an old friend, Sven.

He'd been easy to reach, thanks to the network that now connected the Rinks of this cycle. Our communications were guarded. Short emails, ambiguous in meaning to those not in the know, as we established that each of us was who we claimed to be. We'd agreed to meet in Vancouver. His public profile made it difficult for him to change his schedule or for him to escape the scrutiny of his entourage for a private meeting, but we managed it.

Vancouver was one of the places I'd never been to before. I'd been to Canada, though, one short cycle of unremitting misery. A century or so before, I'd shifted into the consumptive, tuberculosis ridden body of a fur-trapper eking out a pitiful living in the North West Territories. I'd spent a frostbitten, lung wrenching winter in a decrepit log cabin. Alone and scared in the dark desolate landscape until, unable to bear it any longer, I'd awkwardly arranged the musket, manoeuvring it until I could blow my head off and myself back into transition. It was just one of the experiences that drove me to find the secrets of reincarnation. Why had I shifted into such a body? What purpose could there have been in that? There had to be a purpose. The idea that this was all just random was unacceptable.

Sven and I met on Vancouver Island, at the State capital, Victoria. As a junior member of the US Senate, he was on a fact-finding mission to British Columbia, researching global warming. I flew in by float plane from the mainland. One of the many ways I'd travelled, one of my favourites. As we crossed the Straits of Georgia I looked down and saw sailboats criss-crossing between the green forested islands. A wheeling chaotic flock of sea-birds chased a trawler home and I imagined I could hear their raucous cries. As we banked and turned and dropped into our final approach I scanned the seas with the other passengers, anxiously looking out for any semi-submerged logs that might have escaped from the corralled rafts being towed from the logging camps to the lumber yards. Stray logs that every few years fatally surprised even the most seasoned of pilots. It was still one of my favourite ways to travel. The engine roared then died away as the pilot flared-out into the landing. The floats kissed the swell then caught and our seat belts bit as the drag slowed us more rapidly than a ground landing. There are other ways to get to Victoria – ferry, helicopter, regular direct flights to the main airport – but one of the advantages of the float planes is that after a short taxi we disembarked on a jetty at the heart of the city's waterfront.

I'd arrived early to look around and found that it was possible to walk across Victoria in less than an hour. As state capitals go, it was as small as British Columbia is vast. I liked that. Despite my bad experience I'd come to like Canada and its lack of pretensions. Most of the streets follow a grid pattern, some didn't and broke the otherwise boring and predictable symmetry. The architecture was a mixture of quaint and faintly bizarre, some of it almost Disneyesque in character. Curiously, whatever route I took seemed somehow to guide me back to the quay-side and the hotels that lined the esplanade and the shorefront.

Senator Eduardo Torres and I met for a private lunch in his hotel room. His aides and other members of the entourage, dismissed for a few hours, were leaving reluctantly as I arrived.

'They're worried about you.' He grinned as we shook hands, for show really. It's not a Rink habit. The door closed and we were alone.

'Worried, why? What did you tell them?'

'That you're an old friend, now working for one of the green lobbyists. They're worried you'll be able to exert too much influence over me if they're not here to protect me.'

I snorted. 'That's rich. Have they no inkling of the influence you're exerting over them?'

He chuckled. 'Not yet.' He looked me over, still unsure as to why I'd tracked him down. 'You're new in cycle then, Jay? Still on your quest? The search for the end?' I grinned at him. We'd known each other for centuries, not quite as friends but each respecting the other.

'Yeah, I'm newly shifted and yes, I'm still searching. Got any good leads for me?' He grinned back.

'C'mon, you know that's not my thing.' His aides had left us a tray of drinks. He poured and we toasted each other, taking a moment to remember. Through the window I watched as another float plane banked into its final approach then landed with a flurry of water and a roar from its engine.

'So, why are you here, Jay?' he asked quietly, serious now.

I shrugged. 'The honest truth? I'm not sure. But, if you'll agree, I may need your help.' He said nothing, just raised an eyebrow as I tried to explain. 'This is like no other here and now I've ever been in. There's something wrong, things move too fast, there are too many extremes and everything feels out of balance. It's unstable.' I shook my head. 'Sorry, I'm not making any sense.'

He looked at me, puzzled. 'Unstable? Isn't it always? That's the way of the Phems.'

'I know, but it's not just the Phem world, it's the Rinks too. Don't you feel it, this growing tension between the Protectors and the Renegades? And the Seekers, they know a lot more, maybe too much.'

'And you're here to ask me to do something about it?' He looked at me sceptically, his disbelief so apparent I couldn't help but laugh, breaking the tension and dispelling some of the gloom I was casting.

'OK, OK.' I held my hands up. 'Just do me a favour and think about it. Think about it and tell me if you agree, that there's something wrong this time. Then, maybe, we could do something together.' I decided to leave it at that for now. I knew him well enough to know that he respected me for my depth of experience, the lives I'd led, the things I'd seen. That he'd take me seriously. I changed the subject. 'You haven't changed then. You plan to do it again? You're still the "Dark Master"?' It was his turn to shrug.

'It's what I do, it's what drives me just as you are driven. We have different ambitions that's all. And, by the way, I don't like that name.'

'"Dark Master"? I didn't coin it. It was one of your then-self's brothers wasn't it, during your African adventure?'

He grimaced. 'Yeah, Mhlangana, my bastard half-brother; right after he and Dingane killed me.'

'I wasn't around, but I shifted into cycle just after. The world was full of the news of Shaka ka Senzangakhona's exploits – Shaka-Zulu. One of your few failures.'

He looked rueful, held up a thumb and finger.

'I came this close, would have succeeded but for the jealousy of my half-brothers. I should have seen it coming. Still, I've had plenty of successes: before then, and since.'

'So, you'd prefer Sven, then?'

'I like it better.' He tried for nonchalance but failed. He

couldn't help it. It appealed to his vanity. During one cycle he'd broken his own rules and revealed himself to a Phem, seeking to enlist her in one of his schemes. Rumours began to spread of a man who manipulated others and decades later, when he returned in cycle, he found himself fictionalised as Svengali... And so, Sven he'd become.

For him it was a game. In each cycle he sought to unify peoples, build empires. Not maliciously, like the Renegades, or in order to exploit the Phems for his own benefit and aggrandisement. He did it because it was the ultimate test of his skills. I could influence and manipulate individuals but he could do it on a grand scale. He could manipulate whole societies. Sometimes he succeeded beyond his wildest expectations and wrote his name in the Phem history books as yet another great charismatic leader – Alexander the Great, Genghis Khan. More often he failed – Atahualpa, Shaka-Zulu – these too made the history books but were likely to be overlooked by Sven when he regaled others with his exploits.

Occasionally, but rarely, he tried to do it from behind the scenes rather than as the figurehead. He'd had mixed success as Cicero, Machiavelli, Rasputin, but countless times the game had come to nothing. His attempts squashed, snuffed out as he tried to influence and compel his followers but before they could grow to a size that protected him. Shaka-Zulu, the now-self he'd propelled to the brink of unifying first the Zulu nations and then a broad swathe of tribes across Africa during the nineteenth century had been one of his more painful failures.

'I came that close!' He repeated now, but his grin was rueful. 'Still, better luck this time hey?'

I couldn't help it. His grin was infectious and I laughed. 'So, what is it this time?' I saw him tense.

'Who's asking?'

I was puzzled. 'Just me, why?'

He shook his head uncertainly. 'Ah... I don't know, it's just the last few times I've felt there's something acting against me...'

'Something more than the will and common sense of the people you try and enslave to your megalomania?' His head snapped up.

'That's harsh!'

'Is it? Do you really think about the Phems? What you do to them, the wars, suffering, millions of deaths…'

'… Is no different to what they do to themselves! Look at Julius Caesar, Napoleon, Adolf Hitler, I had nothing to do with them. They weren't Rinks and they did more than I've ever done. Phems long to be led, it's a fact. I exploit that, no more than they do themselves.'

He was right. I couldn't argue. Some of what he'd done had actually benefited the development of Phem civilisations. Any collateral misery and suffering were never his intention or aim; I knew that in his heart he was nothing like the Renegades.

'So, this time…? What…? It's time for the Americans to have an empire?'

He gave me a shrewd look. 'You picked up on that pretty quick.'

'I've known you a long time.'

He grinned and shrugged. 'I thought it might be worth a try. Why not? Look at their recent history. There's a pent-up core of Republican nationalists just waiting to be unleashed. Before that, the Bush dynasty might have tried if they hadn't lost confidence. If I don't give them a purpose and aim someone else will. Who's to say they'll be more benevolent than me?'

'Seriously?'

'Why not. Why should they be the only superpower never to have had an empire? Russia had one and is trying to build another – led by a Phem I might add. China has had several and is acquiring another through economic power and cyber-stealth and meanwhile fundamentalist Islam is trying to rise and acquire a nation, maybe an empire… So, what am I doing that's so wrong?'

'Maybe you're using your abilities and influence to lead them down a path they'd otherwise never take.'

'And maybe, if you understood it, you'd know that's not how it works. Hitler and Mussolini proved it in the Second World War, and before them, Napoleon. People follow because they want to be led and they follow most strongly when they're offered their basest needs and dreams. I'm going to offer the American people what they want, they just haven't admitted it to themselves yet.'

'And how do you intend to pull it off? Are you going to be the figurehead or the puppet master?' He pulled a sour face.

'I'm done with that as an experiment.' He hesitated, unwilling at first to share his plans and then shrugged, why not? 'I'm going for the figurehead this time. The new administration won't last. It's got one term at best.'

'And then you plan to stand?'

'No, not as President, I'll be the vice-president of choice!'

'And then?'

'You know what they say, "the Presidency is only a heartbeat away".'

'You'd kill to take his place?'

'Or hers. Not literally, no, but it wouldn't be the first time a President got impeached for some irregularity, or forced to resign through ill-health. That I could and would arrange.'

'You've got it all worked out, have you?'

'No, just the next steps. We both know that acquiring power means nothing. It's what you do with it that matters.'

'But you'll try?'

'That's the fun of it!'

'Fun? You're sure? I'm beginning to understand this world, how fragile it is. By the time you're in position the Russians will be stronger, the Chinese more entrenched. You think they'll stand by and let you make your moves?'

'So, maybe I won't risk coming into confrontation with the Russians or China, and certainly not Europe. South America is where I'd start. It's weak economically and militarily. Drug trafficking and illegal immigration will give us the pretext. It's a no-brainer.'

'You really think the other powers wouldn't oppose you?' He shrugged.

'The Chinese are too busy attacking their primary commercial targets in Europe and too concerned with expanding their influence across into India and Indonesia. If I do it right, they'll protest but do little more. The Russians are too occupied in Europe and the Middle East to react in the way they did in the past, communism is no longer a strength in South America. As for the Europeans stopping me? Well, they'd have to actually unite first!'

I was stunned by the simplicity of his thinking. This really was a game to him, nothing more. 'And you really think you can manipulate the American people into supporting this? For years they've been isolationist, content to be a superpower secure within their own borders. How will you change that ingrained culture? Why would they suddenly become expansionist?' I'd gone too far, challenging his pride, his self-confidence. His glare was penetrating. I'd finally got under his skin.

'You think you know more than the rest of us, don't you, Jay. You think your cycles and years of experience give you greater wisdom. But you forget one thing: great though your powers are in most ways, you're no match for me when it comes to manipulating masses. You call them isolationist, the American people, that's true but only because until recently they have been safe and secure and used their military and economic strength to negotiate access to riches and resources beyond their borders. Tell me, what do you think will happen when Russia, China and others grow strong enough to deny them that access. What will happen when the terrorists penetrate further and destroy that illusion of safety: when the fundamentalists grow in strength and the ethnic minorities grow to majorities within communities already fearful of the challenge to "truth, justice and the American way"?' He didn't pause for breath. His questions were rhetorical. He was in full spate. 'I'll tell you what will happen. They'll be ripe, ready to be led. Hell, it could have been Trump if he hadn't screwed up so spectacularly. And it may not even be me. Who knows, there may be another Phem out there just waiting for the opportunity. Trust me, if it's not me it'll be someone else. It will happen.' I was shaken by his certainty, his utter belief.

'So, a new world order, is that how you see it? A united Americas, a Chinese dominated Indo-china and what, a standoff between Europe, Russia and the Middle East? What about Africa?'

'Still there, still chaotic and still exploited by all comers. Maybe they'll be next, but not this time.'

I was disappointed in him. I let it show. 'Do the people of this world really mean that little to you? They're just pieces in a game of your own making?'

He was exasperated in equal measure. 'Jay, don't you get it? You could kill me tomorrow; it would have little effect. What I've described, forecast if you like, has a high probability of occurring whether I'm around or not! People follow because they want to be led, especially when they're scared, or feeling deprived, or jealous. Just listen to the extreme Republicans and neo-cons in the USA today. They want America out of Europe, out of the Middle East. They want to secure the borders, to reinstate and strengthen those areas of the constitution they believe have been weakened by the liberals. They'd create a USA that would be isolationist, racist and fundamentalist Christian. They claim they'd take the USA back to its origins but, like I said, that would just be the first step because being isolationist is not sustainable.'

'You really believe that?'

'I do, and who knows, maybe I'd be a better leader than some of the crazies I'd be up against!'

'So, you're telling me that if I stopped you, I could be creating a worse future for the Phems?' I was boiling with disbelief, angered by his arrogance. Suddenly he changed, the intensity with which he'd been arguing left him. He cocked his head on one side, grinned.

'Hey, see, now you're feeling my influence. See, I've almost persuaded even you!' It pulled me up short. I suddenly realised he was right, that as I'd sought to reason with him, he'd been manipulating me.

'So…? Everything you just said… you don't really believe any of it?' His grin broadened even more.

'You need to lighten up, Jay. Sure, I believe it could be true, but is the world that simple? No. Of course not. I'm not so warped that I can't tell the difference between the real world and some Xbox virtual reality. But you see what I could do, what others can do? People can be persuaded; they can be led.'

'You can fool all the people all the time?'

'Nope, but you can fool enough, for long enough for it to make a difference. Especially when they want to be fooled.'

I took a long sip of my drink, let the silence grow between us and then changed tack. 'Suppose there was another, a better game to be played? Against a bigger challenge, perhaps the biggest you've ever faced?'

'You think building an American Empire wouldn't be a challenge?' He was looking at me wryly but I could tell I'd piqued his interest. Now I needed him to sell it to himself. I knew the harder I tried to persuade him the more recalcitrant he'd become and that he'd refuse to give up his own plans.

'Think about what I said. The imbalance in the world. Think about all the things you've just told me that are happening. The plans being built by Russia and China. The chaos in Africa. Ask yourself what's behind all that. Or who.' He frowned, truly intrigued now by what I wasn't saying.

'You think there's someone else doing what I do?'

'Maybe not someone, maybe more a group. A faction. Not doing what you do, doing worse. What if it's they who are opposing you? Not just competition. A threat. And there's something else. Have you heard about the Rinks that have gone missing?'

He went very still, his eyes locked on mine, trying to

read what I knew. 'I've heard rumours. Are you telling me it's more than that? I've not heard anything from the Protectors. Surely they'd have sent out a warning if there was some significant movement against us?

I returned his stare. 'Maybe, maybe not.'

'Who are you talking about? The Seekers?'

I held his gaze. 'Same answer. Maybe, maybe not. I don't have all the answers. Yet.'

'So, what are you suggesting?'

'Nothing, yet. Just that you should think about it. And while you're doing that, watch your back, stay safe.' And with that I left him in deep thought, slumped on the sofa. I'd sown the seeds, now all I could do was wait to see if anything would grow.

As I retraced my route – floatplane, airline, taxi – and as I drew ever closer to Geneva and the Institute, I put all thoughts of Sven and my concern for the Phems to one side. I needed to refocus on my own objectives and the plan I'd set in motion when I'd left London. I knew I'd need all my wits about me.

Chapter 18

As we drove through the side streets and approached the Institute, I could sense a change in the local environment. There were vehicles parked, and individuals strolling the streets and sat watching in café's, that somehow didn't fit the pattern that I'd familiarised myself with before I left. I'd deliberately used one of the identities provided by the Protectors when I'd first flown to Geneva. An identity I knew had been compromised and was known to the Seekers. I'd known their search teams would be on the lookout for Joni Salminen and that I'd be detected. Sure enough, it had taken them a while – presumably first to check the airport CCTV footage and to confirm that I was Salminen, then to decide what to do, then to mobilise a team to find where I'd gone in Geneva – but they'd arrived eventually. By then of course I'd left for Vancouver, using one of the IDs they knew nothing about, so the team had probably been growing frustrated as they tried to locate me. It was their sense of excitement that I'd detected as I finally returned and revealed myself to them. They'd found me. That evening, I took Sindri into my confidence. I had no choice, though I hated that she'd be scared for me.

'Are you sure you know what you're doing?' She searched my face for signs of doubt.

'Yes.' I waited while she scanned me, assuring herself that I wasn't lying. I smiled at her. 'Don't worry. You know I'll be fine. When you're sure I'm gone, close this place down. Move to the new location. The transport and arrangements are all made. The security team I've hired will ensure no-one will be able to follow or trace you. Get set up and by the time I return I'm hoping you'll have some answers for me.' Sindri hugged me weakly.

'I may not be here, Jay.' There was resignation but not sadness in her voice. It was the Rink way of looking at things.

'I know, but if I miss you this time there'll be another. We'll sync again, I promise.'

'Even if we find what you've searched for, for so long?'

'I promise.' And that was all that needed to be said between us.

The next day I moved out of the Institute guest house and into a rented apartment from which I exited each morning at the same time and strolled the half mile along the shore-line to the small café where I breakfasted on croissants and coffee before completing the short walk to the Institute. In the evenings I followed a less regular but still predictable routine, emerging from the Institute sometime between seven and eight and then either shopping for dinner in the evening market or dining out in one of the lakeshore restaurants before reversing the journey on foot to my apartment: walking the last few hundred yards in deepening shadows as the street lights became more spaced out. Always alone, never accompanied even in the restaurants.

They took me a few days later. The van slowed beside me, a door slid open, hands grabbed and pulled. I was in and gone from the street in seconds. I knew there would have been no witnesses. I struggled for appearances sake then, outnumbered, I let them hold me face down on the van floor. Cable ties tightened around my wrists and ankles before I felt the sting of a needle in my arm, then nothing.

*　　　*　　　*

The susurration of surf on sand woke me. Bright sunshine from a deep blue sky reflected and twinkled on the ripples as they brushed the shoreline. I was lying on a soft mattress, beneath fresh cotton sheets, but my body felt sore, stiff, as if I'd been immobile for some time and needed to stretch and flex.

For an instant I thought I'd shifted again but then realised there were none of the telltale signs. A light breeze stirred the translucent hangings that made up two walls, a third was open to the sand and sea. I was in a cabana on a tropical beach. I searched my memory for an explanation but recalled only the time in Geneva and my experience in the van. Whatever had happened since then was either lost or I had been unconscious throughout. Judging from my physical state I was pretty sure it was the latter.

Whatever drug they had given me it was gone from my system now. My throat was dry but I experienced no dizziness as I swung my legs out of bed and stood. The decking was polished and smooth beneath my feet. I was naked but freshly laundered underwear, shorts and a T shirt had been left at the foot of the bed. I ignored the clothes and stepped out onto the beach.

The sand was hot, not unbearably so, but the glare from the sun, reflected by sand and sea, was painful. I squinted as my eyes adjusted. I took in the sweep of the beach before me and, behind the cabana, a backdrop of palms fringing the edge of a tropical forest that thickened inland. Was this the "comfortable civilised setting" that Selene had argued for? What else did they have planned for me? I had no doubt that I was being watched, but for the moment I saw no-one. Nor any cameras that I was sure were trained upon me. I stretched, raised my arms high above my head before pausing to allow the sun to wash over me and then bent deeply to grasp my ankles, allowing my forehead to rest briefly on my calves. It felt good. I straightened and turned casually back into the cabana. I was sending them messages, whoever they were. They might have abducted and transported me many thousands of miles to an unknown location but I cared not. If they thought they'd unsettle me, make me vulnerable, they'd failed.

At the back of the cabana, I found a small kitchen equipped with a fridge containing bottles of chilled water. Two satisfied my most pressing need and triggered another, for the bathroom. This, like the sleeping/living area and kitchen, was furnished and equipped to a high standard. Wherever I was, whoever owned this place had not spared any expense creating this slice of paradise. If prison could be called paradise, for that undoubtedly was what it was. I was under no illusions that, having gone to so much trouble to abduct me, I would not be allowed to leave unless it was on their terms. The shower looked tempting but I decided that could wait until I'd exercised properly. However long I'd been sedated and restrained, it had been too long. I needed to flex joints and stretch tendons and ligaments, to iron out the stiffness and allow my muscles to regain tone. I went back out to the cabana's deck and for the next hour I focussed only on myself.

I began with a series of Tai Chi routines, moving smoothly into an increasingly punishing sequence of deep stretches, agility and strength exercises. When I'd finished, I showered and dressed in the clean clothes. Now I was hungry and for the first time the contents of the cabana failed to satisfy my needs. The kitchen was supplied with drinks but was bare of food and, I noticed, any utensil with a sharp edge. Limes and lemons for the drinks were pre-sliced, there were no knives. Returning to the deck I surveyed the beach. A few hundred yards away and close to the sea two palm fronded umbrellas shaded a table and chairs, presumably set up whilst I showered. I could see a lone figure staring out to sea, feet stretched out and cooling in the water as it ebbed and flowed. With a shrug I set off. For the first time since I'd woken up, I was going to do what they expected of me.

As I neared the table at the water's edge, the shaded lone figure was revealed more clearly. It was Selene. So now I knew for sure who'd taken me. The Seekers. Were there Renegades here too? As I approached, she remained motionless, facing away, watching out to sea as if unaware or uncaring of my presence. The soft breeze lifted the folds of the silk sarong she wore over her bikini and ruffled the downy blonde hairs on the nape of her neck. Her skin was lightly tanned, her limbs lithe and elegantly muscled. I wondered what she was meant to be: jailor, inquisitor, reward? All three maybe.

'I assume you're waiting for me.' I took the other chair and settled myself. For a moment we sat in silence, side by side, studying the sea and the featureless horizon, then she spoke.

'And I'm wondering at your calm, your self-assurance. You have been abducted and brought here against your will yet you show no obvious concern or even curiosity about where you are or why you are here.' Still she didn't look at me, her own relaxed demeanour an exact match to mine.

'How would it benefit me if I were to show concern or curiosity? You'll explain in due course, otherwise why bring me here?' She waited a beat and then turned to me, her eyes betraying her inner excitement.

'Let's have lunch then.' As she spoke two figures emerged through the trees bearing trays from which they unloaded plates and dishes of lobster, salad and fresh fruit. A bottle of wine was left in an iced cooler and then they retreated whence they'd come, leaving us alone again.

'This looks good,' I murmured as I filled a plate from the dishes and a glass from the bottle. Then I picked up both, left her staring speechless and returned up the beach to the cabana. I entered without looking back. Your move.

I'd almost finished my meal when she finally followed me to the cabana. She stood uncertainly on the sand, looking in.

'Come in if you're ready to talk,' I said, my tone even, without rancour. 'I assume it would be unsafe for me to attempt to leave here, wherever I am, and whilst it's pleasant enough for now I know I'll bore quickly. So shall we try and make progress?' She tried hard to shield her thoughts but they were obvious. She was angry and impressed. By making her come to me I'd taken a degree of control. By refusing to react to my circumstances I'd raised her concern and curiosity as she'd sought to raise mine. Now I was setting the agenda on my terms not hers. She knew too that I was reading her and that I'd be trying to manipulate her. She thought that by knowing these things she was immune to my control. She was wrong, but I let her think otherwise.

'Thank you.' She gave me her hand before stepping up onto the decking, brushing the sand from her feet before entering. 'I'm Selene by the way.'

'I know.' That made her pause, but she hid it well.

'That was an impressive display you gave us this morning. You demonstrated a bewildering speed and total mastery of the martial arts yet you've only been back in cycle for what… six weeks? How do you develop skills and a physique like that so quickly? It should take years to achieve that level of physical conditioning.'

'In cycle?'

She looked at me, impatient now. 'Can we quit fencing? You are a Rink. Jay, also known as Samson, although there are those who would also identify you as Paul Mason, a software engineer from London.' She paused, then continued when I didn't react. 'I'm here to ask for your help.'

'You have a software problem?'

The corners of her mouth turned down. 'You disappoint me if that was supposed to be amusing.'

I nodded, accepting her admonishment. 'Supposing I am who you think I am. Why would I want to help you? And help you to do what?'

'So, you admit that you are Jay Samson?'

'Nope. Oh, sure I know who you mean, who amongst us Rinks doesn't? But the question is valid whether or not I am the man you're seeking. Why would Sansom help you? To do what?'

'If I tell you, will you tell me who you really are?'

'Who am I telling? Who is asking for help?' I could see her frustration building. It wasn't working. I was supposed to be anxious, ready to answer her questions but I was unyielding. She tried again.

'Again, can we stop this sparring please? Can we just talk, openly and honestly?'

'Can I walk out of here if I choose? Leave now without answering your questions?'

'No.'

I shrugged. 'Then if I am here on your terms, we'll trade information on mine. You go first. Who do you represent?'

'You think you are in a position to dictate terms? Are you not fearful of your position? You know I am not alone. You've been taken by force once already.'

I smiled at her but there was no humour in my gaze. 'Oh I understand my position only too well, my dear Selene.' I lowered my shields, allowed her to see me clearly, and saw a shudder run through her as she felt the full power of my personality, saw the truth in my cold stare. Her step back was involuntary and she raised her hand to her throat in dismay. There was no mistaking the unspoken message. I did not fear her or those she represented. I could not be forced. 'Well?' I was waiting for her to reply and the whiplash of command in my voice compelled her to answer.

'I work for a man called Sandor Pietersen. He's the son of the head of an organisation you may know of as the Seekers.' Shocked she raised her hand again, she'd not intended to reveal this yet, not without first getting confirmation that I was indeed Jay.

'Work for? In what capacity? Are you his whore?' I kept my voice quiet but scything with intensity, projecting a wave of scorn, ridicule, contempt and dismissal that struck deep within her. Forcing her, as I knew it would, to defend and justify herself. I sneered to twist the psychological knife, allowed myself an inward smile of satisfaction as I saw her bend.

She was unable to stop the colour rising in her cheeks but did her best to fight back.

'I'm his Head of Research and Analysis. I'm damned good at what I do and I whore for no-one!'

'And you're here for a beach holiday? Dressed as you are, looking as you do? This whole set up was intended to do what? To lull me? Are you offering yourself as apology for the abduction?'

'I'm trying to be civilised! Yes, we want answers from

you, that's why you're here. I persuaded them you could not be forced, that the only way would be to gain your trust, to explain ourselves and what we are seeking to do. That you would only help if you understood that by doing so, you'd be helping yourself! That's what this set up is for.'

'Be specific, what answers and how do you think you can help me?' I saw her trying to calculate how direct she should be.

'Well, you didn't react when I mentioned the Seekers so I guess it's safe to assume you know all about us, in which case you know that over the centuries our organisation has amassed a lot of information about you and your kind.' She waited, to see if I'd react, then continued. 'We've learned something of the process of reincarnation but not enough. The Renegades are offering to share what they know. Together, with you, maybe we can finally unlock the secret.'

'Wouldn't it have been simpler just to approach me in Geneva, to introduce and explain yourselves there?'

She shrugged. 'That was not my call.'

'No, don't start lying again. The truth is 'they' don't think you can persuade me. They want me here so that when you fail, they can try another way. To force me if necessary.' She nodded miserably. 'And if you fail, am I supposed to worry about what will happen to you? Is that part of the plan. I'm supposed to fall for you?' Her head snapped up.

'I don't care what you think or feel for me. It's your choice. We can do it the easy civilised way, you listen to me explain, talk to me and agree to help us or you can do it their way. The hard way. Either way they are determined you will share your knowledge.' Without waiting for my response, she span on her heel to leave and then stopped, turning her head to look back over her shoulder. 'While you're thinking about it, enjoy the beach but don't try to head inland or stray more than a half mile either way along the shore. The men guarding you are animals. They're waiting for you to try something. You can swim as far out to sea as you wish, the nearest land is fifty miles away. Drown yourself if you like, I could care less.' With a flounce she turned again, stepped down from the decking and within moments had disappeared amongst the palm trees that flanked the cabana. I watched her go, thought about what she'd told me; nothing new so far, just more confirmation that Sora-san wasn't being paranoid. There was little doubt what she was offering, what she'd try next, but as I slept that night it wasn't her that I dreamed of.

Chapter 19

Selene came back as dusk was falling the following day. A day I'd spent exercising and regaining muscle tone and exploring the boundaries of my confinement. I'd tested what Selene had said. The patrols guarding the perimeter around the cabana worked in pairs. As I approached them, they reacted aggressively, raised their weapons and motioned for me to turn back. I had the strong impression they hoped I wouldn't so that they'd have a reason to take me down. Selene was right, I'd seen their type before. She'd called them animals but my guess was they were worse than that. I saw the signs; the scars, the self-made, crude tattoos. On some, old needle tracks traced livid paths along their arms. But those were just the physical signs. Cold, vacant looks, nervous ticks and a naked need in their eyes betrayed their lust for violence and for inflicting pain and suffering. They were merciless killers. Trasker's men I assumed. The ones he'd employ if Selene failed and Pietersen authorised a forced interrogation. I had no intention of giving them a chance to indulge themselves with me. Were they some of the ones who were responsible for the Rinks who'd gone missing? If so, I'd have another score to settle.

Looking back from a long swim out to sea I'd been unable to pick out any landmarks or buildings that gave a clue as to the location. Palms, sand and surf stretched for as far as I could see in any direction. No ships, yachts or other craft passed nearby.

The hidden spycams in the cabana had been easy to find. I'd noted their position but otherwise left them untouched and I'd begun to map those I knew would be located around the outside and the perimeter. Other than that, I was bored. It was all too predictable. I'd just decided to give it one more day, to see what I could learn and then leave, when she stepped up onto the decking.

'You've been busy pacing your cage today,' she said, trying from the off to remind me of my position and her supposed control over my fate. I'd watched as she'd approached along a path leading from the trees. It was obvious she'd dressed carefully, with intent to impress. Her hair was swept up into an artful and apparently casual bun from which stray tendrils escaped and brushed her neck and cheeks. Her long, emerald silk, halter-neck dress, cut low and loose, flowed around her, accentuating her figure. A chiffon scarf shielded her back and shoulders from the light breeze that began to pick up as the light fell.

'This Sandor Pietersen', I said, ignoring her and picking up our previous conversation as if we'd not been interrupted, as if she were of no value than as a source of information. 'Do you always do exactly as he tells you?' She'd set out determined not to show any annoyance but despite herself her eyes narrowed.

'I work for him, he's the boss.'

'But you like doing as you're told. I can tell.' I stared into her eyes, letting her know I could read her innermost thoughts. She licked her lips nervously.

'I like to please my boss, who doesn't?' But I knew what I'd seen on the video feed in London, when she and Trasker had argued about what to do with me. And I could see it in her now, her need to dominate or, if she failed, to submit.

'Oh, I think it's more than that... Much more.' I gave full rein to my powers as I moved towards her. She stepped back under the force of my will, then gasped as her retreat was blocked by one of the thick wooden pillars that supported the cabana's palm-frond roof. I saw a flush deepen her features as she yielded to me.

'He's told you to try again. You're expected to be more successful this time. To get some answers. What's supposed to happen? Dinner and then seduction? Or the other way around?'

'You think I want to seduce you? Or you think you can seduce me?' Blustering, she tried for outrage then sarcasm; she failed at both but I gave her points for trying. I stepped closer, invading her personal space, increasing her discomfort.

'And if you do succeed, if I succumb to your charms, then what, my resolve is supposed to crumble and I reveal all?' I was pushing hard now, dominating her, knowing she'd respond as a submissive – because that was how she was wired.

'I… I…' She was confused and floundering now; any hopes of taking control were gone.

'So, having sex with me… Will it be to please me or you, or maybe to please him?' I was unbearably close now, pressing her backwards but not quite touching her. Her hands fluttered falteringly, rising to push me away and then falling to her sides.

'What makes you think that's going to happen?' But her voice was breathless now lacking conviction.

'This.' I took her hands and raised them above her head, holding them with one hand against the pillar whilst I slid my other gently down her arms and pressed myself against her. 'This is what you want isn't it?' She said nothing but made no motion to resist. 'Isn't it?' My tone was insistent but gentle, not harsh. She said nothing. I felt nothing, but I knew what she wanted, knew what I had to do. I separated her hands above her head and pushed them behind the pillar.

'Clasp your hands and don't move.' Without pausing to see if she'd obey, I released her and, moving behind the pillar, took her scarf and reached up to swiftly bind her hands together. She made no attempt to resist. I leant forward and whispered in to her ear. 'They are watching, aren't they?' She nodded, biting her lip and squirming against the rough wood. Slowly and tenderly, I brushed my fingers across the nape of her neck then tugged and released the tie that kept the halter in place. It fell to her waist. 'Who are *they*?' I breathed into her ear. As she hesitated, my hands moved and she shivered as the sensation became intense.

'Sandor and Trasker', she moaned.

'And?'

'Ah… ungh… just the security team.' I moved in front of her and held her tight as I leant in and kissed her deeply. She was unable to resist as I held her for long moments and then allowed my hands to linger, to stroke and tease, beneath the silk of her dress.

'Where are we?' My fingers began to caress her.

'I can't tell you that.' She was panting now. 'I'm not allowed.' My hands stilled, then started again. 'Ahhhh … Please you have to tell me something first!' She writhed against me, jerking helplessly, pulling at her bindings. When I judged she was ready I tried again.

'OK, I'll tell you this. I *am* the one they call Jay.' I stopped abruptly. 'Now, where are we?' My tone, the command I'd established over her and her need for my fingers to continue overrode her instructions.

'A private island, Central America, off shore from Belize,' she blurted uncontrollably, her head buried in my shoulder. I felt no desire. She was just a tool and I knew they would be watching. I had to behave as they were expecting. She gasped as I removed my hands from her and pulled loose the draw cord on my shorts, allowing them to drop to the floor. She moaned with relief as I hoisted her up and then lowered her gently. Her legs wrapped tightly around me and she gripped the pillar awkwardly with her bound hands as she sought to bear her own weight and raise and lower her body in a rhythm to match mine. As the pace increased, she shivered uncontrollably. We came together, a shuddering shaking climax. I cared not whether I'd given her any pleasure, my own reaction was purely biological. When we'd finished, I stepped back, watching her dispassionately as she sagged against the pillar. Gently I freed her hands and held her, stroking her hair. I felt absolutely nothing for her. She'd served two needs and I still had use for her yet. As she looked up at me, she read only tenderness and caring in my face.

'That wasn't just to please my boss,' she murmured tiredly then, regaining some composure and with another doomed attempt to regain control she pushed me away and retied her halter neck as if nothing had happened between us. 'If you'd care to dress, shall we have dinner now then, Jay,' and she gestured down the beach to where flickering lamps revealed a table that had once again been laid for two.

Chapter 20

She thought that somehow the sex had bonded us, would shield her from me and allow her the opportunity to probe and learn. It wasn't that she was naïve, too eager; she just had no real idea what I, and my like, were capable of. She had no defences as I conditioned her, bit by bit; bite by bite as we dined together. By the time we'd finished, drained a last brandy, she was unknowingly primed and ready. I knew we were being watched, that'd they'd be trying to listen to every word but they couldn't bug the entire beach. I took her for a stroll along the surf line, knowing the tumble and hiss from the waves would defeat any directional microphones.

When she grabbed me, pulled me to the ground, I played my part. Submissive, now, to her dominant. We wrestled, at first playfully, then she began to change. She slapped me, bit me, tore at my shorts, pushed me down and mounted me roughly and urgently. How did it seem to those who were watching? That she was taking her revenge for my behaviour before? That she was satisfying her own needs and using me? I hadn't needed to manipulate her; this was just her base character revealing itself. It was what the watchers would have been waiting to see, so I gave it to them. All the while my mind was elsewhere. Listening to and cataloguing what she was telling me. My body was on automatic pilot. Apparently, it did OK as it was sometime before she rolled off me, sated and panting in the sand. As they watched Selene perform, they were unaware she was telling me all she knew. About the Seekers, the Pietersens and Trasker. About their relationship with the Renegades. The real extent of their knowledge and understanding of reincarnation. It was more than I'd hoped, but less than I feared. I still worried that Piertesen and Trasker might know more, but I'd get to that in due course. For now, Selene had almost served her purpose.

We lay side by side for a while, then I helped her rise. Gently brushing the sand from her and circling her in my arms as if to cherish and protect her. More show for the cameras as I allowed her to lead me back to the cabana. To our bed. They'd see what they wanted to see. That Selene was gaining control. That her way was working. They'd be jubilant, hopeful. Complacent.

Later, as we lay entwined in bed, she was again unable to resist my will or my final questions. Her murmuring was too low for the microphones and her resistance was totally broken. I made her reveal the person she was, her ambition, her proclivities. She told me about those who'd suffered at her hands, the satisfaction she derived from 'hands on' interrogations, as she planned to satisfy herself with me if all else failed. I hadn't needed an excuse, didn't need justification, but any qualms I might have had were long gone by the time I finally allowed her to sleep. I waited for a few hours – for the night, the watchers, the guards to settle.

The carotid sinus, located in the neck just below the jaw and in line with the ear, is the junction between the major arteries that supply blood and oxygen to the brain. It's a highly sensitive area, replete with nerve endings and receptors that control blood pressure and the activity of the heart and blood vessels. The massage I applied to Selene's neck was light enough not to wake her and as I crushed down on the sinus she slipped from sleep to a deep coma-like unconscious state without murmur. A state from which I knew she would not recover for many hours; perhaps never. It didn't matter to me. I'd weighed the balance.

The team watching the screens would have seen nothing untoward as I slipped from the bed and headed for the bathroom. I knew that they were relying on the spycams to track my movements in and around the cabana. The guards were all stationed some distance away, patrolling the perimeter of the zone I was being contained in. But, in the bathroom – as she had told me – the spycam had been disabled at Selene's insistence. I was confident that no-one could witness my departure through the side window. I crouched in the shadow of the cabana, allowing my eyes to adapt to the moon and starlight, checking for movement in case I was wrong and they'd posted extra guards. There were none and as I moved away from the cabana, I followed the zig zag route I'd reconnoitred to avoid the cameras. I was hurrying now in case the watchers began to worry when I failed to reappear in the bedroom.

I'd marked the control room earlier when I'd been testing the boundaries. The location revealed by the poorly concealed power cables and confirmed by the WIFI and radio antennae mounted on the palm roof. Any inkling the watchers had that all was not well was replaced with certainty as I burst through the door. I saw the consternation on their faces as the man they'd searched for on their screens, the man they'd known only as an image, was amongst them in the flesh. It was over in seconds. I was gone before the light had faded from their eyes – eyes which still watched the screens, as if not comprehending that their necks had been broken.

I hadn't killed for revenge, for the pleasure of it. It was logic, not emotion. I'd had to act fast, before they could issue any warning and I knew roughly how many there were in the security team. I'd needed to even the odds. The control room was housed in one of two low bungalows, the other provided accommodation for the off-duty patrols. I listened at a window, heard the sounds of sleeping men. There was no sign they'd been alerted and I decided to risk leaving them undisturbed.

I knew the night-shift consisted of three teams of two patrolling the semi-circular perimeter around the cabana and beach but that, reliant as they'd become on radio warnings from the observation team, they'd be unaware that I'd left the cabana. Moving quietly, I slipped between them. An unmade track led inland and I followed it now, moving at a fast lope, my senses alive as I searched for signs of danger. It felt good to be active, taking the initiative. The palm trees thinned out as I approached a clearing and in it a large colonial-style house with a sweeping veranda and an elegant pillared façade. Two jeeps were parked in the shade to one side of the house; I stood and watched, alert for any signs of movement, but saw none around the vehicles or the house. I ghosted back into the trees and considered the options. I turned on my heel and headed back down the track.

The patrols were easy to find, but they were well trained and I knew they'd be harder to intercept and neutralise than the guards monitoring the video feeds. The first pair made it easier than I expected. They were distracted. Smoking and leaning on the trees that fringed the beach; laughing as they exchanged coarse jokes about what they assumed Selene was doing to me, or vice versa. It seemed that Selene's reputation and appetites had been well known. The afternoon's spycam recordings had provided that evening's entertainment. I listened briefly then approached them from behind, allowing a careless footfall to crunch on the fallen palm fronds, brittle and dry. They whirled, reaching for weapons that should have been held at the ready. Their reactions slowed by the cannabis they'd been smoking. The sweet-smelling smoke that had led me to them. I was pent up and it was all the edge I needed. I used the *nukite*, a variation of the *shito uchi* or "knife-hand strike". Both hands. My fingers tightly extended, compressed together. I leaped the last yard, transferring my weight and momentum into my fingertips as they crushed and compressed the larynx of each man. Cutting off any cries before they could begin to form. Cutting too the flow of air to their lungs as the cartilage broke and their tracheas collapsed, torn and swollen by the violence of the blows. Temporarily paralysed by the nerve shock, they crumpled. I knelt and held them, to minimise the noise of their thrashing as they died. After all movement had stopped, I waited, listening, checking the environment for anything that might suggest the other guards had heard. There was nothing. So far so good.

The routine was for the three teams to regularly move and swap positions. I drifted back through the trees and waited for the next patrol to arrive. It didn't take long. I heard a low voice.

'Can you smell that, Raoul? The bastards are slacking again, fucking dopeheads. Trasker'll string them up if he catches them.' They were moving slowly, in single-file. Weaving their way between the trees, following the rough path their patrols had begun to carve into the subsoil over the past few days. I let them pass me before stepping out behind them. Silent. In my hand I held a knife, taken from one of the dead guards. A knife with a blade blackened and dulled to prevent it from glinting in the moonlight and sharpened lovingly. A soldier's knife, a fighting knife. I tapped the second guard on the shoulder. Surprised, his turn was involuntary. I swept the knife across his throat and pushed him away and to one side, avoiding the splatter. I took another step forward as the first guard, shocked by the sudden fountain of blood that enveloped his head and shoulders stopped in his tracks. I reached around him. Used the knife. Again, I took a step back to avoid the blood. I watched as he fell to join his partner. So far so good.

I hurried back along the rough track. The last pair would be expecting to swap position and I figured that they'd think that any sounds I made would be coming from one of the other patrols. I was only just in time. Again, the voice was low but it carried in the still night and I could hear urgency in his tone.

'Digger? Sam?' I heard the guard click his radio mike. 'Comcheck control… c'mon guys wake up!'

'I reckon they're watching those videos again.' The second guard chuckled.

'No, there's something wrong.' I heard him click his mike again. 'Comcheck all teams…' I was close enough to hear the hiss from his radio as he listened in vain for a reply.

'Shit. They're not answering.' There was a rattle as they both armed their weapons. It was the last thing he said. The last thing they did. They were trying to process why the radios were silent. They were focussed on trying to understand what might have happened when they should have been reacting. I still had the knife and I was moving fast. Too fast for them. It was over quickly and I stood panting hard, flushing the adrenaline that was surging through my body. I'd been lucky. I knew that. Six men down and not a scratch. And no alarms.

I was overconfident as I moved back towards the house. I'd checked, before, for any patrols around the clearing, and hadn't seen any. I heard the movement behind me but before I could turn an arm like a steel bar wrapped around my neck and I was hoisted in the air. He must have been a giant of a man. Not a guard I'd previously seen. He held me, seemingly effortlessly, as I swung and kicked: my feet inches off the ground, the bar across my throat cutting off the blood supply to my brain. I knew I had only moments of consciousness left. I tried reaching back to gouge his eyes but he'd thought of that. His head was bowed forward, pressing into the back of mine, protected and increasing the pressure on my neck. So, I did what he hadn't expected. He'd been even more overconfident than me; he'd relied on his size. He hadn't noticed I was still carrying the knife. I reached up and I sliced through his elbow joint. The steel bar slacked, then flopped as I severed muscle and tendon. I dropped from his grasp, span on one leg and planted my foot deep into his groin as he clutched at his ruined arm. His strangled cry was muted as my rising knee met his descending chin. The force of the collision snapped his head back and I saw his eyes roll in his head. I span again and hammered a heel against his temple for good measure. As I strained to draw breath through my bruised and swelling throat I crouched and listened hard. His cry had been animal like, but stifled. Had my luck held? It seemed it had. I gave it five minutes, the night sounds seemed normal. I looked at the fallen giant, saw a slight movement in his chest but when I checked I could tell he was deeply unconscious. He was no threat. Maybe never would be again if he wasn't found before he bled out. I pulled myself together. I wasn't finished yet.

Moving more cautiously now, I circled the house. There were no more guards outside, of that I was certain. A side door was open. Maybe that's where the giant guard had come from. Perhaps he'd heard something, had come out to investigate. I shrugged, it no longer mattered. It took me ten minutes to check the house. There were no more guards inside either. I found Pietersen and Trasker sound asleep in rooms on the first floor. Above them, in less grand quarters, a couple sleeping together. Housekeeper? Handyman? Whatever, not a threat. I left them in peace.

I took Trasker first: applied only enough pressure to render him temporarily unconscious then used strips of sheet to bind him securely before carrying him downstairs to one of the jeeps. I disabled the other jeep then returned for Pietersen, pausing to grab a few of his belongings that I thought would come in useful, and within minutes had him lying alongside Trasker as we bounced and jolted along the unmade track that ran inland. So far so good. I was coming down from the adrenaline-high now. The end game was in sight. I began to think about what I'd done, now that I had time to think and not just to react. Perhaps I hadn't needed to take out the security patrols, maybe I could have simply disarmed and disabled them but the risk had been too high. And they'd not cared about me when they'd dragged me into the van in Geneva. They'd not cared what my fate would be once captured.

I pushed the thoughts away. Move on.

After a mile the track branched. I paused and listened, heard the sounds of the sea from the left and headed that way. Before long a boat house and wooden jetty appeared, exactly where Selene had told me I'd find them. I turned the engine off and the jeep coasted to a silent halt. On one side of the jetty a forty-foot gin-palace cruiser tugged gently at her moorings as the lazy swell played around her. On the other side a craft of a very different nature lay sleek and gleaming, bobbing skittishly as if impatient to be free.

Trasker and Pietersen were still unconscious as I approached the boathouse. It was occupied. Crouching by an open window I could hear soft snores from within. Two sleepers by the sound of it, boat crew I assumed. I entered silently. They didn't need to die and I was tired of killing. I'd be long gone before they could interfere, so I left them unconscious. Perhaps I did feel a bit guilty about the guards.

I heaved Trasker and Pieterson aboard the larger craft, cast off her lines and the cruiser swung away from the jetty as the off-shore breeze pushed her against the swell. Swiftly I boarded the sleek power-boat moored opposite. A smuggler's craft known as a cigarette boat, though that cargo had long since been superseded. The long, slim, sharp-prowed and rake-hulled craft carried huge twin outboard motors that I knew would be capable of pushing her onto a plane and then exceeding and maintaining forty knots for extended periods. I flicked the switches, checking the tanks were full, and with a throaty roar the engines burst into life. I throttled back, cast off and edged the boat around the end of the jetty before taking a line from the stern to the bow of the cruiser. Once the tow was secured, I fed power to the engines and headed slowly for the reef; allowing the tow line to take up the slack before letting the power build as the two craft got sluggishly under way.

The gap in the reef was wide enough to navigate despite the inertia of the cruiser and the conflicting influences of the breeze and swell on the high sided vessel. Once we were well clear and down current from the gap I reduced power, heaved an anchor and dragged until it dug in. I cut the engine and the two craft drifted then caught and turned line astern. I slumped in one of the padded cockpit seats and ran a mental and physical inventory. I'd used a lot of reserves controlling and manipulating Selene and dealing with the guards. I ached, so I applied some focussed will to ease the pain in my throat and to speed the healing process. I was slightly light headed but that would pass. I wasn't exhausted, but it would take a while for me to recover fully. I stirred myself – it was too soon to relax – and opened the door into the small forward cabin. I found bottles of water, crackers and some fruit. Enough to keep me going. I took a bottle of water back onto the deck and sat sipping quietly as I gathered my energies for what would come next. At the end of the line the cruiser wallowed, twisting and bobbing in the swell. I waited thirty minutes then pulled it close and boarded.

Pietersen had vomited against his gag, was close to asphyxiation as I ripped it clear. He coughed, retched, spluttered. Trasker was awake but seemingly unaffected by my assault or seasickness. His eyes watched balefully as I grabbed him by the shoulders and hauled him onto a bunk. They'd both been sleeping naked when I'd taken them from their beds; it wasn't a pretty sight but I left them that way, vulnerable.

'Joe Trasker, I presume?' I removed his gag but he said nothing. 'The man who believes the only way to get information, the truth, is by torture.' His eyes flickered from side to side but still he said nothing. 'The man who interrogated Ayeesha Rao.' This time his eyes settled on mine as he realised just how much Selene had told me. I bared some of my thoughts, let him see inside me, watched as he cringed back against the bulkhead.

'And now I'm going to interrogate you... We'll do it my way.' I smiled for effect. 'But maybe we'll use some of your ways as well.'

*   *   *

The sun was climbing high before I was ready to leave. I started the engines, hauled anchor then reached back and released the tow-line. Freed from its burden the power-boat darted forward as if with renewed vigour but I restrained her, circling for a few moments and watched the cruiser drift and turn on the breeze and swell until I was satisfied that she would soon be carried down-wind, out to sea and away from the island. I opened the throttles. The deck rose instantly and I braced myself as the boat leapt onto the plane, thrusting its wake to either side. I'd been held on one of the many scattered islands along the Central American coast. Belize City was near enough due west, which meant the Mexican border was less than an hour away at smuggling boat speeds. I set course north west and sped on.

Chapter 21

It took me a week to make my way to New Zealand.

'So? Did you find out?' Sindri had held on, but barely. So weak now she had to be cushioned, supported by a bank of pillows. Her bed faced the long glass doors that opened on to the veranda overlooking the ocean. I opened the doors and breathed in the hot, humid ozone-rich breeze as I considered my answer.

'No, not really. I was able to confirm some of what we'd feared, that's all.'

*   *   *

When I left the island I navigated my way north without incident, aided by the on-board GPS, taking the channel between Ambergris Cay and the mainland until I could put into the harbour at Chetumal, just over the border into Mexico. A search on the smartphone I'd grabbed at Pietersen's villa informed me that this was a main trading gateway between Belize and Mexico, and a duty-free zone for international visitors crossing over from Belize. The port bustled with activity and my arrival was noted by both port officials and others as I tied off on a pontoon in a side channel away from the main bay. I was pretty sure I'd find what I needed here and sure enough it wasn't long before they made their approach.

'Nice boat, senor, had it long?' His Customs official's uniform was crisp and fresh despite the stultifying humidity. He eyed me with something that bordered curiosity and greed.

'Not long,' I answered cheerily. 'I'm looking to get rid of it actually...'

'Get rid? Maybe I can help you with that.' He grinned but it was predatory, not humorous. 'But first you must pay fees.'

'Fees?'

He rubbed his thumb and forefinger together in the time worn gesture. 'Fees… mooring, immigration, Customs…' His hair was lank, greasy and black with dye. His teeth, in stark contrast, gleamed as his grin widened.

'I see.' I regarded him calmly. I had no cash, no papers, but didn't expect that to be a problem. I knew I'd need neither. As we sized each other up a tall, lean figure in jeans and T-shirt sauntered down the pontoon and stood surveying the cigarette boat. The Customs official's demeanour changed, he took a step back, deferential.

'Looks fast,' the newcomer observed.

'She is.' I nodded, waiting.

'Yours?'

'She is now.'

'Seems to me very much like a boat I knew that belonged to some fellows who lived out on the Cays south of here.'

'Well, I can't say if that's so but I won it yesterday. Cards.'

'Is that so?' He was staring down at me, his height and the rise of the pontoon forcing me to look up. He thought he had the high ground.

'Yup, now I'm looking to sell it.'

'Is that so?' We both knew the lies were just part of the negotiation. I shrugged.

'I just need a stake so I can pay my fees,' I gestured towards the customs official, 'with enough so I can move on. Interested?' I knew him for what he was, a hustler: a chancer, always on the lookout for an edge, a cheap score. I watched him as he weighed the options. He knew it wasn't my boat, knew who it had belonged to and knew too what it was capable of. It was a valuable asset. His options were trade or steal. The problem for him was that he didn't know me or what I was capable of. We both knew the Customs official was an irrelevance in this transaction. I changed my stance, fed him some body signals and looked him straight in the eye, encouraging him to make the right choice. He shifted uncomfortably then made his offer.

'Five thousand dollars, cash.'

I paused for effect. It was way, way below value but enough for my needs.

'And you'll take care of the fees?' I grinned at him. He grinned back.

'Sure.'

I would rather have flown but without papers I'd had no choice but to take the bus from Chetumal to Cancun. It was a long hot dusty ride, but I was sure I wasn't followed. In the busy resort I checked into one of the many tourist hotels. A hefty cash deposit allowed the receptionist to accept my explanation that I was waiting for replacements for my passport and other papers that had been stolen. I made some calls then waited impatiently for two days until fresh identity papers, credit cards and cash were couriered to me from the solicitors I retained in New York. They'd no idea of the contents of the package I'd left with them and they were paid well enough not to ask questions. The package was simply marked 'documents, no commercial value'. I used the time to recharge my batteries. By the time the package arrived I was refreshed and ready to move on. The identities provided by the Protectors had served their purpose, from now on I'd be off their radar, independent and on my own. To make up for the bus journey, I'd flown first class to New Zealand.

*   *   *

It was clear that Sindri had few resources left. The move had drained her but a spark shone in her rheumy eyes as she lay collapsed in her bed, willing me to explain. One of her aides, a matronly middle-aged woman, fussed quietly in a corner of the room. Marta, another Rink. We'd introduced ourselves in the formal way. She'd let me know, politely, that she didn't care who I was, that she wouldn't put up with any nonsense, that Sindri was her main concern.

'You got rid of Ulrich then?' I'd seen no sign of the popinjay since my arrival. Sindri laughed. The effort tired her.

'One of my few mistakes.' She smiled ruefully. 'I thought I saw something in him. He seemed to have some kind of potential, for a Phem. Like I told you, I've been too long in this cycle. I'm losing my touch.'

'And this place? It's OK?' I'd chosen carefully. The Coromandel peninsula on New Zealand's north island was as different from the Swiss lakes and Geneva as could be imagined. The cliffs and coves along the twisting coastline sheltered sandy bays whilst, inland, ridges and ravines created microclimates for tropical rainforests where tree ferns and other exotics were gloriously abundant. Once a remote haven for those seeking an alternative lifestyle the peninsula now provided holiday and second homes for wealthy city dwellers. The few staff that had travelled with Sindri were housed in a large private beachfront estate. The locals knew only that an infirm, wealthy reclusive woman had moved there for privacy. Their arrival had generated little interest or comment.

'It's fine… fine. Now quit stalling, what did you find out?' I hesitated. 'Marta, would you mind?' Sindri asked quietly. Marta glanced meaningfully at me but left the room, closing the door quietly behind her. 'Do you know who she is?' Sindri asked.

'No.' I was puzzled as to why it was important.

'She's the daughter of one of my former now-selves. She tracked me down in Geneva. This is her fifth cycle.' She saw the flicker of concern cross my face. 'Don't worry, she can be trusted. She won't tell the Protectors where we are now.'

I relaxed a little. 'So, one of yours? That's amazing!'

Sindri gripped my hand. 'It's something we need to look at more carefully, promise me. We have the data now. Is there a reason that only some of our children become Rinks? Don't forget when I'm gone!

'There has to be something there, Jay. We should look

more closely at now-selves that come from ancestral lines in which there has never been a Rink, and vice versa. Is there a linkage? If so, it can't be genetic. We transfer psyche, souls, not DNA, but then how could it skip generations?' Sindri was thinking out loud, telling me what I already knew. We communed in silence for a moment until a thought struck me.

'You're not telling me Marta's one of ours?' Sindri's eyes twinkled, she snorted.

'Well, that took you a while. No. She's not in your line. Same cycle, but you only gave birth to boys, surely you remember that? I was with her mother before you shifted into the cycle. I don't think you ever met.'

I'd been aware for so long that my memories and selves were, of necessity, stacked and shelved. Available when required otherwise held back in organised self-discipline. I delved and Jaira's memories came to the fore; bringing back the sights and sounds of my life in that cycle with Sindri. Mahandra, as she'd been then, a tall strapping Sikh who'd taken me under his wing, straightened me out, loved me, fathered my children. We'd lived in the Land of the Five Waters, the Punjab, during a time of what, in that region, passed for peace – before the coming of the British – and oblivious to the long years of territorial dispute, partition and persecution that were to follow. I'd never concerned myself with the children of my now-selves, male or female. There had been many, and I'd long since given up being confused by the twists and turns of Rink existence. It was what it was. Jaira faded and I returned to the here and now.

'Now, will you please tell me what you found?' The psyche I'd shared so much with smiled at me through the eyes of a dying old woman; there were few I'd ever been closer to or loved more. I told her what I'd learned but not how. I wasn't ashamed of what I'd done, but I wasn't proud of it either.

*   *   *

The atmosphere inside the cruiser had been rank with the smell of vomit and their fear.

'Get away from me!' Trasker hissed as he struggled awkwardly to push himself upright, to brace himself against the rolling swell. 'You won't get far; they'll be tracking you already.'

'I don't think so. Not your people anyway. The Renegades maybe, but you or Pietersen can tell me about them in good time. Tell me about Ayeesha first.' I couldn't mask the anger that rose within me, now. Anger that I'd held back since Selene had confessed how they'd used her. Trasker was genuinely puzzled.

'What about her? You obviously know she's dead… so what? She's a Rink, she'll be OK!'

'You mean because she'll become reincarnate at some point, somewhere, sometime?'

'Well, your kind can't die, can they?' Trasker sneered. 'So, what does it matter?'

'That's what you thought about the others too?' I saw him hesitate. Trying to think if he could conceal what he'd done, could find a way to negotiate out of it. In the end his inner nature took over, he couldn't resist throwing it in my face.

'Others? You mean the ones we took. The Rinks we've interrogated? They're not all like you, you know. We made them talk. Sometimes the Renegades helped.' He was defiant.

'You're wrong, they are like me,' I snarled. My hands curled and uncurled by my side. I was barely controlling myself as he confirmed the rumours. 'We're people too. You think that because we reincarnate you can treat us as inhuman? That it excuses your own inhumanity?' But I was wasting my breath, I could see it meant nothing to him.' 'And what did you learn? Anything of value?' He shrugged.

'No.' His indifference to the suffering he'd caused, to the waste of life appalled me. It assuaged any last remorse I might have felt for my actions on the island. I was back in control now. Cold and focussed.

'So, you questioned Ayeesha about me and now her now-self is dead, she's passed into transition.' I said it as a matter of fact. 'What did she tell you?' He thought he could wait me out, stared silently, arrogantly, challenging me. I'd had enough so I broke him, without compunction. It didn't take long, just a slight application of will to blunt his mental resistance and some physical encouragement. A refinement of touch that was beyond anything Trasker knew of or could ever had employed, but I'd learned from the best over millennia; nothing crude or overtly brutal, something far more effective.

Ayeesha had told him the legends the Rinks shared about me. He knew about Lela, knew about my abilities. Knew what was said about the cycles I'd lived through.

'What else?'

'The Protectors found out what happened to Paul Mason before you made first contact.' Trasker was spent now, I could ask him anything. He was an open book. 'The time you spent in hospital.'

'So?'

'So, they're wondering what you might have let slip, whilst you were in a coma or recovering.'

'Let slip? About what?'

'Being a Rink!' Did you give yourself away, to the staff, a doctor or nurse maybe.'

'Why? What would it matter if I had?'

'It's what the Protectors do, close down any leaks as they call them. To stop them coming to our attention. They'll do anything to stop the Seekers learning more.'

I felt a cold shiver of concern then pushed it aside. I'd deal with it later. 'They are that paranoid now?' Trasker said nothing. I was asking him questions he couldn't answer. 'Is there anything else you need to tell me?' I already knew, from Selene, why they'd been so determined to track and interrogate me. That they were desperate to know if I'd found the so-called secrets of reincarnation; desperate to learn them before the Renegades, their so-called allies, could control the knowledge. 'What else do you know about the

Renegades? What's their next move? Have they learned anything that will help them achieve their aims?' He rolled his eyes. A thin line of drool ran down his chin. He was powerless to resist, and his silence told me what I needed to know. 'So, last question.' My voice was deathly quiet. 'How did Ayeesha die?'

He couldn't help himself.

'Badly!' He giggled. This time I forced silence upon him, watched as he fought to give voice to his pain and terror. Watched as his muscles bulged, writhed: as his veins pulsed and burst until even I had had enough. I carried his limp lifeless body below, stowed it in the bilges where it belonged. I returned to deal with Pietersen, who'd watched it all, then passed out.

*   *   *

'You're worried about her, aren't you?'

I sighed; Sindri was only asking to be polite. She could read me like a book. I delayed my answer, tucked a blanket around her shoulders. Marta had looked in moments before and I'd renewed my promise to make sure Sindri was comfortable.

'Who?'

'Don't be obtuse, Jay, not with me. The nurse you told me about. Meg. Are you worried that the Protectors might treat her as a potential "leak"?' I sighed, again.

'I'm not sure why she's so important to me, but yes. She's one of the reasons I have to get back to London.' Sindri gave me one of her penetrating stares.

'You need to be more honest with yourself, Jay. You're worried because you care. I'm worried about *you*. You've created a false self-image. You're not as callous, cold, calculating and focussed as you'd have yourself believe.' She shifted awkwardly against the pillows. 'Don't try and make yourself be something you're not. You lost your humanity once before. Don't risk that again.' I turned away, made uncomfortable by her stare or her words. Maybe both. 'And don't be so hard on yourself. The rest can wait. If you're worried and care for her then of course you must go. What's the other reason?' I turned to face her again, glad to be able to change the subject.

'Because of what Pietersen told me, about the Renegades.'

*   *   *

Extracting what Pietersen knew had been easy, once I'd revived him.

'Tell me about the Renegades.'

'What do you want to know?'

'Who you've been dealing with, what they know, what they want from you. That'll do for starters.'

He swallowed hard, struggled to work out what he could conceal and what he couldn't, realised it was hopeless.

'They call the leader Dandy Tom ...'

'I know that. I saw him. And Iril Karzan and a bunch of others when you met in London. That's new, they've never been that organised before. Why are they organising now?' But he was no longer listening to me. He'd gone into a world of his own.

'He's evil... They're all evil... I didn't realise... Didn't know–' The crack of my palm on his cheek snapped him back. He focussed blearily on me, replaying my words in his head. 'You saw us? You knew? Even before we took you?'

'And I sent you a warning which you ignored.'

He gulped. 'What are you going to do with me now. Why don't you just get it over with. I saw what you did to Joe.'

'Tell me about Dandy Tom and Karzan. They scared you. Why?'

'Everyone in the room was scared of Dandy Tom. Karzan is a vicious bastard too but even he defers to Dandy Tom.' He paused, shuddering as I forced him to remember. 'They know everything about us.'

'Us?'

'The Seekers. Our organisation, who we are, our families, our strengths, our weaknesses.'

'So why do they need you?'

'Because of our numbers. There's only a few of them, maybe a hundred or so in cycle at any one time. We've thousands of members now, spread around the world.'

'You've become their *army*? Kidnapping and torturing Rinks for their knowledge?'

'Yes.' Pietersen shuddered again. 'We sold our souls to them.'

He'd surprised me. Despite it all he finally knew the truth of what they'd done.

'So why did you imagine you could trust them, or protect yourself from them?' Pietersen's laugh was rueful, embarrassed, ashamed… pathetic.

'They were desperate for answers, for the secret. We thought that as long as they thought we knew something of value that we could trade with them.'

'Did you really believe that? You must have been pretty desperate to think you could somehow strike a deal with the Renegades.'

'It was my father. He's been terminally ill for years. He saw this as his last hope.'

'To do what?'

'To discover the secret of awareness. To find a way of bringing back his psyche, his soul, after death!'

'What did you get from the Renegades so far?'

'They gave us the locations of the Phoenix Centres, identified key Protectors. Because of them the total Seeker knowledge of the Rinks had increased tenfold in the last few years.'

'In return for interrogating Rinks and for capturing me if I returned?'

Pietersen nodded miserably.

'The deal was that then we'd trade you for whatever they know about the secrets of reincarnation.'

'And you agreed but decided you'd first try to learn everything you could from me?'

'The whole Rink world talks about you. They say if

anyone knows the secret, you do. And even if you don't know everything, we figured that a combination of what you and the Renegades know might provide the answers.'

'Do the Renegades know anything?'

Pietersen groaned. 'I don't know. They hinted, something perhaps.'

'And did they tell you why they want the secret? Why they care? They are Rinks, they already have the capability. Did they tell you why they are so desperate to find out what makes it happen?'

Pietersen shook his head wearily.

'No.'

The cruiser rolled and wallowed in the swell as I pondered his answer. So, the Renegades were still hiding their real motives, interesting.

'What's their next move?'

'They're waiting for us to deliver you to them.'

'They know for sure that you had me? Did they know where you were holding me?'

'Not where.'

'And when you don't deliver me? What will they do?'

Pieterson shook and shivered. 'They made it very plain; if we don't deliver then they know enough to destroy us all.'

*   *   *

'Sora-san was right, then? There is an alliance, Seekers and Renegades.' The news energised Sindri, but only briefly.

I shrugged. 'Alliance? Not really. They have the same goal but very different reasons for wanting to understand how to control reincarnation. Would either side share with the other if they discovered the secret first? I don't think so!' My laugh was mirthless.

'What did you do with Pietersen?'

I smiled at her. She'd never admonished me for the things I did but I knew she was softer than me.

'I left him on the boat. Alive.' She raised an eyebrow.

'He did what he did for his father. He at least tried to control Trasker and Selene, to curb their worst instincts.'

'You weighed the balance? You gave him a break? You?'

'I figured that he was someone else's problem. If the police find him with Trasker's body he'll have a lot of explaining to do. If he gets out of that he'll have the Renegades to deal with. Either way he won't be our problem again.'

'And I thought you'd lost your touch. Maybe there's hope for you yet.' Her smile was back, briefly, then she grew serious again. 'Tell me the truth. Are the Protectors right to be worried?'

'We should all be worried, especially now we know Dandy Tom is involved.' I was more than worried but shielded it so Sindri couldn't pick up on it. I knew what the Renegades really wanted and not even I could predict what would happen if they got it.

Sindri was fading fast now, her powers ebbing. 'I wish I could stay, to help.' She squeezed my hand. I squeezed back. In one sense Trasker had been right. In the long run Rinks had little to lose; there was always another cycle. There was nothing more to say between us. We held hands and watched as the sun set over the southern sea.

*   *   *

Sindri died a week later. We'd said our goodbyes with sadness, not because it was the end but because we had no way of knowing when it would begin again. I'd never been able to detect a pattern. Sometimes I'd be in transition for as little as a few months, other times for decades. It was the same for Sindri: when – if – she returned, she'd look for me. Maybe I'd be there, maybe not. Though I was sad, I was also free again.

I wanted nothing more than to retreat from the world and to immerse myself in the search for understanding: to reviewing what the Institute had learned and to mining the data from the Protectors to see if the answers I sought were there. I'd long since tried to convince myself that I'd seen, done, experienced everything the world had to offer. I'd tried to convince myself that, aside from Sindri and Lela and maybe one or two others, there were no relationships, psyches or souls, no joys or cares that would ever be worthy of distracting me from my goal. It seemed, however, that no matter how I tried I couldn't isolate and control the emotions that kept me engaged with the world. Since I'd shifted, I'd been on the move almost continually. Driven to act, to react, by the actions of others. In her last week Sindri had helped me map out several promising lines of investigation and Marta had proved to be more than just Sindri's aide. She had been well trained; would carry on the research and analysis where Sindri left off. The work was in safe hands. If there was anything to be found she'd find it. I desperately wanted to stay but had stronger needs. I'd had to accept the reality that I couldn't yet disengage from the world. I had other work to do that couldn't wait.

I flew back to Europe that night.

Chapter 22

My return journey was convoluted. Despite my confidence in my new papers, I wanted to avoid any direct flights. I flew via Dubai, partly because of the anonymity afforded by the vast international hub but also out of fascination to see what had been built there. I'd watched many of the world's major cities grow from villages to towns to vast urban sprawls, in every case over decades, centuries. But not so Dubai – it seemed to have appeared in the blink of an eye.

I arrived in the afternoon and, after booking an onward flight to Turkey with a different airline, gave myself the evening to explore. From a skyline cafe I sat gazing out across a city of lights many of which marked the soaring crane towers that were a constant hazard to the helicopters that crisscrossed the city even at this time of day. Where once there had been nothing but desert and shoreline there now had emerged a harbour and one of the world's largest container ports, artificial islands, a forest of skyscrapers, malls, theme parks, marinas and to support it a vast infrastructure of roads, metros and utilities. I'd seen many wonders at the time of their construction or at the height of their fame and glory: the Pyramids, Angkor Wat, China's Great Wall, Machu Picchu, Imperial Rome, the magnificent cathedrals of Europe, the soaring skyscrapers and bridges in America... the list was endless but did any match this as a display of man's endeavour, ingenuity and determination to mould the world as they saw fit, despite the cost, the labour required? I mingled with the crowds thronging the malls late into the night. One even contained an indoor ski resort. In the desert!

Dubai was a statement. The Americans had built casinos in their desert city, Las Vegas, but in Dubai, beyond the glitter and glamour of the hotels, malls and beaches the Arabs had built satellite business parks and offered incentives to businesses to relocate there. The city had become a global business centre as the world watched, wondered and dismissed it as a tourist destination. It reeked of money, success and power. I wondered what the Arabs planned to do with that power; wondered if others recognised the challenge they would face.

The next day I flew on to Turkey and then a shorter hop to Tallin. I did it because it amused me to do so, after my experience with the Estonian thugs in London, but also for practical reasons; the country, one of the European Union's smallest members, is a signatory to the Schengen agreement that allows travel free of controls throughout the EU once you've crossed her borders. I entered without problems then travelled with no restrictions by ferry from Estonia to Denmark and then by train through Germany and the Netherlands. I finally re-entered the UK as a foot passenger on the passenger/freight ferry that plies back and forth between the Hook of Holland and Harwich. The border controls at Harwich were far more relaxed than at the major UK airports. I was travelling on yet another set of papers, using an identity that I was sure was unknown to the Protectors, Renegades or Seekers. I'd also altered my appearance and mingled with a crowd of football fans returning bleary eyed and foul mouthed after watching their team lose in the quarter final of the Champions League. I couldn't be sure I'd avoided detection but took further precautions as soon as we docked. By the time I arrived in London I was certain that even if my return to the UK had been detected I was, for the moment, free from any tags or followers. I only needed it to stay that way for a few days – that was as long as I was prepared to allow myself. I had four things to do, would not allow them to take longer.

*   *   *

The café was as I remembered it. The same barista, same

mirrored wall, same bustling turnover of customers. The same awful, tasteless coffee – how had this become a global brand? I pushed my cup to one side. I didn't need the caffeine while I waited. If she didn't show today, I'd return tomorrow. But I didn't need to wait long, she was sticking to her usual routine. I watched her as she queued to buy her coffee. She was alone and no-one seemed to be paying her any particular interest. As she turned, looking for a seat, I half rose and beckoned. I watched with inner delight as signs of surprise and then pleasure lit her features. She came over.

'Well, well. Should I be pleased to see you again or not? Twice we've had coffee. After the first, the next time I saw you was as a patient; after the second you vanished. When was that now…?' She pretended to think. 'Ah yes, weeks ago, and not a word since.'

'I don't know about "should" but I know you are…'

An eyebrow arched dangerously.

'Pleased.'

'Jeez, you're a cocky one.' I thought for a moment I'd over played it but she grinned and pulled out a chair. 'So, go on, convince me… you just happened to be here?'

'Nope, I was lying in wait.' I grinned back, I couldn't help it. She pressed all the right buttons.

'And how long can I expect to enjoy your company this time?' She sipped her coffee, grimaced, put it down and shucked her coat from her shoulders onto the back of her chair. I liked watching her, liked how she moved. I nodded towards her cup.

'Why do you come here? Why do you drink this muck?'

'It's an acquired taste, I'm still working on it and it's like I told you before, this is somewhere to come to unwind.' She gave me a professional once over. 'You're looking disgustingly healthy. You've obviously recovered well. So, I assume you've not come looking for a nurse. Why are you here?' She picked up her cup again. Her hair fell forward, shielding her face as she bent to sip from it.

'Does there have to be a reason?' Her hair fell back as she straightened in her chair and stared me full in the face.

'"*Once is happenstance. Twice is coincidence. Three times, it's enemy action, Mr. Bond.*" My dad was a huge James Bond fan, he encouraged me to read the originals. *Goldfinger* was my favourite.'

I recognised the name, but not the quote – I let my confusion show. 'Well, I've never read it… but, I'm not your enemy.'

"Ah, but I don't know if I can trust someone who doesn't know *Goldfinger*," she said with a grin. Her eyebrow jerked. 'So, again, why are you here?'

'To be your friend? Maybe I could buy you dinner?' I hadn't planned this. I'd intended just a quick coffee, to make sure she was OK and that there was no reason to be concerned about her. I'd made the offer before I knew what I was saying. She sighed, exasperated.

'And we're back to my original question: how long can I expect to enjoy your company this time?'

'Honestly? I don't know, but as long as I'm in London I'd like to spend some time with you.' She gave me a long, considered look, her head cocked to one side, then she gathered her coat and bag and stood looking down at me.

'OK, last chance. Dinner, eight o'clock. J. Sheekey's… You'll need to book.'

'I could pick you up if you like?' She shook her head.

'One step at a time, Mr. Bond.' And with a grin she was gone. I smiled to myself, took an absent-minded sip. It spoiled the moment.

Chapter 23

I probably wasn't being smart, was doing the wrong thing but Sindri had warned me not to lose my humanity again, and that was easier said than done given the fire that burned within me.

I could no longer pretend to myself that I was detached from the here and now.

I had business with the Renegades and questions for Sora-san and the Protector leadership but I had other needs too. I was in sore need of some sense of normality and so now I was going to have dinner with a beautiful woman. It would be a time-out with someone who was ignorant of the increasingly dark world of the Rinks.

I told myself there was another reason: that she was an innocent in danger of being caught up in the machinations of the guilty and that I shouldn't let that happen. I tried to ignore my other feelings, but I couldn't. Try as I might I couldn't deny the attraction I felt for Meg.

I hadn't stopped thinking about Lela. The cycles we'd spent apart hadn't reduced those feelings. Sometimes at night I ached so much for her that I'd conjured her so clearly it was if I could feel her next to me. The caress of her breath on my neck, the intoxication of her scent. I still longed to find Lela again, but I'd had centuries learning to live with the loss and now, inured to being without her, I was finding it hard to resist the charm and challenge of another beautiful and vivacious woman. I chose not to feel guilty; it was what it was.

Since returning to London, I'd kept a low profile. I'd avoided the Savoy, just in case, and taken a room in a small down-market hotel in an unfashionable part of the West End. I returned there now, made the restaurant booking as Meg had instructed and took time showering and changing. A grey silk suit, plain shirt and tie, hoping I'd chosen right. I wanted to look good for her, not for me.

With more than an hour to kill, and despite my best intentions, I decided I could afford to at least reconnoitre enemy territory. This time the cabbie was one of that rare breed – the non-talking kind. In silence we headed back into central London and completed a swing past Cockspur Court. I'd no idea what I expected to learn, and I learned nothing. Number 13 was just another door. There was nothing that revealed whether there were Renegades there. I thought it unlikely. The street was well chosen; central yet a backwater, discreet and with no through traffic. I would be hard to penetrate undetected but I doubted the risk would be worthwhile. I'd already decided I'd have to find another way to confront the Renegades.

Next, we headed for Knightsbridge and cruised past Selene's house in Ovington Place. It was dark but I could see the curtains were open, suggesting it was unoccupied. It offered no clues as to Selene's fate or what the remaining Seekers were up to, now that I'd severely disabled their organisation.

Finally, we reached Curzon Street and I directed the cabbie to a side street and to park where I could see the Phoenix Centre. If he had questions about what we were up to he kept them to himself. Again, I wasn't sure what I'd expected to see and after five minutes or so of boredom I was about to tell the cabbie to head back to the Strand when a chauffeured car pulled up outside the centre. Moments later Sora-san emerged, got in and was whisked away.

'Follow that car please.' Still no questions, the cabbie just did as he was asked. It was unnatural. I checked my watch as we headed west, skirting Hyde Park, but decided the risk of being late was worth it. I had thought that Sora-san would be heading for a dinner engagement and was surprised when, a few miles later, the car entered the leafy avenues of Holland Park and then pulled into the drive of one of the more secluded mansions in the exclusive enclave. The front door was opened by suited doorman – a butler in this day and age? – and Sora-san swept inside. His home?

As the cabbie pulled away and we headed back toward the city I sighed to myself. I'd killed some time but learned nothing of importance. Sometimes life's like that.

*   *   *

I wasn't late but I cut it close. I'd only just been seated when Meg arrived a few minutes after eight. Despite its age I'd not been to Sheekey's before. The décor, service and staff uniforms seemed anchored in its one-hundred-year-old origins. I wasn't sure if that was good or bad. It certainly seemed to be a characteristic of the current era – more than just nostalgia, a sense that true quality was a thing of the past – and one that was at odds with the technological and social advances of the new millennium. I'd chosen a secluded table for two so that we could talk in privacy. Whatever it signalled to Meg it was obviously an OK choice. I rose as she approached the table and she greeted me with a broad smile and a peck on the cheek before taking her seat.

'Hi. Nice table.' She glanced around. 'I hope this is all right for you, I hope you like seafood, I should have asked.' She was nervous, bubbling with energy. I grinned at her, taking time to admire and enjoy her glow, her vitality. She was dressed to kill though I suspect she would have denied it had I suggested it. She'd piled her luscious hair in a tumbling cascade, loose tendrils caressing her ears and neck. Simple earrings and a single-strand necklace set with onyx accentuated the highlights and her dark, dark brown eyes. The neckline of her plain but perfectly fitting dress revealed rather than plunged and the colour, neither blue nor black, somehow hinted at hidden depths. Mine hadn't been the only eyes that had tracked her progress from door to table, had noted the sleek, athletic figure, accentuated by her high heels as she'd glided effortlessly across the room. She gave me a sharp look.

'You brush up quite well yourself,' she taunted, 'but close your mouth, it spoils the look.' I couldn't help the burst of laughter that escaped me.

'My apologies, but it is your fault after all. You look stunning. Thank you.'

She'd exhausted her cool and a blush of pleasure swept across her cheeks. 'Well, you made an effort too, so, thank *you*.'

'Shall we call it honours even and toast ourselves?' I signalled the waiter to bring the bottle I'd ordered earlier. It popped, he poured and we clinked glasses as the bubbles settled. As we sipped, our eyes questioning each other – where was this going? We relaxed, content for now to enjoy the journey. 'And this is fine, I love seafood.'

'Great, then I'm ordering for both of us.' With total assurance she engaged with the waiter, checking the specials and ordering from the menu she clearly knew by heart. I raised an eyebrow.

'Do you always insist on being in control?'

She chuckled. 'No, but with you I suspect it may be wise.' We were both grinning.

'You eat here regularly?'

'Nope, never been here, can't afford it. I've heard about this place and browsed the menu online waiting for someone to treat me. I adore seafood. You are going to treat me, aren't you?'

I felt the stirring of emotions I'd long suppressed. Buttons were being more than pressed by her brazen flirting as she leaned towards me, her elbows spread wide, fingers interlaced palms down on the table, a challenge and an invitation. She was the opposite of Selene. Open, without artifice. Warm and generous. Unselfish. I told myself this was a woman I must never use, or abuse. I had reservations – fears for her if she associated with me – but for now I set them aside. This was a journey I wanted, needed, to enjoy.

We retreated from the flirting, content, I thought, to test, explore to find out more about each other. The conversation was light, about the food, living in London, as we attacked the stacked dishes of Fruit de Mer that she'd ordered for us to share. I'd asked her how it was going at work. She'd asked me where I'd been. I made up some tales. Said I'd been travelling on business. Then…

'So, what's your real name?' A change came over her. Her previously relaxed demeanour replaced, now, with a wary suspicion. It was as if she'd been holding it back, reluctant to challenge me but could wait no longer. She'd taken me completely by surprise. I half choked as I inhaled rather than swallowed the fragment of lobster I was sucking from a cracked claw. She waited calmly as I sorted myself out, physically and mentally.

'What do you mean?'

'I mean you're not '*uh, Paul Mason*'.' She played back my hesitation and slip – the way I'd introduced myself to her the day I'd shifted. There was certainty in her gaze, in her voice. And some anger, some fear that I was going to hurt her somehow.

'What makes you say that?'

'Well, let's start with who's Jay?'

Shit!

Now I was really shaken. For a moment I phased out, had to force myself to focus. She'd ambushed me. I gathered myself, pulled myself together. I had to limit the damage before it got worse. 'Where did you hear that?' I asked quietly, focussing on her, reluctant to do what I feared would become necessary.

'From you. At the hospital, while you were drifting back from the induced coma.'

'And what did I say exactly?'

She frowned. 'To be honest, I'm not sure. It didn't make sense. It was if you were talking to yourself, fighting with yourself. You repeated certain phrases: *"I can't be gone"*; *"enough, Mason"*; *"I will be Paul!"*; *"get over it, you're one of us now"*; *"there are other lives to live"*. And then there were streams of names. Some you repeated: Jay was one, Samson another. Several times you said *"we're all Jay now"*. I was going to ask you about it when you were recovering but you disappeared before I had a chance.'

My mind churned as I tried to work out what to say. I

remembered how the residual elements of Paul's psyche had attempted to re-assert control over the now-self as I'd lain weakened but I'd no idea that anyone else had witnessed our struggle.

'Look,' Meg continued earnestly, 'it was obvious when I first met you. You hesitated when I asked your name. You were hiding something. Why?'

'I was ill, that's all. Remember? I fainted because I hadn't eaten.' I put a lot into it; compelling her to believe, to accept it. It didn't work. That's the trouble with getting to know – to like – someone. Compulsion works better when there's no emotional link, no respect, no care.

'Don't try and fob me off, Paul or whatever your name is, it was more than that.' She was frowning now, disappointed in me. Growing defensive as she feared the worse. That she'd been wrong to like me, to trust me. I tried a winning grin.

'C'mon, what would I be hiding?' That didn't work either. I watched in dismay as she shook her head and pushed back from the table, prepared herself to leave. Her voice was quiet now, serious.

'No, Paul, or whatever your name is. Tell me now, what's going on or that's it. I mean it.' She was hurt and angry, reluctant to go but I could see the determination within her.

'Who else have you mentioned this to?' I asked, scared for her now. The change of tack confused her.

'How's that relevant? What do you mean?'

I stopped trying to compel, tried honesty instead. 'Look, trust me for a moment. I can explain, but first it's important I know if you've said anything to anyone else.' I saw her wrestling conflicting impulses, trying to decide whether to leave or to give me one last chance. I held my breath then released it slowly as she relaxed a little. Around us the bustle of waiters and clatter of dishes brought us back from the edge. She pulled her chair back toward the table.

'I didn't say anything but there was a reporter who pestered us some weeks after you discharged yourself. He said he was doing a follow up on the mugging, the attack on you. He came to me and asked me to confirm what Tim had told him. You remember Tim the ICU nurse?' I nodded.

'What had Tim told him?'

'Pretty much what I told you, plus some more he'd heard you say about 'past and future lives', 'who are the Seekers?'… Other stuff that made no sense.'

'And you confirmed all this?' I was thinking aloud. The "reporter" would have been a Protector. Of that, I was sure. She glared angrily; ice crept into her tone. I saw I'd been clumsy, offended her.

'No, I sent him away with a flea in his ear and had an almighty row with Tim for breaching patient confidentiality. I threatened to report him if he didn't donate the payment he'd received to charity.' Her palm slapped on the table as she drilled me with a look that brooked no further delay. 'Now you come clean. What's this all about?'

With great timing our waiter stopped by, refreshed our drinks and then, sensing now was not the time, moved away without leaving the dessert menus. It had bought me enough time to cobble together a cover story that I thought would hold for now. It had elements of truth in it, hopefully enough to convince her. I took a deep breath.

'Ok, you're right, I'm not Paul Mason. Well, not now anyway.'

'What does that mean?'

'Paul Mason was a cover name I was using.'

'What, you really are a spy then, *Mr Bond*?' Her words dripped with scorn. I was seeing her tough, defensive side now.

'No. I'm a cop. When I first met you, I was undercover, investigating drug dealing. When you helped me in the street I was recovering from a warning. I'd been roughed over. I'd got in the way of one of the gangs.' Her glare softened as I saw doubt creep into her eyes. Her hand rose to her mouth before she caught herself.

'And I should believe that? Why?'

'Because it's the truth.' I said it simply – and some of it was true. I wasn't trying to compel her but most people can recognise a truth when it's given openly and honestly. It's just lies that we're bad at detecting. I saw her doubts deepen, that maybe she'd been wrong to distrust me.

'And the next time you saw me it was because I hadn't backed off enough. The dealers hadn't made me for a cop, but they thought I was a competitor trying to muscle in on their territory. So, they gave me a proper beating. If it hadn't been for you, I might have died.' This time her hand made it to her mouth. She'd wanted to believe. Otherwise, why would she have agreed to dinner? Now the shock of what I was telling her and a growing relief that she might be able to trust me were striking home. I felt good and bad about that. I pressed on before she asked for more proof, maybe to see my badge or some official identification. 'Think about what happened next...' I was winging it now, making it up on the fly, but I could see it was working. 'The police came to see me in hospital, yes? But there was no follow up. That's because the locals were warned off, to protect my cover. They were told to leave it alone. There was no investigation.' Meg nodded.

'That *was* unusual. No-one even asked to interview us, which happens with most assault cases. No-one that is until the journalist started asking questions.' She was thoughtful now. She wanted to believe me and I'd given her a credible story. Her subconscious was telling her to accept it.

'Look, I'm sorry if you think I've been lying to you but I had no choice.'

'So, that's why you keep disappearing... Is it over now?' She reached across the table and grasped my hand as relief replaced her anger and distrust. 'Is it really OK for you to be telling me this now? And the other stuff you kept saying, about past lives... Seekers and so on, what was that? Delusion and memories of other undercover jobs? Is that right? And Jay, is that your real name? Can you tell me?' She was bubbling again and I hated myself for what I was about to do. Hated that it meant more lies. Hated that whatever journey we'd been embarking on was over, but it had to be. I shook my head.

'No, it's not OK that I've told you.' I saw the first flickers of concern in her eyes. 'I shouldn't have and I can't tell you any more details. It's not a life that I can share with anyone.' I was back to the real truth. I'd learned the hard way. I couldn't share my life with a Phem. I should have known better, should never have given in to my emotions. Dinner had been a mistake. The bubbles burst as she picked up on what I was really saying. She withdrew her hands.

'So why the invitation to dinner? Why did you come to find me?'

I steeled myself and gave her the lines that I knew would drive her away. 'Because I'm human. I wanted to see you again. I couldn't help myself, even if it was just one more time.' I didn't need to pretend to be miserable.

'One more time? So, what, you thought maybe third time lucky? A one-night stand? Is that what you came for?'

I shrugged, made myself seem callous. 'I never promised anything else.'

'You never promised me anything, but you seemed to be offering me something. You know you did. You led me on.' She was gathering her things for real now, clutching her bag defensively against her. 'Thanks for nothing. Don't try a fourth time. I'm not as easy as you think!'

Secluded or not, by now our table had attracted attention from several others. This time the looks I received as Meg stormed out were scornful and pitying, not envious and admiring. I signalled the waiter. It could have been worse. At least I knew she was safe. Whatever I'd blabbed in my coma shouldn't have been enough to concern the Protectors.

As for what might have been?

I'd just have to get over it, as I'd gotten over so many others before.

Chapter 24

I'd returned to the UK with four tasks to complete. The first hadn't gone entirely to plan but I was at least satisfied that Meg was safe. She could continue as an innocent: ignorant of the dangers that had threatened her. I put her out of my mind, as best I could, and spent the following day planning my next moves. The last three tasks would not be so easy and I was anxious to get back to the Coromandel, to Marta and her team. It was time to take some risks because it wasn't just the Coromandel that I needed to get back to. I had no idea how the knowledge that Sindri, and now Marta, were compiling would help us, but the ubiquity and consistency of a belief in reincarnation could surely only mean one thing. Either mankind was uniformly deluded or the "between world" really existed.

With every passing cycle I became more and more jaded with the here and now. I knew – but couldn't say why – that wherever I went during the transition times was where I was meant to be. I knew, too, that I could always choose to end each cycle as soon as it began, to force my psyche back into transition, but I also knew – again without knowing why – that the secret to existing permanently on Plato's plains of forgetfulness could only be found in the here and now. Each time I had to stay for as long as I could, to search for the secret. I was sure there were clues in the data we'd amassed. It couldn't just be that there were transgressions I needed to make amends for – there were so many. Or that I should do something to better the world – there seemed so much that needed doing. So, I had to keep looking.

I knew, now, that the Seekers had found nothing to add to our store of knowledge but that they believed the Renegades had made progress. Before I could tackle that, however, I decided my next task should be to make sure the Seekers had been neutralised for at least some time to come. They had become too active, too powerful and too uncaring. I now knew I'd cut off the head, but the tentacles would still be writhing. Of that, I was sure.

The next day, I was on my way to Ovington Place when I saw the headline: '*Amnesiac Identified as Nurse*'. I would have missed it if it hadn't been repeated on every newsstand. I grabbed a free sheet and turned to the story, searching urgently for a picture, a name. I found it. Tim. There were few facts. He'd been found wandering the streets, confused and unable to give his name or any other details. Admitted, by chance, to his place of work, and identified by his colleagues, he was now under their care but his loss of memory appeared deep and profound. I rammed the paper into a bin, venting some of the fury that swelled within me. The bastards! What they'd done wasn't just unnecessary it was callous. They'd grown indifferent to anyone's needs but their own. It was that realisation that suddenly allowed everything to click into place. I finally understood what had been happening since I'd shifted, how I'd been manipulated and played. My every move plotted and orchestrated. That's why I'd been in react mode. Constantly on the go. I'd been an unwitting pawn, but no longer. Change of priorities, change of plan; I headed to Holland Park.

*   *   *

Sora-san was calm, he'd expected me, I could tell. The costumed flunky – butler or whatever – opened the front door before I had a chance to knock. With a murmured greeting he led me through to an elegant drawing room where Sora-san was waiting. He posed with studied indifference; leaning against a floor to ceiling bookshelf, book in hand.

'Jay, this is a surprise.'

'Really?'

Sora-san sighed, gave me a world-weary look. Was I going to be that tiresome? He turned and led me towards some easy chairs, waving his hand, bidding me to take a seat.

'When we last met you made it plain you wanted nothing more to do with me, with the Protectors. So, why are you here now?'

'You really want to play it that way, Sora-san? Bewildered innocence?' I'd had time to think it through some more and time to reduce the feelings of anger that surged within me. Anger and frustration at my blindness and humiliation that they'd played me so effectively. Calmer now I drilled him with a glare. 'You used me, set me up. You and the other council members.'

Sora-san sank into a chintz covered armchair, crossed his legs, picked idly at a piece of lint that marred his otherwise immaculate trousers. 'My dear Jay, what on earth do you mean?' he purred, not attempting to conceal the smirk that soured the atmosphere between us even more than his words. I looked down at him with contempt.

'You did nothing about the Seekers watching the Phoenix Centres, knowing that when I eventually returned, they'd track me. You knew I'd have to react, would be drawn in. That play with Ayeesha Rao was just that, a play to distract me. How many others around the world did you have ready to sacrifice as you sacrificed her? You knew she'd been approached by the Renegades, that she was sympathetic to their cause. Did you also know the Renegades would sell her out to the Seekers or did you just not care?'

'You've never understood have you, Jay?' Sora-san was genuinely frustrated. We care, but we care about one thing above all else. We've never lied to you. We will do whatever is necessary to protect Rinks from exposure and to prevent the Renegades from achieving their goal. We believe it's for the greater good, even for the Phems.'

'And this greater good means that the rights, the lives of innocents are yours to use or abuse as you see fit? You claim that moral high ground?'

'Innocents?'

'The nurse whose memories you've taken. Tim. How was that necessary?'

'You speak to me of a moral high ground? How many men have you killed in your time, Jay? How many already in this cycle alone? Are you a moral man?'

'I've never claimed to be. Those I kill have crossed a line, from good to bad. Yes, that's my judgement, but it's at least consistent and one I can live with. I don't hurt the good, the innocent. I don't sacrifice unknowing pawns and claim some twisted justification and absolution for doing so.'

'Ayeesha wasn't entirely unknowing and, when she returns, she'll be stronger and wiser.'

Any doubts I'd had slid away as his cold indifference hardened the resolve that drove me. 'And Tim? He was what, a potential danger that was better neutralised?'

'That was unfortunate. The Protector we sent to remove the nurse's memory of your time in hospital was poorly trained. He exerted too much power; hopefully he'll do better next time.'

'Tim knew nothing! Nothing that could be construed as a danger to any Rink!'

'You said too much when you were in a coma. He heard enough. We can't allow more Phems to become aware that we exist. The Seekers know too much about us already. They are learning about us at a rate we can no longer control!'

'And that's why you've been using me? You knew that if they drew me in, I'd act against them? Why not take direct action yourselves?'

'Because we also needed to find out what the Seekers have learned about the secrets of reincarnation. We knew you'd be motivated to find out and you're the best person to truly judge how much they know.' He was telling me nothing that I hadn't worked out for myself but as he spoke something was nagging at the back of my mind. I grew colder still as I realised what it was. 'You said *"hopefully he'll do better next time"'*... against who? Who have you sent him after? Meg?'

'You shouldn't have met her again, Jay.' Sora-san looked away, checked the clock on the wall, looked back, stared me in the eyes. 'Yes, we decided that it was necessary. By now it should be done.' He was still looking me in the eyes as I broke his neck. It was pointless – he'd told me he was going to end his life, this cycle, soon anyway.

But it made me feel better.

Chapter 25

Removing a memory requires finesse but can be completed in a matter of moments once a subject has been isolated and suitably prepared. I'd done it many times. The process – a combination of psychoanalytic, hypnotic and psychotherapeutic techniques – was developed over decades by Rinks working with successive Phem scientists and philosophers – the likes of Leibniz, Hegel and Fechner. It would have been published by Freud, and later Jung, if the Protectors hadn't intervened and selectively removed some of their memories. Since then, the process had been kept a closely guarded secret. Whoever had been dispatched to clear Tim's memories had clearly botched the task, probably by rushing the preparation. In the worst instances subjects could be left as little more than drooling imbeciles.

Frantic with worry I called Meg as I drove. Voicemail. I texted her. No reply. From our conversation at dinner, I knew the shifts she was working and knew that by now she would be just about finishing at the hospital. I halved the normal journey time, punishing the BMW I'd taken from outside Sora-san's house and provoking repeated flashes from the speed cameras as I tore past. I dumped the car, doors open and keys swinging invitingly, about a block from the hospital and ran the remaining distance.

There was the usual melee of patients waiting to be seen in A&E and harassed staff dealing with them as best they could but there was no sign of Meg. I scanned the room again, my pulse quickening, before weaving through the crowd and pushing to the front of the queue at the desk.

'I'm looking for a nurse, Meg Jackson.' The receptionist looked at me wearily, was about to launch into a sarcastic put-down when he saw my face. He swallowed hard as I exerted enough will to reinforce the request then answered.

'Cubicle three. She's with a patient.' He pointed across the room to a corridor lined with curtained cubicles. I grunted my thanks, ignored the protests from the queue and eased my way back through the crowd. The first two cubicles were empty. The curtain was closed on the third and I could hear a soft murmuring within. It stopped as I slipped through the opening. The short, overweight patient sitting upright on the bed dropped Meg's hand, startled. I saw her head droop as he let go, her legs buckled slightly and she swayed before catching herself.

'Who are you?' The patient blustered, indignant. 'This is private. I'm receiving treatment!'

I rested my hand on Meg's shoulder as she steadied herself. 'It's OK, Meg, I'm here. Relax.' I loaded my voice with reassurance, felt the change in her as she took a deep breath. She turned to me, confused, still dazed.

'What…? What are you doing here, Paul?'

I heaved a sigh of relief, if she recognised me, I was in time. 'I'm here for you.' And as I said it, I finally acknowledged the simple and honest truth of my feelings for her.

'Well really!' The patient slid to the edge of the bed, swung his legs down and tried to sidle past, 'I'm going to report this!'

I checked him with my hip, blocking him against the wall. 'You can stop pretending, we both know you're not here for treatment.' I looked him in the eye, let him see that I knew. Let him see the fury boiling within me. Let him know what I really, really wanted to do to him. He shuddered and looked away as I shoved him with my palm. 'You're lucky I was in time and you're lucky I'm going to let you go.' I saw the relief in his eyes. 'Don't get me wrong, I'm letting you go because you're just a foot soldier, but don't let me ever see you again. Tell the ones who gave you your orders that I'll be calling on them, tonight. Tell them if anything happens to Meg, they answer to me.' I stepped back and he brushed past, anxious to get away. I wanted nothing more than to hurt him, to crush him for what he'd tried to do to Meg but I needed him to deliver the message.

'What was that all about?' Meg was looking at me curiously. She slipped past to look after her patient who scurried out the doors without a backward glance. 'Where's he going?' Confused she turned back to me. 'And what are you doing here? I thought I made it plain I didn't want to see you again?' I ignored here, checking her over, looking for signs. Saw nothing bad. 'Well? You're doing it again!'

'What?'

'Ignoring me! You're off in your own world. And what did you mean about that patient being a foot soldier? Why did you warn him…? And why should anything happen to me?' She was shaking now, a combination of anger at me and the after effects from being prepared to have her memories wiped.

'Sit down, Meg.' I guided her gently towards the bed, urged her to sit, poured more calming reassurance into my voice. 'I'm really sorry this happened.' I extemporised fast, struggling to find a plausible explanation. 'He wasn't a patient, he's one of the gang of drug dealers that I've been working undercover to catch.' It was the simplest lie, one that I hoped would be easy for her to swallow.

'Why was he here?'

'Some of my colleagues have been trailing him. We think he came here trying to find me. We're pretty sure he attacked Tim but learnt nothing, so they came after you instead; hoping that you might know something that would give them a lead. They thought they'd left me for dead, now they need to silence me.'

It was thin, very thin, but – in her shocked and dazed state – she bought it.

'Oh my god.' She sank back, hand on her chest. 'And you came here to protect me?'

'You know me. The others need to stay out of sight until we can round up the whole gang.'

'And that thug?'

'He'll be followed, watched. I've no doubt he's done what I said, returned to report to his bosses.'

'Am I safe now?' I nodded, sat beside her and gave her a hug.

'I'm sure of it.'

She leant against me. 'And you? Are you safe?'

It felt good, but, reluctantly, I moved away. Preparing myself. It was getting harder every time.

'I'm as safe as houses. Now, are you done? Is your shift over?' She looked at me quizzically.

'Yes, I just have to sign out. Why, what did you have in mind?'

'Just to take you home, to make sure you get there safely.'

'I thought you said I was safe now.'

'You are, it would just make me feel better.' She looked at me, trying to read my real intentions. She hesitated and then nodded.

We rode in silence, together but apart, in the back of the cab. Once she opened her mouth as if to say something then stopped. I didn't press her. When the cab drew up outside her apartment I stepped out, held the door for her as she slid across, gave her my hand to help. Hers was soft and warm. She looked up at me, questions in her eyes but still said nothing. I followed behind as we climbed the steps and she used her key.

'Well, are you coming in?'

I wanted to say "yes", but I couldn't.

'I know what I said, about never wanting to see you again… But I've been thinking about you…And now…' She turned towards me, one hand on the door, confused. I took her hand, leaned forward, kissed her briefly and wished it could be different.

'I know…But I have to go.'

She dropped her eyes, 'You know I don't want you to, don't you?'

I nodded miserably. 'Yes, but it's how it has to be.'

Her head came up as she stepped back into the doorway. 'Bye then.' Testing me. But I wasn't bluffing.

'Bye Meg.' I said and I turned and left. It was a long walk to the corner of the street. A long way to walk without looking back.

Chapter 26

As I left Meg's flat, I felt my resolve weaken. I kept telling myself it was for the best. I couldn't deal with it again, the pain of a lost relationship with a Phem, but that didn't make it any easier. I almost turned back. How different would things have been if I had? I pulled myself together and decided that I needed a distraction before confronting the Protectors. I headed towards Ovington Place.

As I'd travelled back to the UK from New Zealand, I'd spent the hours between flights and during layovers finding my way through the network of servers and databases that supported the Pietersen business empire. I'd finally tracked the location of the data the Seekers had accumulated. It had been impressive and now it would take them a long time, maybe decades, to rebuild it. There were no backups. I'd found them too.

More recently, I'd seen the news reports of the death of the elder Pietersen, Viktor. His gamble hadn't paid off, he'd died before finding the secret he craved. That, and the arrest of his son, Sandor – found aboard a drifting cruiser with the body of his business associate, Joe Trasker – and the accompanying scandal, had severely dented the company share price and with it the financial resources of the Pietersen empire. The investigators I'd hired had confirmed that the contract with Connor Security, for surveillance on the Protectors' Phoenix Centres, had been cancelled. They'd been unable to find any trace of Selene, however. The house and facility on the island offshore from Belize had been sold and the new owners had no discernible connection to the Pietersens or any known Seekers. Whatever had happened to Selene she hadn't returned to London. I doubted she ever would.

My visit to the Ovington Place house was belt and

braces. I needed to confirm what I already knew – that the Seeker organisation had been rendered ineffective for the foreseeable future. When I got there it still looked deserted so I dispensed with my previous cautious entry. No-one passing by would have seen anything suspicious as I climbed the porch steps, picked the lock and slipped inside. I listened hard for sounds that someone might be waiting for me. There were none. The house was empty. It had that feeling of a prolonged vacancy. There was nothing to suggest the occupants would be returning imminently. I checked the alarm. It hadn't been set. There was no need to rush as I searched. There was clothing in some of the wardrobes but too little for someone who was a permanent resident, and no toiletries in the bathrooms. The kitchen was clean and tidy. No dishes in the sink, not even a teaspoon. There was no mail, no newspapers on the mat. A side room, one which had obviously been used as a study, yielded little of interest. No computers, empty file drawers, empty waste bins. If this was still a Seeker base it wasn't an active one.

It was close to midnight by the time I finally got to Curzon Street. The Council members were waiting for me as I'd expected they would be. It wasn't just that I'd sent them a message via their foot soldier, I'd done more than enough to make them worried. They had to know what I knew. There were seven of them, so not the full Council. Sora-san would have been an eighth. The ninth was missing. Maybe, like Sora-san, he or she had recently transited and they were still appointing a replacement.

'We got your message, Jay.' The speaker, I took her to be the current chairman, was a lithe, physically twenty-something brunette. I looked closely, then more deeply.

'I greet you, Angelica. It's been many cycles,' I responded calmly. 'Greetings also to your fellow Council members.' Six heads bowed in formal acknowledgement. If Angelica Klein was surprised at my ability to identify her, she didn't show it and continued smoothly.

'It's been a long time, Jay, but I see you haven't changed. Was it necessary to deal with Sora-san so harshly?'

'Harsh? Not by my measure and I only hastened what he had planned anyway. Perhaps when he returns it will be with a greater sense of humanity.'

Angelica shrugged – I doubted she'd had any real concern for Sora-san – then fixed me with a glare. 'You've been busy since your return, Jay.' I shrugged back, waiting for a question; guessing, but wanting them to confirm why they had assembled in wait for me. 'And tonight, what did you find out about the Seekers?' That made me pause. I'd been unaware they had been following me, or tracking my movements somehow. That, I didn't like. I kept silent, waiting to learn more. 'We know you were at their London house tonight; your entry was noted.'

"Noted": an interesting use of words. I thought it through: guessed that I may have triggered some hidden alarm at the Ovington Place house. Maybe they'd even reactivated the webcams I'd left behind, as motion detectors. So, they hadn't tracked me, I wasn't losing my touch. I studied the chairman, saw her hidden anxiety and wondered at its cause. The lights in the club-like office were turned low. There were no street sounds to disturb the tense silence as they waited for me to answer.

'What were you worried I'd find?'

'Why should we be worried?'

'Why else would you gather to wait for me?'

Angelica sighed, niggled by the jousting. 'Are the Seekers still a threat to us? Have they managed to find out anything about the secrets of reincarnation? If so, have they passed that to the Renegades? Come on, don't be obtuse, Jay, you know what we want.' She was good, but not good enough, the tell was there.

'And…?'

She sighed again, 'And what?'

'And don't you want to know if I found evidence that someone in the Protectors has been feeding information to the Renegades?'

Angelica stiffened. 'We already know about Ayeesha, and that she paid for that folly.'

'You think she was acting alone, a naïve Rink in only her third cycle?' I felt rather than saw a stirring amongst the other Council members.

'What are you suggesting, Jay?' Angelica's anxiety was clear now, despite her apparent icy calm.

'I'm not suggesting anything. I know exactly what's going on. My return was a godsend to you. The Protectors have become weak, you've been losing your grip. Most Rinks want as little to do with you as possible. They want your continuity services, yes, but otherwise they want to be left alone, to enjoy their lives. The more so since you developed this consuming paranoia about the Renegades and Seekers. My return came at just the right time for you.'

'Weak? I don't think so, Jay. Fewer in number maybe but not weaker. You're right, not many Rinks want to become Protectors and some are being seduced by the Renegades, but there are still enough of us.'

'Enough for what? To brutalise innocent Phems? To sacrifice unwitting Rinks?'

'Enough to ensure our mission is fulfilled, by whatever means. We protect Rinks and our secrets and, with your help, we'll prevent the Renegades achieving their aims.'

'You don't know who's betraying you, do you? Ayeesha was passing information to the Renegades, but who gave her the information?'

'Do you know who?' I ignored her and asked my own question.

'Sora-san told me you've had no contact with Lela but he pretended to lie. He was trying to manipulate me into collaborating with you. Later Ayeesha was told to threaten me, was told to tell me that you have had contact and that you could help me find her. But I didn't believe her. So, which is it? Have you had contact?'

'Will you believe whatever I tell you now?'

I shrugged. Outwardly calm I was shielding my emotions. This was what I'd come for. I was trying not to hope. 'Probably not, but I won't know until I hear it.'

Angelica sighed. 'Sora-san truly believed that someone

in the Council had been in contact with Lela. I told him that so he could use it to try and manipulate you. It was a lie.'

It was what I'd expected. I used every ounce of my powers to read her. If she was lying now then I couldn't tell. I had to accept her words. A part of me died inside. It was time to go, I had what I had come for. I stood up, looked around the assembled Council and caught their eyes one by one.

'I've destroyed the Seekers. Their organisation is shattered in this cycle and they are leaderless. I've erased their databases, their records of Rinks. They'd learned nothing of value about the secret of reincarnation. I'd guess it will be generations before they can rebuild. Before they can ever again become a threat.'

A collective sigh of relief ran around the room. 'Thank you, thank you, Jay!'

'I didn't do it for you. I did it to stop their madness: as I shall stop yours, and the Renegades'.' A still silence came over the room. Angelica got to her feet.

'What do you mean?'

'I mean that it's over. The paranoia, the persecution, the plotting. For generations Rinks lived alongside Phems in harmony. Rinks couldn't help being what they were, they knew to keep their secrets from the Phems and, except for a few, refrained from exerting influence or power over the Phems or their affairs. That changed. I watched it change and did nothing. I was at fault for doing so.'

'What do you mean you'll stop us?' Angelica's voice was icy with anger.

'Not, will…have. I've taken away your power. You too will have to rebuild. You'll be faster than the Seekers, but you'll have time to think, to learn from your mistakes. Maybe next time you'll get it right and if not… Well, I'll be back. Sometime.'

'What the hell have you done, Jay?' Angelica didn't doubt my words, she was shaking with fury.

'Your power comes from your knowledge and your

ability to control the accumulated resources of all the Rinks who use your services. You can no longer access any of it. In the time I've been back I've done what you should have done. I've learned from this here and now.

'With its strength has come its greatest weakness. Amazing technologies underpin everything these Phems do. You too have become dependent on them and vulnerable to their loss. There's only one truly effective form of warfare now, cyber warfare, and I've learned how to wage it. I was late getting here because I had more to do than just reconnoitring the Seekers house. I warned you to take precautions but you didn't take me seriously enough. When you look, you'll find your databases are gone. The systems you've used to access Phem systems and databases have been disabled. Your bank accounts have been emptied.

'You still have your physical records – enough to continue providing your continuity services – and you may still have Rinks in places of authority in the world of the Phems but they'll have to compete on equal terms now. Good luck to them, and to you.' I strode to the door and flung it open.

'We'll come after you, Jay!' Angelica screamed.

'Be my guest.'

I closed the door quietly. One more task and I was free.

Chapter 27

I'd moved again, this time choosing a hotel that I'd never used before, the Shangri La at the Shard. It was higher profile, but I didn't care if they came after me now. The Seekers and Protectors were so weakened they were unlikely to be much of a threat and I planned to be long gone before they rallied. I'd chosen the hotel on a whim, because of its name, a fictional paradise inhabited by immortals. Sindri had believed that the description of Shangri La, in James Hilton's novel, had not just been the product of his imagination. She'd been convinced that Hilton had either been an unrecorded Rink, with a memory of the transition – the between world – or he'd spoken to a Rink who'd told him about it. I too wanted to believe, to agree with her. If she was right then somehow it was possible to retain memories of the transition times and I was right to keep looking.

I slept most of the morning, spent the afternoon exercising and trying to relax; gathering my resources, my drive to continue. I had one more task to complete before returning to the search for the peace I was so desperate to achieve. I had to deal with the Renegades. Far more dangerous than the Seekers or the Protectors they sought the power to destroy the world of the Phems and to replace it with one of their own devising. A world which they would dominate and plunder, to satisfy every one of their warped desires. I still had hopes that Sven would throw his weight behind my efforts, but, if not, I'd find another way of dealing with them. I figured that at the very least I could do enough on my own to seriously disrupt their ambitions.

I was planning how as I stared out across the sprawling lights of London, watching the pulsing crawl of the early evening rush hour, streams of red and white lights criss-crossing the capital, when there was a knock at the door. I considered the probabilities – housekeeping or threat? – decided there was only one way to find out and swung the door open. I wasn't often surprised and for a moment I stared dumbstruck until he spoke.

'Good evening, Jay.' He had the same air of supercilious superiority but it was overladen now with a smugness so thick it invited a smack. So, I gave him one, deciding in an instant that since he couldn't be here for any good purpose, I had no reason to be reasonable. The crack of my open hand wiped the expression from his face and I watched as it was replaced with an ice-cold anger. I grabbed him by the lapels, dragged him into the room and shoved him roughly against the wall. He brushed the back of his hand across his face, checked for blood, there was none. I'd hit him hard enough to bruise his ego, nothing more.

'This is not going to help you,' he sneered, blustering to regain face.

'And why would I need help, Ulrich? Is it still Ulrich Fanderl or have you changed your identity?' The effete young man I last met at the Institute in Geneva glowered at me. He'd expected shock and concern; I was displaying neither.

'And it's not going to help her either…'

He had my attention now. I felt myself go cold. 'Her?'

'Can't you guess?' Regaining his composure, he tugged his jacket back into place as he studied the effect his words had on me. I didn't need to guess. I forced myself to be calm, began to do what I should have done from the off when I found him standing there. I began to scan him, reading him for every clue. Took what I saw and began building on it.

'So, you fooled me in Geneva,' I acknowledged, playing on his vanity. I saw his subconscious reaction; he couldn't help but preen. 'You used your arrogance, your behaviour to distract me. I didn't read you as a Rink. You fooled Sindri too which tells me you've had many cycles to develop such skills. You're a Renegade.' It had all come together in my mind in another moment of blinding revelation. 'You were sent to discover what secrets, if any, my Institute had uncovered. And now you're here. To threaten me.' It all made sense, but I hoped desperately that I was wrong.

'Very good, Jay. I'm almost impressed.' He stepped past me, gave himself some space, in case. 'Threaten? No, I'm here to offer you a deal.'

His self-assurance took away my hope. 'My knowledge for Meg's life?' I guessed. Now it was his turn to bow his head in acknowledgement.

'You're fast, they told me you would be.'

'They? Dandy Tom? Iril Karzan?'

'Amongst others.' He was more cautious now. I could see I'd surprised him by my knowledge of Renegade affairs in this cycle.

'Are they here, in London?'

'Waiting for you as we speak.'

I pondered his words. 'Convince me you have her.'

His look was sly, leering as he answered. 'Shall I describe the touching scene, yesterday, as you said goodbye to her at her apartment? The lingering look she gave you as you walked away?'

My heart sank as he confirmed what I'd feared. But he wasn't finished.

'You should have seen the look on her face when we knocked and she answered. She thought it was you, returning to her!'

I held myself back, despite my instinct to do anything but.

'She tried to run, poor girl, but Iril was too fast.'

I went cold.

Cold at the thought of Meg in the hands of the brutal Mongol, but I knew this was not the time to show it. I forced my fears aside and turned away to grab my coat and bag before brushing past him to open the door.

'Let's go then.'

He'd been expecting more – a demand for an explanation, counter threats – was surprised when none came. I used that surprise now. It weakened him, exposed him to my powers. He was unaware of my influence as he grabbed my arm, patted me down and then pointed at the bag.

'What's in there?' I opened it to show him my laptop. He glanced in but made no move to search the bag as I spoke, compelling him to believe me.

'It contains what the Renegades want. I assume they're expecting to trade?' I saw the effect of the influence that I'd been able to exert. Saw as he accepted my words. Then another thought flashed behind his eyes, his muscles tensed. I shook my head wearily at his stupidity.

'Don't even think about it. It's encrypted and only I have the key.'

After a moment he shrugged, then led the way.

Chapter 28

Fanderl took me to a rundown townhouse in the east end of London. The interior, knocked out into one vast open plan living area, was a chaotic mess. A den, not a council chamber. There was no sense of déjà vu, but once again I was facing an assembly of Rinks intent on using me, my knowledge, for their own purposes. But, unlike the Protectors – with their Council, their formality, their self-righteous and uptight beliefs in their 'duty' – the Renegades were dissolute, hedonistic. They had no real organisation, no structure other than a leader, Dandy Tom. Fanderl presented me like a prize then waited. I could see he was expecting, craving, praise. Dandy Tom was sprawled in a chair. A half-naked girl curled at his feet.

'Did you search him?'

'Yes,' Fanderl nodded. 'He's got a laptop in his bag; says it's got some encrypted data on it.'

Dandy Tom stared at him for a moment longer then dismissed him with a casual wave of his hand. 'You can leave us then.'

I saw Fanderl bridle with anger and disappointment, but wisely he kept his peace as he drifted off into the shadows to join the other Renegades scattered around in the gloom. At Dandy Tom's feet the girl slowly uncurled. Her eyes were open but unseeing, pupils blown wide by whatever drugs she'd been fed. It wasn't Meg. I looked around, couldn't see her anywhere in the dimly lit room that swirled with smoke from candles and incense burners, pipes and joints.

'Nice place you have here, Dandy.' I glanced around, counting the opposition, trying to gauge their strength, doubting they were all as drunk or drugged as they pretended.

'It serves,' he drawled, 'pull up a chair.'

'How did you find me?'

'You were followed tonight. From Curzon Street.'

'One of the Protectors tipped you off that I was there?' He ignored the question.

'Sit down. Can I offer you anything?' He gestured at the girl, the bar, the lines of coke laid out on the table before him. I took a chair, pulled it away from the table so I could move freely and sat with my bag resting against my leg, within easy reach. I thought about his offers, rejected them, made my own.

'Sure, you can offer me Meg safe and sound and I'll agree not to send you and your friends back to the between world.' Something flamed in Dandy Tom's eyes. He pushed the girl aside; she crumpled without a murmur. He stepped over her, came close, gave me a hard stare.

'Oh, she's worth a lot more than that, Jay. You'll give us copies of the Seeker and Protectors' databases, you'll tell us what you've learned, what you know about controlling reincarnation and then you'll beg me for her. How's that for an offer?'

I let him bluster, swagger. I needed to build his anger to increase the tension between us. I watched as he came to the boil, spoke before his anger crested. 'What makes you think I have copies? And why would I beg you for something I can just take?'

We'd confronted each other before but never like this. We'd both cycled endlessly. He knew me as I knew him. Neither of us had what a Phem would have called a conscience; we were past that. We both lived, took, used as we saw fit, the only difference between us was a deviation in moral compass. We set our own very different boundaries. He was a devil and whilst I was certainly no saint, I'd never sink to his depths. In terms of powers, we were about equal. Close enough, certainly, that neither of us was keen to put it to the test: but he had his followers and I was alone. He thought that gave him all the edge he needed and I was counting on that. He laughed in my face, brought himself back under control and sat back down, overconfident.

'Take her? Just like that? Would you like to see her?'

'That's why I'm here.'

I didn't see the signal but one of his acolytes untangled himself from the pile of semi-naked bodies sprawled on mattresses in a far corner and slouched out of the room. He came back moments later pushing a bound and gagged Meg before him.

The sight of her, her helplessness, brought back the fear and anger I'd forced aside when Fanderl had told me she'd been taken. Now I fought to control the adrenalin surge as my pulse raced and every muscle tensed in readiness to fight for her. I held myself back as she stumbled; unbalanced by her hands bound behind her. I could see her fear but no outward signs of injury and, in the moments before she saw me, her defiance. Anticipating the next shove, she turned on her escort and kicked out hard, catching him full in the groin. He sank with a groan as the others hooted and cackled. She span back to face Dandy Tom and saw me for the first time. I saw the fear and confusion build, and her defiance fade, as she tried to work it out. What was I doing there?

'Satisfied?' Dandy Tom grinned at me as he grabbed her, sank back in his chair and held her struggling beside him. He grabbed her hair, forced her head back and ran a lingering leer along her body. 'She looks like she could satisfy me…'

For a moment I lost control. I was out of my chair and took a pace towards him before I caught myself. I held myself rigid, watching as Dandy Tom prepared himself for my attack and then sneered as he saw I wasn't going to. I ignored Meg's pleading looks, ignored my own surging fury and focussed all my attention on Dandy Tom. 'Are we here for games or to trade? How do you want to do this, Tom?'

From the corner of my eye, I saw Fanderl, watching catlike, waiting to see if the mouse would run. He and Iril Karzan, seated at a table, looked to be the most alert. The greatest threats after Dandy Tom. I'd worry about them later. Dandy Tom released his grip on Meg, rested a hand possessively on her shoulder as she tried to move away from him.

'You're ahead of yourself, Jay.' He was enjoying himself now. 'You can start by telling me what you know, then we'll decide if there's a trade to be made.'

I shrugged, feigning nonchalance. 'That's easy. I know the same as you.' It was a lie but he wasn't going to find out.

'OK, then, start there.'

I stepped back, grabbed my chair and sat down, this time with my bag on my lap. I gathered my thoughts for a moment then began. 'For many cycles now there have been rumours that some Rinks can control how they reincarnate, can control the gaps between each cycle. You've heard those rumours and more. You've heard that it might be possible not only to control the "how" but the "when".' Dandy Tom grunted. I was saying the right things. Meg stared at me, confounded by my words. I continued. 'No one has ever questioned it before. In every reincarnation myth and belief, confirmed by every Rink experience, we die, time passes and at some future time we are reborn – but you believe the opposite is also possible: to reincarnate backwards in time, to occupy a now-self in some previous era. You believe this and will do anything to acquire such a power.'

'And do you know why we believe this? Why we'd want this power?'

'You believe it because there are historical anomalies that are difficult to explain. You claim these anomalies are evidence.'

'Such as?'

'How did Leonardo Da Vinci know so much about anatomy, engineering, chemistry so far in advance of his contemporaries? Was it future knowledge or a flight of imagination that led him to sketch designs for helicopters and hang gliders? Could he have been a Rink who reincarnated backwards in time? A 'Retro-Rink' as you've named them. Or maybe Leonardo was just a Phem who met a Retro-Rink who was travelling back through time and gained his knowledge that way.'

Dandy Tom leaned forward, nodding: his desire to believe writ large on his features.

'There are others... What about Nostradamus and his prophecies? Or other scientists who've showed remarkable advances in thinking and learning? As far back as Pythagoras, he actually claimed to be reincarnate, or before him the Chinese who developed advances in civilisation and technology centuries, millennia even before the equivalent in Europe. Or more recently Newton... Or perhaps very recently the fiction writers, Clarke and Orwell, how else could they have foretold so accurately developments in science and society?'

I shrugged, shifted dismissively in my seat. 'You've made quite a study.'

Dandy Tom gave me a sly look. 'So have you, Jay.' I returned his stare, refused to blink first. 'Don't deny it, Jay. It's what caused your row with Lela. It's why she left you. When your search for the secret of reincarnation first began to consume you and you almost came over to us. You lost your sense of balance, your humanity. For a while you stopped at nothing in your search for knowledge. When she left you, it shocked you out of it. Your balance returned, but the drive is still there... Isn't it? It's still consuming you and you're no closer to the truth, are you?'

The silence between us was absolute as he waited for me to respond. I couldn't deny what he'd said, but neither would I give him the satisfaction of admitting he was right. Lela's ultimatum had been absolute. Choose between her or the path I'd been following. I hadn't chosen fast enough and, though I'd changed path since, she'd never returned to me.

He broke first, pressed me for an answer. 'So? Don't you believe it?'

With a monumental effort I made myself shrug, forced indifference into my tone. 'You've some of it right, Tom.' I conceded. 'But you're fundamentally wrong, as deluded as you ever were. I believe that through the ages there have been men, and women, with vision and imagination. Does there have to be another explanation? Was Nostradamus different from any other seer? He foretold events in such obscure and general terms that the gullible, the willing to believe, have been able to interpret his sayings as they see fit. You call this evidence. I see curious anomalies that's all.' I was telling the truth. It was what I'd reluctantly come to believe as I'd found no evidence otherwise. But that didn't stop me wondering.

Dandy Tom waved his hand in sour dismissal. 'Deny it all you like, but I'm not wrong.' He squinted at me. 'And why are you so quick to dismiss it? Is it because you know what we would do if we found the secret? You know the power we would have?'

'I know what you *imagine*. You want the ultimate control. You want to reincarnate yourselves way back into pre-history, taking with you today's knowledge of science and technology. Then you plan to start again, to mould the development of the world's civilisations to fulfil your own plans and ambitions. Ruling as virtual immortals, controlling each forward re-incarnation. Discarding and adopting new bodies without any gaps or periods lost in transition. The world as we and the Phems have known it would simply cease to exist. The history we have known obliterated, re-written. Everything replaced by a Renegade controlled world tailored to deliver only the Renegades' wants and desires.'

Dandy Tom guffawed. 'Very good, Jay! We wondered if you'd really understood... but you do!'

'But *you* don't. It's all rubbish. There is no real evidence that retro-reincarnation is possible and even if it were, it would be paradoxical to suggest that there could be any effect on our history or the reality as we've known it. If you found the secret, went back in time and started all over again then the events that led to you finding the secret would never have happened. That's the paradox!' I was wasting my time arguing with him. I was applying logic to a dream that had too much emotional appeal. Dandy Tom scowled.

'We disagree.'

'That's your problem. Not mine. If you want to waste your time chasing myths and dreams, be my guest.' I wasn't as calm or disinterested as I made out. Inwardly I was heaving huge sighs of relief. No matter what the Seekers had believed or the Protectors had feared it was obvious from Dandy Tom that the Renegades had made no real progress in understanding the processes of reincarnation, retro or otherwise. He was so sure he had control of me he was making no effort to screen his thoughts. I could read him clearly. He was desperate to know if I'd learned anything of value.

'And are you still looking to end it all, Jay?'

'Yes.'

'So, you're still searching too? You've not learned how?'

I didn't have to fake anything to convince him. 'I'm still searching.'

'You want to die, and we want to live for ever...' Dandy Tom pondered the fundamental difference between us. 'You're a fool.'

I said nothing, he was entitled to his opinion.

'I don't believe you've destroyed the Seeker and Protectors' databases.' He continued, 'You haven't been back long enough to analyse what they contain. You spirited your Institute out of Geneva but I know you've relocated it somewhere! It can't stay hidden from us forever. They've got copies, haven't they? Where is it?'

I smiled at him. Dandy Tom had no way of forcing me to tell him. He couldn't threaten me physically, I could resist any torture and, if they went too far, they'd have to wait until my next cycle and start all over again. He thought he could use Meg as leverage, but I was about to take that away from him. My smile only enraged him further, as I'd known it would. He wasn't thinking straight. He thought himself safe, confident that his powers were a match for mine and that he had more than enough backup in Fanderl and Karzan and one or two other lesser Renegades guards who were watching soberly from the shadows. His thinking was flawed. He assumed I'd be relying solely on my own skills and resources. I'm not that proud. He'd misjudged Fanderl. Misread the Renegade's arrogance and ego. Hadn't realised how Fanderl's overconfidence had allowed me to deceive him when he'd searched me.

I reached into my bag, removed the gun I'd hidden under my laptop – the gun I'd taken from the Estonian drug dealers, weeks before – and shot Dandy Tom between the eyes. Fanderl and Karzan were hampered by the table so I took out the sober Renegades next, firing before they'd barely had chance to launch themselves towards me. Iril Karzan's eyes blazed in defiance and furious impotence as I swung back towards him, he and Fanderl both realised they could do nothing. I sent them to join Dandy Tom and the others in the between world.

Smoke from the gunshots thickened the already foetid atmosphere, the stench of cordite was rank and pungent. The other Renegades had barely moved but it scarcely mattered. Drunk and drugged they were no immediate threat. I dropped the gun. I had no need for it any longer.

Meg was slumped beside Dandy Tom's chair, shaking with shock. Gently I helped her to her feet, used a smashed glass to cut the ties that bound her hands, and carefully removed her gag.

'W… what… how…?' She stuttered, unable to form a coherent sentence. I wrapped my coat around her and held her tight, waiting for the peak to pass. After a few moments the shaking subsided and she drew several deep shuddering breaths as she started to regain control. I judged it was time.

'Meg, I need you to trust me now. No questions. I will explain, I promise, but later. Now we have to move. OK?' I felt her head nod against my chest. Keeping my arm around her I led her carefully away from the carnage and out into the night.

Chapter 29

By the time we got back to the Shard, the shuddering had passed; leaving Meg pale and drawn. During the cab ride back to the hotel she hadn't asked where we were going, hadn't raged about what had happened to her or asked to call the police. As we walked through the lobby, my hand on her arm guiding her, she neither leant on me nor pushed me away. She'd closed down. Overwhelmed by what had happened, by what she'd seen and heard, unable to process it. We rode the elevator in silence, walked the corridor to my suite without speaking. I ushered her in and closed the door. In the lounge, she stood, listless. She made no comment about the room, the view from the floor to ceiling windows. I turned on the lights and wondered what to do next. Eventually she stirred.

'Am I safe here?' she asked.

'Yes. I promise.'

'Even from you?' There was a confused bitterness in her voice. She meant it. She genuinely didn't know what threat I was to her.

'Totally safe, I promise.'

'You told me that before.' She was staring now. Through, not at me. At something she was trying to grasp, to understand. 'Can I leave if I wish? Would I be safe if I did?'

I ignored her last question, not ready to answer it yet. 'I'd like you to stay. So I can explain.'

She hesitated; knew I'd dissembled. 'Will you tell me the truth?'

'Yes.'

'Really? All of it?'

'Yes.'

She shook her head in confusion, unable to decide. 'You killed those men!'

'They would have killed me, and you.'

'That's it? That's all you can say?'

'It's part of the truth.'

She covered her face with her hands. I wanted to move, to hug her; knew that it would be wrong. Eventually she lowered her hands, too exhausted to fight anymore.

'In the morning then: the truth, all of it.'

I nodded. 'Take the master bedroom. I'll be here when you're ready.' I watched her walk away. She didn't look at me as she closed then locked the door behind her. I spent the night staring out at the lights: waiting, hoping.

*   *   *

She slept until soon after dawn and woke full of fears, questions, challenges and distrust. Now, she was curled on a sofa, wrapped in a thick towelling robe, her feet tucked beneath her. We'd been talking for a couple of hours. I'd provided answers and truths. Slowly trust was being rebuilt between us. Disbelief and confusion were being replaced by the beginning of an acceptance that what I had told her might be true, but the questions kept coming.

'So, how many Rinks have there been over the millennia?'

'The Protectors had records of tens of thousands. Those are the known Rinks. I think there are probably more. Some who wish to remain hidden, some who have simply not made contact with the Protectors. Some who in their first few cycles were driven mad by the experience and never recovered, living each cycle in delusion or seclusion. Who knows how many we really are – at any one time there are maybe as many as twenty thousand Rinks whose cycles are in sync.'

'And you just live amongst us? No one knows you exist, except a few Seekers?' She was trying to accept it but I could tell she hadn't got there yet.

'We've occasionally revealed ourselves to Phem leaders – politicians, royalty, presidents – when we've thought we should help them to control the worst excesses of Renegades like Dandy Tom. It's never been very satisfactory.'

She raised an eyebrow.

I sighed. 'They always want what they can't have. Immortality, reincarnation for themselves.'

'But I've never read anything about this. Why haven't they exposed you?'

'Who'd believe them? They have no evidence, can offer no proof that we exist and though we're relatively few in number we exercise considerable control. The Protectors ensure that a number of those in cycle occupy positions of power in the Phem world. It's even easier in this cycle with the aggregation of so much power in the hands of the mega corporations and global media empires.'

'Are you saying that actually you rule the "Phem world", as you call it?'

'Rule? No, the Protectors exercise only enough control to guard the secret of our existence. Most Rinks are not Renegades, we've no desire to control Phems. Why would we? New Rinks, in their early cycles, are helped to get established. Those of us with more experience have access to riches and resources that allow us to do as we wish whilst we're in cycle.'

'You're rich?'

I nodded. 'Probably richer than any Phem who has ever lived.'

'That's boastful.'

'It's a fact, nothing more.'

'And you've lived through sixty cycles and now you're searching for the secret of how to die, to end it all?'

'That's the simple version, but yes.' I stayed calm in the face of her scepticism. She was fighting acceptance but I could see she was weakening now.

'What's the complicated version?'

'What you call death isn't exactly what I'm seeking. I want to return to the between world, where we go in the transition time between cycles. And I want to be able to stay there, never to return to this here-and-now world. Never to occupy or absorb another now-self.'

'What's so good about this between world?'

For a moment I didn't know what to say, but I'd promised her the truth. 'I don't know.'

'You don't know?' there was shock and disbelief in her voice, 'But you'd banish yourself there?'

I reached for a better explanation but I had none. I gave her the only one I could. I nodded. 'Yes. I guess you'd have to call it faith. I just know that's where I'm supposed to be. It's where I'll find lasting happiness.' It was as honest a truth as I could give her. It was a truth of which I was certain. But I had no idea why. I saw the questions bubbling inside her but she chose to leave it, for now, she changed tack.

'Tell me about those cycles, the lives you led. Who have you been? What have you done?'

'Will you listen for more than a few minutes? It would take hours, days… In a shorter time, what could I tell you about thousands of years of living – some in cultures, countries, civilisations that no longer exist – that would have any meaning for you?'

'You could tell me that you've done good, that you're not an evil man.' She paused, considered, 'Are you even a man? A human? What are you?'

'I'm a person. I have a psyche, a soul if you will, just like you or any other. When I'm in the here and now I'm human, sometimes as a man, sometimes as a woman. When I'm elsewhere? I don't know. That's all I can tell you.' I waited, knowing there was little more that I could say, knowing what was to come. How could I not know? I'd been through it before, more than once. I'd broken my vow, never again to become involved with a Phem. Now I had to be patient. All I could do was hope.

'How do I know you're not mad, delusional, making this all up? Maybe what you told me before is true. You're just some seedy undercover cop caught up in some gang war that I've somehow been dragged into. Everything else is just bullshit.'

I waited to see if there was more but she'd subsided and I knew that, no matter how much she wanted to disbelieve she'd finally begun to accept. I watched as she pulled her knees close, hugged them and turned her face away, unable to look at me.

'Why would I construct such an elaborate lie? What would it serve? If I was really that delusional, would I be functional?' I sighed. 'I've told you the truth, fantastic as it must seem to you. And when I lied to you before it was to try and shield you from this. I can and will tell you more, show you more, but now is not the time. I'm not an evil man by my standards. When you know more, you'll have to judge me by yours. That and safety is all I can offer.'

'What do you mean, "now is not the time"?'

I took a deep breath. It was time to give her the bad news.

'Because you're right about one thing. You have been dragged into something.' I paused, not liking what I had to say next. 'I told you I'd tell you the truth and nothing but…'

She uncurled, looked at me, sensing that what was coming was not good.

'I also said you were safe here. I should have added, for now. You know about us – the Rinks – and the Renegades and Protectors know about you. More importantly they know about your relationship with me. You can't extricate yourself from the affairs of the Rinks and that will always put you at risk.'

'We don't have a relationship.' Her voice was bitter.

'OK… They know your importance to me.' Her head snapped up, she gave me a sharp look as if to say, "don't you dare!" I raised a hand to forestall her outburst. 'It doesn't matter what you say. They know it's how I feel. As long as I'm in this cycle they'll always have you to use as a lever against me.'

'Use me for what?'

I shrugged, 'To get to me. The Protectors and the Renegades will both be after me for the data I've stolen. The Renegades for the simple act of revenge too. Even the Seekers will come looking if they can rebuild fast enough.'

'So, do the honourable thing. If everything you've told me is true just take yourself out of the equation.' It wasn't her fault that she didn't know, had no way of understanding what she was asking.

'Suicide? You want me to return to the between world, to enter transition, to wait to begin another cycle?'

'Why not? You've done it before, many times. You'd lose nothing. I'd no longer be of any value; I'd be safe again.' I looked away then gave her the simple answer first.

'I can't do that.'

The silence between us grew. When I looked back, I didn't need any powers to read her confusion and her hurt – to sense her guilt that she'd asked, and her fear when I refused. I searched for a way to explain how my guts churned at the prospect of dealing with yet another shift. The sense of loss and despondency that would descend upon me if I had to start yet another cycle. I did my best.

'I'd lose the chance to find what I've been searching for. The data that's been accumulated in this cycle is like nothing that been available before. I've only just begun to analyse it.' I saw her curl tighter as she heard, but was unwilling to process, to accept, the implication of what I'd said.

'So, you're selfish. I'm at risk because of what you need and want.'

I heard the truth in her words and had no counterargument. 'At least it's honest. I promised you the truth.' But I knew I hadn't told her the whole truth. I pushed the thought aside. Once again, we sat in silence for long minutes. Eventually she sighed, stirred.

'So, what's your solution?' I let out the breath I hadn't realised I'd been holding.

'If we're together I can protect you. At least until the immediate danger has passed. I have the skills, the resources. And then I'll help you to build a secure future. Whatever you want that to be.'

She was still, silent. I tried not to hold my breath again. I didn't try to read her. I made myself wait. When at last she spoke, her voice quiet and resigned, she didn't capitulate but she opened a door. 'How would it work? Where would we go? How would we live?'

*   *   *

It wasn't easy but we talked and worked it out, the beginning at least. I'd use my financial and other resources to isolate us from the world of the Rinks and she'd accept my protection. But the easy familiarity between us was long gone. Whatever we thought we'd felt before was no longer there – or if it was, the barriers we'd both raised hid it from us.

I hired a car and we slipped away from London, drove north and holed up in a remote guesthouse in Scotland. Meg wrote to the hospital apologising that, for personal reasons, she was taking her accrued vacation at short notice and emailed colleagues and friends to say she'd be away for a week or two. I prepared our disappearance, obtained new papers and identities for Meg, and found a safe house to use while we planned a safer, longer future. She maintained a distance between us and I saw her waver, hesitate, reconsider. I did nothing more to persuade her. It had to be her decision. To my relief she didn't change her mind and when, finally, we left the UK I hoped that we'd left everything that had been a threat to her behind.

Chapter 30

I don't think she ever came to fully accept what I was. Sometimes, when I was reading or working on my research – trying to give her space – I'd catch her watching me. In her unguarded moments I could read her uncertainty. I tried not to read her too much. She knew my capabilities. It was part of the trust between us, unspoken, that I would never again abuse them, or her. It was a trust I promised myself I'd keep, unless I couldn't – it was the best I could do.

Some months after what we'd taken to calling "the escape" she finally began to thaw towards me. We were staying on one of the properties I'd kept secret from the Protectors. An estancia, a cattle and sheep ranch in the centre of Uruguay, owned by me through an obscure and hidden subsidiary of my main holding company, PP&F.

For decades the ranch had been managed through a law firm in Montevideo, leased on long term to a succession of tenant ranchers. The last lease had lapsed at the right time and I'd instructed the lawyers to have the main house refurbished and prepared, the land and stock to be contracted out to a neighbouring ranch.

*   *   *

We flew to Buenos Aires on one set of papers, dumped them, and used another to board the ferry to Colonia. Crossing the murky brown waters of the River Plate estuary beneath blue cloudless skies. In Colonia we collected the 4x4 I'd purchased through the solicitors in Montevideo and began a three-day road trip, north through Uruguay.

We stayed off the beaten track and the roads ran long, straight, and dusty through endless softly rolling, almost flat, verdant rangeland. Whenever we stopped – for a picnic lunch, a drink on the shaded veranda of a village store – I'd check for signs that we had been followed. There were none. No familiar vehicles, no dust trails on the horizon. As we headed deeper into the rural interior, staying overnight in small and basic guest-houses, I began to relax. Meg did too. Smiling more as the excitement of the journey replaced her fears. The final track from the road to the ranch house was a little over twenty kilometres. Rutted and potholed, that last leg took almost an hour to drive. Jorge – the ranch hand – and his wife, Maria – our housekeeper – had plenty of notice of our arrival: warned by the noise and dust from our vehicle, and the cackle from the geese that patrolled the house compound.

It took only a few days to establish a routine. Jorge and Maria had prepared the house. The pantry was well stocked. They'd laid in gas supplies for the lights and fridge – there was no electricity – enough for several months and piled seasoned logs for the range stove and open fire to keep the evening chill at bay. With water from the well we were self-sufficient.

Maria came in each day with supplies of fresh salads and vegetables from her garden. Mostly we cooked on a barbeque, lamb and beef steaks from the neighbouring ranch. Occasionally one of our own chickens or a wild turkey, from the many that gobbled and scuttled through the surrounding scrub. Jorge told me that the imperious Rheas, that strutted and pecked without a care for our presence, were protected and, with a wink, that they didn't taste good anyway. I eyed the sow and her litter of piglets that roamed and scavenged through the compound but was warned off by an outraged Meg and Maria. The pair had become firm friends; Meg coaxed the shyness from Maria's two young daughters and they gave her a focus in life that was not me, or the world we'd left behind.

Each day I rode out a mile or so to the nearest low ridge and scanned the horizon. There was nothing to see other than undulating rangeland, grazing cattle and sheep, an occasional Gaucho, blue skies and scudding clouds. There were no signs that anyone had found us. On the way to Uruguay, I'd used the internet to monitor the activities of the Protectors and Renegades as they attempted to rebuild their networks and capabilities, but they were a long way from recovering from the chaos I'd caused them. The Seekers were equally in total disarray. I was as sure as I could be that we were safe.

As I'd hoped, the landscape and lifestyle captivated Meg. She loved animals, she came to love horse riding and most of all the vast open ranges that gave her the space to adjust, to reflect and to come to terms with it all. In the evenings, while the gas lights hissed and the logs crackled and sparked, I told her about my lives. Told her what had been good, what had been bad. I didn't try to justify what I'd been, the things I'd done. That was for her to judge. My other selves watched and I felt their approval. I was doing the best I could. Only time would tell if I was doing the right things. I watched her eyes widen in wonder as she realised just how old I really was and all the things I'd seen. I blushed as she'd laughed at me, for the times I told her about when I'd struggled with my gender or orientation. When she heard things that made her go quiet, made her look askance at the man she was sharing her life with, I walked away to give her time. One morning, as we returned from a dawn ride, she said to me, 'You're not an evil man. I know that now.' That was the start of the thaw. I made her a promise that she could leave whenever she wanted. With a new identity, wealth, whatever she needed. But she stayed. She began to trust me, we became friends. Eventually we became lovers.

Once I asked her, 'If I find the secret, could show you how to reincarnate, would you want to?' We'd just made love, were lying in bed. Dappled sunlight, filtered through the gently waving branches of the apple trees that shaded our windows, cast light beams on the walls. A gentle breeze dried the beads of sweat our exertions had left on her soft tanned skin. She looked at me, head to one side, considering the idea.

'To live the lives that you've led? To become like you?' She looked away, not wanting to hurt me. 'No, I don't think so.' Then she nudged me. 'But I'm glad *you* have.' Her tone was playful, wistful.

I leaned on my elbow, looked down at her. 'Because?'

'You've been a woman, you know what pleases a woman, you know what pleases me… Now, can we do that again… please?' Her grin almost broke my heart. I obliged.

I don't think we ever spoke of it again.

Six months later we knew it was time to move on. It was time to resume living with a purpose. The ranch would be leased again but it'd be there if we needed it, if not there were others … and so we left.

We crossed the world, sometimes settling for a few months, at other times for only a few weeks or days. We did our best to engage in what Meg called the real world but I kept us moving, partly for security but also as my research led us far and wide. It proved fruitless; I found no clues to the secret of reincarnation as I revisited supposed centres of enlightenment and interviewed mystics, religious leaders and philosophers. I struggled to maintain my optimism when I spoke regularly with Marta and the team at the Institute, but it became increasingly clear to me that we were not going to find any answers in the data obtained from the Protectors' files.

The team had tried coming at it from every angle, cross-referencing every pattern that emerged from the beliefs contained in the legends, myths and philosophies that we'd found in the world's religions and folk memories. We'd come up with exactly nothing. Nothing that would explain why there were such variances in time between dying, ending one cycle, and shifting, beginning the next. Nothing that explained why one shift would be into a youthful body and the next into an ageing one, or vice versa. Nothing that would explain why gender or sexual orientation changed seemingly at random or why a cycle would end in one continent and then begin again in another. There was no hard evidence, only anecdotal, that any Rink had ever retained memories of the transition, the between world.

I'd put my faith in science, the application of logic and analysis, to provide some answers. I hadn't overlooked the true nature of science, the need for experimentation, but to experiment I needed two things: a hypothesis to test, and the ruthlessness of the Renegades – and I had neither. I could never do what I now realised the Renegades had begun – a random slaughtering of Rinks just so they could monitor how and when they returned, to see if they could learn anything from that.

I was no closer to even speculating what controlled the process of reincarnation, or transference if that was what it was. Marta tried to stay positive. Pointing out that if nothing else they'd ruled out some theories; that it now appeared there was no controlling mechanism and that the incidence of reincarnation and the timing of shifts and transition periods was entirely random. That wasn't my definition of positive. It wasn't the answer I was so desperate to find and I began to realise that I had to stop before once again it could become destructive – an obsession that would tarnish anything that was good left for me in this cycle.

It was time to stop the search for answers, just as – if I was being honest with myself – I'd stopped looking for Lela: because it felt disloyal to Meg. I thought of Lela sometimes but it was being with Meg that kept me from the depression that might otherwise have claimed me. I'd committed to myself that I'd live trying to find answers but the reality was that for some time all I'd been living for was Meg.

It wasn't just fulfilment and contentment we found with each other; it was deep, deep love. She constantly surprised me. Her independence of spirit, her ability to take whatever came and to make the best of it. Her care for others, her sense of fun, her sense of adventure. When she could, she continued the work she loved: caring for other people. She didn't need to, of course, but that was part of her. It's what made her who she was. It was her reason for living. Protected by an appropriate identity she'd worked in hospitals, refugee camps, remote clinics wherever we'd moved. It wasn't all work. Occasionally we'd treat ourselves to a week or so of idle luxury but that wasn't the life Meg wanted full time.

It was her needs that eventually drew us back to Europe.

Chapter 31

Meg had been drawn irresistibly by the need to do something to help the millions of refugees. The mass exodus of asylum seekers and economic migrants fleeing to escape the chaotic fallout from the pandemic: from poverty, famine, persecution and oppression by their own governments and the forces of religious fundamentalists in the Middle East and Africa. For years refugees had coalesced in immense camps in Turkey, Jordan and Syria. More still were trapped at waystations in Greece, Albania, Austria and France as they were denied onward passage to safe havens in Great Britain, Germany and Scandinavia by governments fearful of terrorist infiltration and uncontrolled immigration.

We landed one evening in Montenegro. It was late autumn and the small country was once again becoming a bottleneck for migrants who'd survived perilous Mediterranean crossings in the summer and had made their way through Greece and Albania only to be blocked by the Serbian and Bosnian governments' refusal to allow them passage through to Western Europe. We were there to meet with "Care First", a new charity that Meg had helped grow into a major asset – working alongside Médicins Sans Frontières and the International Red Cross. For some time now she'd been channelling funds to them from PP&F Assets. We'd originally managed the donations through cut-outs, to protect our anonymity, but Meg had been insistent that she had to meet the charity's organisers and to see the chaos at first hand. She was determined to do all she could to help. All they knew was that she was a reclusive, wealthy donor and that I was simply her partner.

We'd arranged to meet Brad, the Care First co-ordinator, at Podgorica airport – just twenty kilometres from the camp at Nikite Vale that the Montenegro authorities had set up to house the refugees entering through the Bozaj crossing from Albania. He was just finishing up a press conference and the harsh camera lights revealed dark shadows under his eyes and deep wrinkles. The stress of his job all too clear.

He shook our hands and led us away from the reporters and journalists who were jostling for a last comment. He had a Jeep waiting outside and before long we were alone and working our way through the back streets to the small hotel where he'd established a temporary base. As dusk fell, and the temperature with it, the leaden skies began to produce first a thin drizzle, then a flurry of sleet and finally a dusting of snow.

'Great, that's all they need,' Brad groaned, tiredly – they being the migrants. 'It wasn't so bad a month ago, but since the weather's turned their lives have become even more miserable. Few of them have cold or wet weather clothing and the tents we have are barely adequate.' He wasn't complaining, just stating facts.

'Will you be able to cope?' Meg asked.

'We're on it, but it's taking time to get the supplies here and the flow of arrivals shows no sign of decreasing.'

As far as I could see the various governments were doing little other than to create the conditions for a perfect storm. In the face of the wave of terrorist attacks that began in Paris but soon spread to every major city, the European nations, supported by North America, had stepped up the supply of arms and other resources to Israel and other allied countries to try and contain the forces of a resurgent Islamic fundamentalism. As a result, the flow of refugees increased just as, also in the face of the wave of terrorist attacks, the European Union enforced strict border controls and suspended the Schengen agreement to create temporary internal border restrictions. Controls and restrictions that effectively penned the refugees in the camps. Camps that had grown and filled beyond crisis point. The simple truth was that no matter their skills, dedication or resources, international aid organisations were going to be swamped unless the mass migration of people could be reduced or even halted. The waystations, the transit camps could be emptied quickly if the haven countries opened their borders – but that would require a significant change in social attitudes in many of them – and they'd refill equally quickly if the horrors in the refugees' home countries weren't dealt with.

'You know what I heard on the radio today?' Brad said wearily. 'Some government spokesman claiming that migrants constitute a high and growing percentage in the crime statistics, and so immigration has to be controlled. They know full well that it's the underprivileged who are over-represented in crime statistics, and that by virtually ignoring newly arrived immigrants, instead of supporting them, they're just adding to an underclass that turns to crime. It's their policies – forced on them by their electorate – that cause the problems, not the migrants. Sometimes I just want to give up.'

'You don't mean that, Brad,' Meg said gently. He considered it for a moment then sighed.

'I know. But someone needs to do something.' I saw him glance at me in the rear-view mirror, looking for support but I said nothing. Meg saw the look on my face, gripped my hand and gave it a squeeze.

'OK, I hear him.' She whispered to me. 'But let's not go there again, not tonight. OK?' she said, her voice tired. I nodded and as Meg leant gratefully against me I could feel her concern, her despair. It was something we'd discussed. I'd argued that we should somehow use our resources, my skills, those of other Rinks, to influence and change government policies and actions. Meg was scared for me, for the life it might lead me back into, but I could see her resolve weakening – her sadness deepening – as the plight of these refugees worsened. I knew there'd be no simple solution but I had some ideas and I was determined to try, as much for her sake as the poor souls shivering in the cold and unfriendly dark.

*   *   *

The next morning Meg left early with Brad to see just how bad it was in the camps. I lazed in bed a while longer, scanning the news whilst finishing a room service breakfast. The image on the screen – Meg, with me beside her, caught on the edge of a shot by the press conference cameras the evening before – sent a cold shiver down my spine. I reached for the phone. It had been a fleeting shot at the end of what was becoming increasingly yesterday's news as the refugee crisis moved into yet another month without visible change. I could hope that no-one of any concern would have seen it. But I wasn't about to take that risk. When we left Uruguay, I'd arranged a constant security coverage. It was provided by a worldwide agency that was well versed in the needs of the wealthy, both those who were famous and those who didn't wish to be. For the most part, a small team shadowed us. It could provide an immediate presence, should it be required, but otherwise they maintained a discreet distance and remote surveillance. There had also been times when I insisted on close protection for Meg. Not from the threat of the Renegades or Protectors but because of the places she insisted on visiting – to help, to care for others. The current team leader, Raisa Talanov, was one I'd met before, she arrived within minutes of my call.

'Your wife's fine, Sir.' She sought to reassure me. 'We've an agent with her, travelling in the same Jeep, and we're tracking her locket back here at our base. We know where she is at all times.' It was something else that I'd insisted on. That Meg should wear a locket that broadcast a signal whenever she travelled in high-risk areas. In turn she'd insisted I wear one too.

'OK, that's good. But I want to increase the coverage for the next month or so.' I explained why, the risk that the TV broadcast might have revealed our location and movements to those we were seeking to avoid.

'I see. I'll arrange it.' She paused, coughed. 'It would

of course help us do our job if we knew who you were trying to avoid, Sir.' But she said it with a weary resignation. We'd had the conversation before. I grinned at her.

'I know. Sorry, Raisa. Can't help you. Just accept there is a real and unspecified risk and be ready when we need you.'

'Yes, Sir.'

I liked her. She never had much to say, just got on with her job, but I really couldn't help her. If, when, a move was made against us it was unlikely to be someone I'd recognise and I couldn't explain who they might be or who they'd represent to the security team. It wasn't perfect but it was the best we could do, short of hiding ourselves away for ever, and neither of us was prepared to do that.

Whilst I waited for Meg to return, I watched a CNN special report and caught up with what was going on in the USA. A thought that had been brewing in my mind began to take shape. I spent the rest of the day thinking it through. Since I'd reluctantly come to realise that I had to stop my ceaseless quest for answers I'd become increasingly introspective. Now, I gave space to the idea that I'd wasted endless cycles in the here and now. That I'd lost perspective and respect for Phems, their lives and ambitions. A respect that working and living with Meg had re-introduced me to. The thought took shape, became a drive, a desire for action.

* * *

If I was quiet during dinner, that evening, it went unnoticed by Meg and Brad. I might as well have been invisible, so wrapped up were they in their own issues and concerns. We'd planned to stay for three days in Montenegro but already I'd had enough. I needed to do my own thing. As Meg and Brad talked more over dinner, I excused myself with an explanation that I needed some air. The low clouds that had so depressed on our arrival had lifted and the night sky was for once clear and sleet free as I stepped outside of the hotel. I think that was when my mind finally cleared and I made my decision.

'Jay…' I heard Meg call out. She'd followed me from the dining room. I turned and gave her a smile and, though she didn't have my capabilities, she read me with ease. 'What is it, Jay?' I saw her smile falter. 'Why did you leave? I'm sorry that Brad and I have been so pre-occupied. Is that it?'

'You think I'm angry at you? That I'm disappointed?' I shook my head. 'It's the opposite. I'm jealous. Jealous of what drives you, jealous that you feel what I haven't felt for a very long time.' She tilted her head; not understanding but wanting to hear more she leaned against me, holding my arm as we walked through the streets.

'What is it that you think I feel, Jay?'

'You care for others; you want to help them, to improve their lives.'

'You care for other people too. I've seen it.'

'For individuals, yes; for people close to me. But that's not the same.'

'You said, "haven't felt for a long time" … Has that changed?'

And that was the question I'd been pondering. Why now did I feel some care, some concern for the world of Phems? I'd seen social groups, communities, kingdoms, empires, even whole civilisations rise and fall before so what was so special about this generation? Why did I feel driven to interfere, to try and counter the forces that were threatening to destabilise the civilisation of this here and now? And I'd come to realise the answer. It was because of the pace of change, the achievements I'd witnessed and marvelled at since my previous cycle. It was as if the Phems of this here and now had reached a new level of awareness and capability. They'd developed to a point where their potential for future development was exponentially greater than ever before. They had developed skills, tools, resources that might, just might at last allow them to tackle the major threats to humanity, not just war but also poverty, injustice and disease. And it was because that potential had been threatened, weakened by the activities of Rinks.

Renegades, acting as warlords, were fomenting unrest in the Middle East, Asia and Africa. As crime lords they were driving the trafficking in refugees, drugs and sex-slaves that was overwhelming the processes of law and order and stable societies in the developed world. The Protectors, manipulating the media to hide the worst excesses of the Renegades, had blunted public reaction and hence the response of Governments until it had become almost too late. The balance had to be redressed somehow. I didn't tell her any of that, then. How could I? I hadn't yet fully understood it myself, so my answer was, as usual, inadequate.

'Yes… it has.' With a squeeze of my arm, she let me know that was enough for now and gently led me back towards the hotel. She knew me so well.

*   *   *

The next day, Meg left Brad to his own devices and she and I talked.

'So, you're off on another mission? I'm no longer enough for you?' There was a twinkle in her eye that told me she knew that wasn't what I meant.

'No, you're not.' I had the same glint in my eye. 'In the same way that I'm not enough for you. You need me, but you have other needs. To help others, to help Care First make a difference. I too have other needs. I thought I needed to find the secret of reincarnation so that, when I was ready, I could leave the here and now and never return. Now, even if I had that secret, I wouldn't use it. Not yet anyway. Because of you. And because I need to do something else first.'

'What? What is it you need to do?'

And so, I told her. Not the specific details but the general. I explained my need to help Phems achieve their potential. To somehow undo the damage that Rinks had done to them. There were some things I couldn't explain. The sense of fulfilment that had come over me when I'd made the decision to turn my back on the search for the secrets of reincarnation and to begin a new quest. I couldn't explain to her why, suddenly, it felt as if I was at last fulfilling my destiny, because I didn't understand it myself.

The next day I checked that the extra security was in place and once I'd satisfied myself that Meg was in safe hands, I left Montenegro and flew to the USA. I knew I'd only need a day or so: either what I had in mind could be started in that time, or it couldn't and I'd need to find another way.

Chapter 32

The roads from the airport became increasingly treacherous as they climbed higher and higher into the Rockies and what had been a tentative flutter of snow became a more persistent downfall, settling and drifting at the sides. I was glad when, a mile or so from the highway, the track I was following finally ended at a gate. As I approached the security detail blocking the entrance to Sven's mountain retreat in Colorado, I wondered about his state of mind. I was here to find out if he and I could work together. I wound the window down, presented the guards with my ID and then shivered whilst they checked the trunk and the underside for anything untoward and the cold thin air replaced the comfortable fug that had built up in the car. Eventually satisfied, they waved me through and I followed the track for another quarter mile until my headlights picked out the lodge that was just one of the homes available to Sven: better known to Phems as Eduardo Torres, the former Senator from Wisconsin and now Vice President of the United States of America. Sven's predictions had been good, and his boasts hadn't been idle. I'd watched from afar as he'd done exactly what he'd said he'd do.

'I hadn't expected to see you again during this cycle, Jay. The word was that you'd disappeared, most of us thought you'd gone back into transition.' We were sprawled in arm chairs around a glowing log fire, large snifters of brandy and plates of canapés in easy reach on side tables. His staff, attentive to the point of intrusion, had been dismissed and we were alone.

'Not yet. There's still something I need to do.'

'So, where've you been? Still questing?'

I shrugged. 'Yup, still searching.' I was deliberately playing it down; I didn't want to share the disappointment that I was still coming to terms with.

'You may have heard I had a disagreement with the Protectors and a run-in with the Renegades?'

'Disagreement? Ha! You've upset a lot of Rinks. They'd taken for granted the services the Protectors used to provide.'

'It had to be done.' I'd known that most Rinks would be OK when I'd destroyed the Protectors records. None of us relied entirely on the Protectors services and the continuity papers they managed. We all kept some assets secure and secret from the Protectors. Assets that were buried, cached in places only we knew. Old family vaults in obscure remote cemeteries were a favourite. I looked around. 'I can see you've been inconvenienced...' He had the good grace to laugh.

'It's not like you to hide though, Jay.' It was a shrewd insight.

'I wasn't hiding, I was protecting someone.'

'I heard about her. Is she your new Lela?'

I bridled at the suggestion. it was clumsily put but he was just trying to understand.

'No, she's just someone who became very special to me.'

'Became?'

'Still is.'

'Ah... So, what brings you here? Why the urgent request to meet?'

'I want to know if you've thought about what I said at our last meeting.'

He looked at me, trying to evaluate the meaning behind my words, then leant forward to add a log to the fire and sat back. 'Remind me. What did you say?'

I shook my head, exasperated. 'Neither of us have time for these games, Sven. You know full well what I said, and I know you've been giving it a lot of thought. It's written all over you.'

He sighed. 'OK. Yes, I've thought about it. And I've been doing my own research. Now that I've looked into it, I have to agree with you. There is opposition. Not just to what I'm doing but against governments, administrations. Opposition that is over and above the fundamentalist and terrorist activity. A kind of organised anarchy movement – if such a concept makes any kind of sense.

'And you can see who's behind it?'

'Yes. Renegades, using the Seekers as well. It seems they'll do anything for a promise of immortality, no matter how vapid that promise is.'

'You know that it's the Renegades who're behind the number of Rinks that have gone missing?'

Sven scowled, almost spat with disgust. 'Yes. They're out of control.'

'And the Protectors…?' I left the rest unsaid, to see if he'd pick up on it. He scowled again.

'Have been corrupted. Someone on the Council has been working with the Renegades. Feeding them information and arguing against direct action by the Protectors.' There was anger in his voice now. I let the feeling build within him, waiting for the right moment. I was making him face up to – acknowledge – something he'd known but had put to one side as he focussed on his own ambitions, his own game. Sparks whirled as the logs shifted in the hearth. I judged it was time.

'Years ago, I asked you when the game would end: when would you have had enough?'

'I remember.'

'And you had no answer other than to tell me it was the game that was the challenge, not the outcome.'

'I remember that too.'

'So, suppose I suggested that the ultimate challenge is not just in playing a game for yourself. It's about playing it for others.'

His eyes gleamed in the firelight as he leaned forward to refill my glass. 'Are you accusing me of being selfish, Jay?'

'No. I'm just offering you a chance to be self*less*. And to discover how great that can feel. I want you to change your plans, Sven. I want you to change them for a bigger, better game.'

He snorted. 'Bigger? What could be bigger than building an American empire?' He sensed what was coming, was resisting me. I took a sip of brandy.

'C'mon, Sven be honest with yourself. You never really believed you could pull it off. An American empire? You were in it for the fun of it, there was no realistic chance you'd make it happen. And you've already been distracted. Why else have you been doing your own investigation? And now you're angry about what is happening. Maybe just because of how it's affecting you, but maybe – again if you're honest with yourself – because of how it's affecting and destabilising the here and now. And you're angry at the Renegades.' He was hunched, staring at the fire. Hearing everything that I was saying, but not yet willing to yield.

'So, what's your proposal?'

'What could be bigger or better than stopping the Renegades, avenging the Rinks they've abused and doing something that will help the entire Phem world?' The glass clicked as I placed it firmly on the table between us and stared him in the eyes. 'You and I working together to make it happen.'

'You've already beheaded the Renegades, destroyed the Seeker organisation and taught the Protectors a lesson. What's left?'

I played the only card I had left, an appeal to his vanity. 'The opportunity to shape, define, design what comes next, before the Renegades can regroup. I beheaded them, yes, but they're still strong and active, wreaking havoc. They'll get ever stronger as they draw more Rinks under their spell. Then there's the opportunity to fix things before the Seekers can rebuild, they'll find more sponsors, their numbers will swell. Together we can ensure the Protectors never again forget their original purpose, to support the newly aware and Rinks returning from transition. I'm offering you the opportunity to be remembered as *the* Rink – the one who made it happen.'

*　　　*　　　*

The snow that had fallen, as we talked and debated through the night and into the morning, lay deep and crisp as we trudged a furrow from the lodge to the ridge and its breathtaking view down across the valley. On the far side the slopes were crisscrossed with lifts and pistes but as yet few skiers; it was still early. Around and behind us the VP's security team hovered out of earshot but in easy reach if needed: their positions marked by cloudy breaths as they cooled after the exertion of the climb.

'You're asking a lot, Jay. I've worked hard to get to where I am.'

I nodded. 'I know that. But it's because you're where you are that I think we could do this. It hasn't been a waste. And I'm offering a lot too.'

'Offering? What?'

'Satisfaction, fulfilment. If we pull this off, you'll feel like you've never felt before.'

He gazed out over the slopes, gauging the truth and weight behind my words. 'Why now? You've never before shown any inclination to involve yourself in their affairs.'

I shrugged. 'Maybe I should have done? Maybe I realise the time I've wasted. Maybe it's because now I could make a real difference, at a time when it matters?'

And maybe, though I didn't tell him, it was because of what a young, newly aware Rink called Ayeesha had told me, and because her words had finally made sense. *'Are there none who would use this gift we have for a better purpose?'* she'd asked, and I'd fobbed her off. Maybe it was time to make amends for that.

'And you'd really play your part if I do as you ask? You'd use your capabilities to complement mine? Between us we'd manipulate the key players as well as the masses?'

'As long as you agree to the plan, to the outcome, yes.'

He held out his hand and we shook – it was as good a way of sealing a deal between Rinks as any other. And that's how it started. It was still a game for him, I never expected that he'd truly share any lofty ideals, but I'd give him a bigger challenge and he couldn't resist. Even if he – if we – failed in this cycle I knew I'd sown the seeds and when and if he recycled, he'd return to the challenge. I'd launched him and I'd committed to be there to help. I'd once again made a commitment to live trying.

This time it felt better.

There hadn't been a lot more to discuss after that. We both knew what had to be done and each other's role in it. We agreed he would take the lead – after all he did have more experience – and that when he needed me, he'd call and I'd come. So, I left and headed back to Montenegro, more at peace with myself than I'd been for as long as I could recall. Even the inevitable delays at the airport didn't puncture the feeling. When the departure's body scanner beeped and I got pulled over I removed the tracking locket that I wore beneath my shirt and tucked it into my bag on the X-ray conveyor before passing through again.

It's the little things that bring you down.

Chapter 33

The overnight flight from the United States to Amsterdam had been peaceful and I'd slept, but the onward connection to Montenegro had been delayed and it was early evening before I arrived. Although I was tired, I'd called ahead to tell them I'd get a cab and not to bother meeting me at the airport.

It was my own fault. I'd known the TV broadcast might put us at risk, but I'd worried more about Meg than myself. I'd not taken anyone with me on the trip and I'd allowed the thought of the extra security cover in Montenegro to dampen my own instincts. Distracted by tiredness and the relief of being out in the fresh air after hours of breathing recycled guff, I paid little attention to the traffic and the passers-by, or the cab that pulled in ahead of the line that had been waiting patiently. I sank back in the seat as we joined the stream of traffic, barely noticing as the driver turned off into a side street with a muttered, 'Short cut…'. Even when the doors were yanked open, I was slow to react and by the time I'd begun to berate myself for my stupidity the sting from the needle that was plunged into my neck had faded along with my senses.

*   *   *

I had a throbbing headache but there were no other indications – stiffness, muscle weakness – to suggest I'd been unconscious for long when I came around. I was blindfolded and bound at the wrists and ankles to a chair. I suppressed a surge of fear, knowing it for what it was – an instinctive reaction, but one which offered little benefit. I needed to be cool and calm. I used some focussed will to reduce the throbbing and started gathering information.

From the sounds, the echoes, I was in a largish room with a hard floor. The sounds came from footsteps, shoes with leather soles, not trainers or anything similar. There were no obvious odours, just the normal domestic smells of the kind you'd encounter in any home. That was all I processed in the first few seconds. It didn't tell me much, other than that my thought processes seemed to be working fine. I was trying to work out how many there were when one of them spoke.

'He's awake.' Voice One was male, probably young. He spoke in English but it wasn't his first language. From his accent I guessed he was some kind of Slav so maybe he was a local. I tagged him as 'the Montenegrin'.

'Good. Now, Jay, tell me, do you know why you're here?' Voice Two was also male and he too addressed me in English, but with an American accent. There was something familiar about him that I couldn't place, yet. But he'd told me something important. To the world at large I was whoever my current ID said I was. The Care First team knew me only as Josef Schoorl, a wealthy but reclusive South African. Meg and I had kept a very low profile, there'd been no media stories about us. Very few people knew that the Schoorls were sponsors of Care First. To those who did know, I was to Meg as Dennis had been to Margaret Thatcher – a relative nonentity, in the shadows. My captors knew me for something else, for what I really was.

Only Meg and other Rinks called me Jay.

I considered the situation before answering, decided to play it my way. I ignored the question and carried on processing. 'You've kidnapped me, why?' I thought some more, working it out. 'You're Rinks, the only question is which faction? Are you misguided idealists, Protectors? Or Renegade thugs?' As I finished, I heard a sharp intake of breath and angry muttering in a slurred guttural language.

'Careful, Jay, my friend here is not as well disposed towards you as I am.'

I listened hard, searching for clues. Why was Voice Two familiar?

He continued, 'You're right, Jay, we know exactly who you are. So, I'll ask you again, do you know why you're here?'

I was still trying to work out who he was. I had nothing to say so I said nothing. It wasn't much of a strategy but it was all I had and I figured he wouldn't be able to keep quiet. I wasn't wrong.

'It's simple, Jay. If you're here, then you're not there, protecting her, Meg. Your security teams may not be enough, she's vulnerable now. Without you beside her we can take her whenever we want. Do you want us to, Jay? Shall we take her? What would you trade for her? Not just for her life... Let's call it her "wellbeing".'

It took every ounce of conditioning and self-control to fight the terror and fury that threatened to overwhelm me. I heard Voice One chortle sickeningly as I tensed and tested the bindings around my wrists, desperate, willing them to tear but it was useless. I forced myself to relax, to focus and replay the conversation so far. No amount of panic was going to help Meg. I processed what I knew and listened again to Voice Two in my head, until I was sure. I couldn't show fear and I had to somehow establish a degree of control. I needed to impress them. Right now, I had only one weapon, my ability to think. I could guess what they wanted but who were they?

They were acting as individuals; of that I was pretty sure. The Protector organisation was still in disarray. The Council had been dismissed; a conference of Rinks had declared them "extremists".

There were no signs I'd been able to discern that Dandy Tom or Iril Karzan had shifted back into another cycle and, without them or their like, the Renegades acted largely as individuals.

The Seekers had managed to retain a semblance of a network but, lacking the financial and organisational resources that the Pietersens had provided, they were toothless. I'd watched carefully to see if another Phem would emerge as their sponsor but so far none had. So, if it was not an organisation that was after me that just left some individual who knew me as a Rink.

But why threaten Meg? That was easy to answer – to make me do something. They knew I wouldn't respond to violence, would simply resist until they went too far, so what'd be the point? So, they'd threaten Meg instead, knowing I'd be unable to bear that. I put it all together and gambled.

'No, you won't take her. Let me tell you what I know, and what's going to happen.' I kept my voice even, calm, matter of fact. I needed to use everything I'd ever learned to manipulate their emotions, to compel them. I turned my head to where I'd heard him last.

'You, the one who sniggered at the idea of taking Meg, you're Montenegrin, a low-level Renegade. You'll be the first to die if anything happens to her.' I willed him to believe that what he was hearing wasn't a threat, that it was a cold statement of his fate. I paused as I heard him move and the brief tussle as he was restrained. Maybe it was working, maybe not. It was too soon to tell.

'You, the other one, you were a Protector, a former Council member now discredited and dismissed and gone over to the Renegades.' I'd sensed I'd known his voice when he first spoke but it had taken me a while to place it; one of the members who confronted me that fateful night in London. 'It was you who fed information to Dandy Tom and the others and now you've thrown yourself in with them. You're also the one who used Ayeesha Rao and then gave her to the Seekers. For that you also deserve to die.' Another bold statement. To convince him he couldn't hide from me. But this time there was no sign it had had any effect. I kept trying.

'You tracked us here when you saw the news, the shot with Meg and me in the background. It was luck, not skill that allowed you to find us.' Disparagement – they thought they had the upper hand; thought they'd been clever. I was telling them otherwise.

'At the moment we're in the kitchen of a private house, not far from Montenegro.' A pure guess but it didn't feel as if I'd been drugged for long. They wouldn't have had time to take me far and the acoustics seemed right. 'You're about to offer me a deal but we're going to trade on my terms not yours.'

I was telling them I knew everything. That they couldn't surprise me. That I was still in control. There was a long silence and for a while I allowed myself to hope. I knew I had to keep them off balance. To delay. They'd expected fear and compliance and instead I'd given them a cold implacable analysis and threats of my own.

It wasn't much but I thought it was a start until, without warning, the blindfold was whipped from my head. As I squinted in the harsh light, the Montenegrin wrapped his hand around my throat and forced me back against the chair. His spittle flew in my face as he crushed down, venting his frustration and anger, but as I read him, I could see more than that. I could see triumph and I didn't know why. The Protector dragged him away and I sucked deep breaths, watching them carefully as they argued before the Protector regained command. He turned to me and the way he returned my stare told me I hadn't done nearly enough.

'Very good, Jay, but no more than I would have expected from you. Now that's out of the way, can we return to the matter in hand? I take it that you understand the deal on offer?'

'You want the data I took from the Seekers and the Protectors and in return you'll leave Meg alone.' I did my best to sound confident, in control. I still thought all I needed to do was delay. I couldn't see my bag; it was probably still in the taxi – and with it my tracking locket – but although I'd been stupid, I still hoped my abduction had been seen by the security team. They should have been waiting to shadow me from the airport and I was sure they'd have at least followed the kidnappers.

The Protector nodded. 'Good, Jay. So why do we need terms? It seems pretty simple.'

He was confident, too confident and I realised I'd made

a mistake. When I'd been blindfolded, I'd thought I'd heard fear in their voices, but I'd been wrong. I could see now it was excitement. I fought for calm.

'Terms, guarantees, call them what you like. I know who you are, what you've proved capable of in the past. Why would I trust a Renegade? We're not going to live the rest of our lives looking over our shoulders.' I was searching for something, anything that would explain their excitement and give me something to negotiate for.

'What choice do you have, Jay. Are you in a position to propose an alternative?' I opened my mouth to answer but he held up a hand and moved behind me and swung my chair around. I was facing a desk with a screen; on it the image was stark and clear. It was Meg, bound and gagged in a chair much like my own.

'Sorry, Jay, I lied a bit. By the way she can see you but there's no sound, either way. Miklos was sniggering because, as you can see, we've already taken her.'

My resistance drained away. They'd played me beautifully. I'd wasted energy and emotions believing that I could somehow take control of the situation and keep Meg safe. I'd been considering the options: planning, scheming and in one fell swoop they'd taken all my hope away. It was classic conditioning, designed to make me panic, to agree to whatever they demanded, and it was working. I tuned them out, focussed instead on Meg's image. She couldn't hear me but I mouthed words of comfort, hoping she'd lip read some reassurance. As far as I could tell she was unharmed. Gagged she couldn't even mouth a response but I saw her thumbs rise as she did her best to signal that she was OK.

Miklos's giggling brought me back into the room. I made myself concentrate. I had to keep trying. I took a deep breath.

'OK, so we do it on your terms. Get rid of the giggling idiot and let's talk. What's your name. Let's start with that.' The giggling stopped and I tensed, waiting for the blow but it didn't come. Instead, I felt a hand on my shoulder, a brief pat.

'I like you, Jay, but be careful. I don't control Miklos and when this is over, you'll have to deal with him.' I ignored the warning and continued staring at Meg, trying to transmit strength to her as we locked eyes. Another pat. 'Touching as this is, I think we'll leave further discussion until tomorrow. We'll leave you two to think it over. Think hard. By the time you realise you're out of choices we'll be back. When we return be ready.' The Protector paused, chuckled. 'Oh, and if you were expecting your security to come bursting in at any moment, sorry. We knew they were there. We used a second car to block them when we took you. They didn't follow us.'

Behind me I heard their footsteps, then the door as it was opened, closed and locked. I listened hard but there were no more clues, no street noises. As far as I could tell I was alone. Except for Meg's image. We stared at each other in wordless desperation, communicating hope and love, willing each other not to give up. After a while I saw her head fall as stress and then sleep overcame her. I couldn't take my eyes off her. As I watched I considered the Protector's words. The options were obvious, the choice wasn't. By the time I'd decided, the night was almost over and, try as I might, I could keep my eyes on her no longer. I slept, fitfully.

I was awake long before I heard the click of the lock behind me. I'd reviewed the options again: they hadn't changed, nor had my choice. I heard the familiar footsteps; the rustle of snow being brushed from their coats. I smelt fresh coffee and sensed them sipping from their cups as they looked me over. They kept me waiting, presumably they thought it would intimidate me. It didn't. I ignored them, gave my attention to the screen and Meg's image. She was still asleep, slumped awkwardly in her chair, but finally I could see it, what I'd hoped and prayed for. As she'd moved in her sleep, the scarf she'd tucked inside her blouse had shifted. I could see the chain that had been hidden from view. I knew what I had to do now. Eventually the Protector spoke.

'Well, Jay, have you decided?'

I knew exactly what they'd figured, that I'd have three options: one, I could have killed myself during the night – those of us who've lived enough cycles know the secret of death by autosuggestion – that would have left Meg vulnerable but ensured they'd never recover the data from me; two, I could refuse to trade – and take the consequences for Meg and myself, gambling that, somehow, we might survive; three, I would agree to trade. I'd ducked option one – confirming my need to protect Meg – and that told them option two was out for the same reason. So, three it was. Now they just needed to hear me say it. But I needed to keep him off balance, to begin the negotiation on my terms.

'Yes, I've decided…' I left a lengthy pause, let their tension build. 'I'll take my coffee black, two sugars.' I gave it a few more beats, let their emotions swing from anticipation through frustration and into anger and then as I heard them draw breath I continued. 'And when you've brought it, I'll tell you how and when I'm prepared to transfer the data to you. You'll have until midday today to make the arrangements. Before then you'll bring Meg here. If we've not completed the trade by midday, if I'm not convinced that Meg is safe and will remain so and unharmed for the rest of her life then I will assume I cannot protect her and though she may die I will not transfer the data. There will be no second chance.'

Now it was my turn to wait. It didn't take long. Without warning my chair was spun around and I braced for the blow that never came. The Protector leant forward, offering a cup with a straw for me to drink. Miklos stood to one side smirking.

'A wise decision, Jay… and I'm glad I guessed right about your coffee.' His eyes were bright with triumph. 'Now, take a sip and let's talk details. How do you propose to make the transfer.'

It seemed that no matter what I tried he was keeping a step ahead of me. For want of anything else to do I bent forward and sipped. I knew immediately where he'd got the coffee from, it was awful but at least it eased my dry throat. I glanced at the watch on his wrist. From now on it would be important to keep track of time.

'Bring her here first, then I'll tell you. I can make the transfer from any internet connected computer but the data will be encrypted and I'll retain the key until I know Meg is safe.'

'Make him do it now! He can use this one!' Miklos pushed forward, shouldering the Protector aside and swivelling me back to face the desk and screen. I counted to three, felt his breath on my neck as he bent to snarl instructions in my ear, and then snapped my head back as hard and as far as my bindings would allow. I gave full vent to the frustrations and anger that had lay tempered, damped down within me, for too many hours. I was rewarded with the crunch of rupturing cartilage, a tortured howl and a warm gush of blood. It felt as good as anything had for a long while. From the corner of my eye, I saw the Montenegrin sink, semi-conscious, to his knees. One hand out in support, the other clutching at his ruined nose as he tried to stem the flow. On the screen in front of me I glimpsed Meg's eyes bright with worry as she watched what was happening, before I was swung around again to face the Protector.

'That was stupid, Jay. I warned you already that I have trouble controlling Miklos.'

'And I warned you that you've until midday to make this trade or it won't happen. That's in just over two hours from now. I also told you my terms. They're not negotiable, no matter what your thug friend thinks. Now, again, when Meg gets here I'll give you the rest of the details, until then keep him away from me.' The Protector hesitated, looked uncertainly at Miklos' groaning figure then nodded. I heaved an inward sigh of relief and gave mental thanks to Miklos. His intervention had created the conditions I'd needed. The Protector had dropped his guard momentarily and I'd been able to exert a degree of compulsion. He'd agreed my terms, would follow my instructions.

For now.

*　　　　*　　　　*

I was still bound to the chair when they brought Meg to the house. The Protector and Miklos had stayed with me so that meant there were at least one, more likely two others working with them. Meg still had her hands tied but before they could stop her, she ran over and knelt beside me. They pulled her away, but in that moment I could see it. I heaved another sigh of relief. She was still wearing it. Now we had a real chance.

'Jay! Are you alright?'

I nodded urgently. 'I'm fine, Meg, fine. Relax, it's all going to be OK. Don't worry. It'll work out.' I was signalling in every way I could. The last thing I needed now was for her to try anything heroic. I watched the doubt flicker in her eyes before she saw something that made her trust me. For long seconds we shared a look, emotions and understanding and then she nodded. I turned to the Protector.

'OK, so this is how it's going to work. You're going to take us, Meg and me, to an internet café in town. By now it'll be busy, crowded. There'll be plenty of witnesses so you'll have to free us but I assume you'll all be armed and that you'll have others in or around the café so I'm not going to risk Meg's life by trying anything stupid. OK so far?' The Protector nodded warily. I sensed that Miklos wanted to interfere but he was silenced with a look. 'OK, so then I'll transfer the encrypted data to any address you give me. The files are large so that'll take a few minutes to complete. I assume you have someone who can check that they do transfer, OK?'

He nodded again.

'Right. When you confirm the data has transferred, you'll release Meg. She'll walk away from the café and, when she's safe and certain none of your men have followed her, she'll call you. Give her your number.'

'And then?' The Protector was sceptical.

'Then I give you the encryption key and we wait while you check the files have decoded.'

'And then?'

'Then you let me walk out of there.'

'And then?'

'Then we all go our separate ways and hope our paths never cross again.'

There was silence in the room as he considered my terms. I glanced again at his watch. It was almost eleven. Ten minutes since they'd arrived, probably thirty since they'd moved Meg from whenever they'd been keeping her. It should be soon now.

'What if you refuse to give us the key after we've let Meg go?'

'You'd still have the data. It would take time, years probably, but a good expert would decode it eventually. And you'd still have me.'

'And why would we let you go after we have the key?'

I shrugged. 'Because that's the deal and I'll have to trust you. What's the worst you can do? Kill me?' I watched the thoughts flicker and flash across his features. He wanted to accept the deal. It sounded simple but at the same time too easy. He was searching for the catch, was wary of my lack of concern and my willingness to trust him. And of course, he was right. None of what I had described was going to happen, but he couldn't read me as I could read him. Now I'd penetrated his defences I nudged him some more and watched as he decided.

'Alright. We'll do it your way.' He turned to the man who'd brought Meg. 'Get the others and head for the café, check it out and when you're sure it's secure set a perimeter around it and then get back here.' As the man left, he scowled at Miklos who was holding a blood-soaked rag to his face. 'Clean yourself up or you're not going anywhere. You'll attract too much attention. We'll be leaving in fifteen minutes.'

Meg shuffled over and sat beside me. She rested her head on my thigh. I should have kept my promise and kept her safe. Now I just prayed it was almost over.

Chapter 34

When the man returned, he spoke briefly with the Protector and they cut my bindings. I was free to move and I could sense they were wary, wondering if I'd control myself or make an attempt to escape. I was tempted, but inside the house the odds were against me. They were armed and I was stiff from being held tied for so long. Once we got outside, I was hoping that the odds would be in our favour.

I nodded that I was ready to go. Meg's hands had been freed too. The Protector held her close at his side, his other hand on the gun in his pocket, as we filed out through the back door and down the steps to where a car was waiting. Its exhaust spewed fumes in the cold air. A black saloon with darkened windows. The driver sat, waiting.

Though it was midday, the sky was darkened by snow-laden clouds scudding low across the city. I took it all in as we approached the car. Searching for signs but seeing none. I breathed deeply, bracing myself for action. Tensing and relaxing my muscles, easing their stiffness. The Protector led the way to the car, still holding Meg. I was next with Miklos. The other man brought up the rear. I could sense that Miklos was itching for me to try something, anything that would give him an excuse to hurt me badly. I held my breath: waiting for what I hoped, had gambled, would happen.

It did.

As the Protector reached to open the rear door it swung back and Raisa Talanov stepped out. She did it so casually it made it somehow even more unexpected. For a moment we all froze and in one smooth move Raisa pulled Meg from the Protector's side before he could draw his gun. Coiled with tension from the long night, I was whiplash fast. He was helpless as I grasped his wrist with one hand and clamped down on his bicep with the other. The elbow joint is complex, strong and powerful in one plane, delicate and weak in the other. I tore the joint in the wrong direction. The Protector collapsed, whimpering and cradling his arm as I sensed Miklos make his move behind me. I span, adrenalin and anger fuelling my need to take him down. A palm strike is a terrible blow and it drove what was left of his nasal bone deep into his brain. I watched Miklos fall. The other man fell too, knocked senseless by a second security agent who'd waited patiently below the stairs, and then trailed silently behind as we descended from the house. Panting, I nodded to him. He gave me a thin smile. It was like he did this every day.

After hours of fear and uncertainty it was over that quickly, that simply. More of Raisa's team appeared and took control of the driver. Conscious of the guns trained on him he'd stayed silent and immobile throughout. I was aware of Raisa's men bundling Miklos's body, the Protector and the other man into a van as I held Meg. She'd begun to shake. When yet another of the security team's Jeeps raced into the courtyard, I helped her aboard. My own body was beginning to feel the effect of the control I'd placed upon it. Controlling my fear and emotions when I was captured. Staying cool when I'd realised Meg had been taken, forcing myself to be patient and the explosive release of anger and then relief at the end had drained my reserves. As I was about to join Meg in the Jeep I felt Raisa's hand on my arm.

'You're a surprising man, Mr Schoorl.' She smiled quizzically. 'If I'd realised what you can do, I'd have brought fewer men. We'll talk at the hotel. For now, I need to know one thing. These men' – she indicated the van – 'can they just disappear? Is that what you want? Would it cause you trouble?' She'd surprised me again.

'You'd do that? Your men would do that if you ask?'

She nodded. 'We lost one of our own when they took Meg. We screwed up. We owe you and my men want revenge.'

'You'd be putting yourselves at great risk.'

She shrugged, 'Not really. Here, at this time, in this chaos, many people are disappearing.' She looked at me. 'You and your wife… you're good people. These people' – again she nodded at the van – 'they aren't. So…' I was tempted to go along with it. Her approach to life – to good and bad – was not so different to my own, so who was I to tell her she was wrong. But I couldn't let her do it. Couldn't let her do what I should do myself.

'No. Put them somewhere safe. Let me know where and I'll come later.' She looked me in the eye, checked that I was sure and then shrugged again.

'You're the boss.' She closed the Jeep's door and tapped the roof to signal the driver to take us back to the hotel. I held Meg, squeezed her tight but felt her body stiff and trembling. Resisting me. I closed my eyes and held on. Hoping that, somehow, we'd get back to how we were.

Chapter 35

Meg was distant with me. The barriers were back. At the hotel she resisted when I insisted that she should get checked by a doctor.

"Why? They didn't touch me beyond tying me up. What's the treatment for that?'

'I just thought…'

'Well don't.'

I couldn't break through so I stopped trying. For now, I didn't know what else to do. She retired to our bedroom, closing the door quietly but firmly. When I checked later, she'd finally succumbed and was sleeping deeply but fitfully. I left her with some of the security team keeping watch in the corridor and hotel lobby and followed the directions Raisa had sent.

*   *   *

The renegade Protector and his men were lying bound and gagged on the hard packed bare earth floor of the barn. I didn't ask Raisa how she and her team had found the place, or whether it was safe for us to be there. Nor did I ask about Miklos' body. They were professionals.

'Thank you, Raisa. And your team.' I looked at her, making sure she realised that I was giving her my heartfelt thanks for everything she and her team had done. Not just for the current arrangements.

'It's what we do. And, as I said, we owe you. They should never have taken you or your wife in the first place.' I think it was the first time I'd seen real emotion in her face. She blushed, ashamed at the thought that they'd failed us. I nodded.

'Consider the debt settled.' I saw her relax a little, but knew it would be a while before she'd fully forgave herself.

'And now?'

'Now I take responsibility. Can you forget you ever saw these men? That you were ever here?'

'What men? Where, boss?'

The barn door swung closed with a groan. I heard her vehicle start up and then accelerate away. We were alone.

*   *   *

The following morning Meg had thawed a little, enough that we could at least talk.

'It was the locket after all then? When they didn't come at first, I thought it must be broken.' She was worryingly calm now and I couldn't tell if it was an overreaction to the traumatic events or whether she was masking some other emotion.

'Yes. Raisa's team couldn't track it until they moved you. Its signal must somehow have been blocked, maybe by the buildings around the first location where you were held.'

'And why couldn't they track you? Where was your locket?'

I grimaced in embarrassment. 'I took it off to go through security at the airport check in. Put it in my case and forgot about it. They dumped my bags soon after they took me.'

'After all the arguments you made about the need to wear them?' There was an iciness to her calm now.

I could only nod and soak it up.

'When no-one came to our rescue, I'd thought that, like me, you'd somehow forgotten to wear it. Then when I saw the chain I began to hope.'

We'd had problems before with signals being blocked and that's why one of my terms was that they should move her. I'd known that by then the security teams would be on full alert and would act swiftly if they picked up the signal. We were sitting on one of the sofas in the suite living area. Together, but not close. Meg shifted now, increasing the distance between us as she changed tack.

'What happened to the kidnappers?' Her voice was quiet, still outwardly calm. 'You left the suite last night. Where did you go?'

'I went to talk to them. To find out how they'd tracked us down. I needed to know how many more there might be who could find us. I needed to make sure we'd be safe from now on.'

'You talked to them? And they told you? Just like that? Her voice dripped with doubt and disbelief. 'And? Are we safe?'

'They told me because I gave them no choice. And yes, I believe we're safe now, so long as we don't reveal ourselves like that again.'

'And where are they now?'

'They were Rinks – Renegades – they're gone now, out of cycle. Back into transition.'

'You killed them.'

'Yes.' I wanted to lie, to somehow deny it, to make her believe and make it right between us but I couldn't. 'What would you prefer? We had to know and I couldn't just let them go. We'd have been hunted by them for the rest of our lives.'

She shuddered and sighed. 'You really don't feel anything, do you?' She wasn't disbelieving, she knew what I was capable of. But once again, she was scared of me. Scared of the man I could be when I needed to be.

I thought about it. 'About them? No. They were Renegades, but they were also Rinks. You know death has a different meaning for us. But I feel! I was helpless with fear that you were in danger and I feel an overwhelming relief now that you're safe. I feel immeasurable gratitude to Raisa and her team for the way they handled it. I feel, Meg, just not about things and people that don't deserve it.'

We teetered on the edge of the arguments we'd had many times in the past, but we stepped back, both of us. There was no more to be said that hadn't been said before. Meg had accepted it once before and now she chose to accept it again. Accept but not condone and she accepted only because the alternative was that otherwise we could no longer be together. Neither of us wanted that.

Raisa asked a few questions but tactfully ignored the paucity of the answers I gave her: about who the kidnappers were and why they'd threatened us. She didn't ask about the Protector or the others. She stayed on our security team but never learned of the existence of the Rinks, and, though she often looked at me with curiosity, she never questioned me again.

It was surreal, but within days it was if it had never happened. Brad assumed Meg and I had taken off for some time together and we allowed him to go on believing that.

Meg insisted on staying in Montenegro for several weeks. She spent time working as a volunteer nurse – carefully shadowed and guarded of course. I think it was partly her way of paying something back on my behalf. I helped too, but mostly to be with her. To check that what had broken between us was really mending. It took time but it got better day by day. Eventually there was little that we could do that others couldn't and the Care First teams needed to be left alone to get on without our interference and presence. We arranged more funds and left them to it.

Chapter 36

For a while we retreated. We chose a small town in the mid-west of the United States as a base, to rest and recuperate. By day we hiked, fished, rafted on small, slow-moving rivers; picnicking on the banks until the winter drew too close. In the evenings we read or sat in companionable silence watching the fire, thinking: all the time testing, probing, each reassuring the other that all was well between us. And then we talked about the future. Meg, try as she might, couldn't shake a feeling of vulnerability. The kidnapping had left scars.

I saw how unsettled she became when strangers appeared in the town. I knew she was asking herself could she resume the life she'd led before? Was she ready? Was she up to dealing with, and adjusting to, working again in dangerous places and with people that too often were filled with pain and suffering? I knew how much it had cost her to return to working in the refugee camps after the abduction. She'd done it, in part, to prove to herself that she could. But it had shaken her to discover how much of her self-confidence had been taken from her.

And what about me?

Meg knew that I'd come to accept that I wasn't going to find the answers I sought but I had told her nothing of my discussions with Sven, nor the new commitment I'd made to myself.

*   *   *

'So, what's next?' She was leaning against the counter, her hands in her jean pockets and her head cocked to one side as she watched me. We were staying in a small lodge, beside a lake. There were security teams nearby, but we were alone in the lodge, enjoying our self-sufficiency. Meg had washed up and I was drying and stacking the dishes after dinner. The sink gurgled as it drained and I paused, giving myself time to think as I registered that behind her apparently casual pose and question there was an intensity that had been missing from our talks until now.

'Coffee?'

I winced as she leant forward and punched me hard on the bicep.

'Don't do that!' Her voice was earnest. 'You know I was being serious, don't make light of it.'

I rubbed my arm. Lesson learned.

'OK.' I gave her the look that said I meant it, that I understood her – that I'd behave from now on – and was rewarded with a half-smile. I saw some of the tension leave her curled shoulders. 'But, seriously, let me make coffee and then I've something to tell you.'

'About what you went to discuss with Sven? About what you and he decided? I wondered when you'd think it was time to tell me.'

There was a nervousness in her voice and it tore at me. She'd told me that she trusted me, but I could see the doubts were still there, flickering uncertainly behind her eyes. I vowed to myself, once again, that I'd do better: that I'd never again be a source of hurt for her. I pulled her toward me and held her close as I sighed.

'I've not been keeping it from you. Events kind of took over... Then, after, it just never seemed to be the right time.'

'And it is now?' The nervousness was still there. She couldn't disguise it, wasn't trying to.

I searched for the words that might re-assure her. 'Yes. It's time for us to decide what we are going to do next, together.'

I felt her hesitate, then:

'And what about Lela?' And I knew then the real reason for her nervousness.

'What about her?'

'Have you been thinking about her? Isn't that another

reason why you became so introspective... Before... in Montenegro?'

I cursed my stupidity, my insensitivity as I held her, tighter. 'No! No. Not in that way. I think about her, yes, but not in the way I think about you. If we meet again in this cycle, it will not be of my doing. I'll not search for her again.' I said it as positively as I knew how. After a long moment I felt her relax a little and then she pushed me away, gently, so she could look me in the eye. She seemed to find what she was looking for.

'OK then.' She pressed her palms against my chest, 'I'll take it black, please, and bring us some of those cookies I baked earlier.' She kissed me lightly, slipped from my grasp and settled herself on the sagging sofa by the fire. Her legs and feet curled beneath her. I heaved a sigh of relief and went to do as I'd been told.

'You do realise that emptying frozen cookie dough into a dish and shoving it in the oven isn't baking...' I said as I placed the tray on the table and poured coffee. She reached forward, said not a word but one eyebrow was raised dangerously. Too soon I thought, would I never learn? 'Well, um... Anyway,' I continued, 'About Sven. I have a proposition for you.'

'Go on.' She sat back, dunking a cookie in her coffee, eying me expectantly.

'Before I left to go and see Sven, we talked. But you were pretty engaged with what was going on in Montenegro, in the camps. Did you really take in what I was saying.'

She sat back, considering. 'Well, I think so. You told me that you wanted to do more with your time in this cycle. That you wanted to find a way to help us, Phems, achieve our potential. Also, that you wanted to undo some of the harm that the Renegades were causing. But you didn't say how you could do any of this.'

I nodded as she was talking, realising how much more there was to say. Through the open door I listened to the sounds – bird calls, fish in the lake, a breeze in the trees – that filled the silence as I wondered how to explain.

'Do you remember when we arrived in Montenegro, Brad was talking about the need for Governments to solve the refugee crisis by dealing with the root causes?'

'Yes.' She finished her cookie, reached for another. 'And you and I have discussed it before. But it's such a huge task, what can we do?'

'It's a huge task when you think of it in Phem terms. Not so much when you look at it as a Rink.' She looked at me quizzically. I hurried on. 'Look. It's a huge task that may take generations to achieve. That's hard for Phems to contemplate, easier for Rinks. It's a huge task because of the numbers of people, whole societies that will need to change how they think and behave. That's daunting for Phems, they've too much bitter experience – seen too many failed attempts, diverted or derailed by deranged or self-interested politicians and leaders. It's easier for Rinks, we have skills – powers if you like – at our disposal that the Phems lack. And there's another reason that will make it easier for us to achieve. Much of what is wrong – is going wrong – is because of the activities of the Renegades.'

I was on my feet, pacing: energised by the ambition that had gripped me. I told her what I believed had been happening, driven by Renegade warlords in the developing world and crime lords in the so-called developed world. 'If we can stop them, and mobilise and motivate the Phems back onto the right path, then we can make a real difference.' I stopped pacing, suddenly self-conscious as my arms fell back to my sides.

She put the cookie back on the plate, sat motionless and said nothing for long moments. Staring at me. The silence grew. Now I was nervous.

'Well? Say something… Please.'

She looked away then looked back, uncertain, her turn to search for the right words.

'I… I don't know what to say, what to think. As you said all of that, there was a fervour within you I've not seen before.'

'And…? So? You think I'm dreaming, that it's an

impossible task?' I flopped onto the sofa beside her. She shook her head.

'No. I'm scared that you do think it's possible. And I'm wondering what makes you think that you have any right to interfere in our world. Or what makes you so sure that you know what the right path is?' She placed her cup carefully on the tray. Her movements stiff, as if she was having trouble controlling herself. She stood, began pacing and then stopped and stared at me. Now it was pain and confusion I saw flickering behind her eyes.

'I need to think about this.' She turned away, heading for the bedroom.

'Meg, wait…!' But I didn't know what to say. I'd been so convinced, so carried away with my plans, my ideals that I hadn't stopped to think. She was a Phem, I was a Rink. Like it or not, we thought differently. 'Meg…?' I tried again, but I was talking to her back. She paused but didn't turn.

'I'm sorry, Jay. I can't talk any more for now. Tomorrow maybe… Goodnight.' Once again, a door closed softly behind her and I was left alone, wondering what would come next. Her words rocked me. I'd not even considered this reaction. I'd expected anger – because of the Renegades – and doubt that what I proposed could be achieved, but I'd just assumed she'd agree with me, and trust me. I realised I'd been a fool.

*   *   *

The sagging sofa proved as uncomfortable as I expected but I was nonetheless in a deep sleep when the sound and smell of sizzling bacon woke me.

'One egg or two?' She was at the stove, looked well-slept; spoke as if all was right in her world. I scrambled to pull my own thoughts together, to try and catch up with the change in her mood.

'Two please.' It seemed the safest answer for now. I knew she'd explain in her own time. I left her in the kitchen, singing quietly to herself, as I had a quick wash and found fresh clothes. When I returned, breakfast was on the table and she was waiting for me to join her. I waited for her to take the lead as I took my seat and she served me a plate of eggs and bacon, offered toast, poured coffee. Eventually she was ready.

'I've come to a decision,' she said.

I tried to swallow as my mouth went dry. I wasn't trying to – couldn't – read her. I'd no idea what was coming next but I knew how much I wanted it to be right, for us.

'If I believe you to be a good man – which I do – and if I trust you – which I do – then I have to trust you with this. You will do what you think is right, because you think it's right. Not because you have some other motivation.'

I began to hope, began to breathe more easily.

'If you really think you can do this then I will help you, if I can, and I will be with you.' I started to speak, but she held up her hand. 'I'm sorry about how I reacted last night. I promise you this. I don't ever want to doubt you again – so I won't. But I know too, that in future I will be tested. That you may be compelled to do things that I will struggle to accept. Just promise me that you won't abuse my trust, Jay. That's a pain I will *not* endure.'

She was opening her heart, herself, to me in a way that transcended even what we'd had before. I was a lucky man. I'd brought fear, upheaval and the unknown into her life and yet she'd forgiven me. I'd repeatedly tested her faith in me and yet every time she repaid me with her trust. I was a lucky, lucky man.

I promised. What else could I, should I have done? The frown lines that creased her forehead, as she waited for my reply, smoothed as the tension that had gripped her ebbed away.

'OK then.' She lifted her knife and fork. 'Eat. And tell me what happens next.'

Once again, I did as I was told.

*   *   *

We talked for an hour or so. I gave her the basic outline of the strategy that Sven and I had discussed and she tested and probed to find the flaws.

'So, you don't really have a plan, just an objective and some idea how to get started.' She said finally. I chewed thoughtfully, then nodded. She was right.

'Hard to plan to achieve something that's never been attempted before,' I said, trying not to be defensive. 'We'll make a start, see how it goes and build on that.'

Meg placed her knife and fork carefully on her plate. The creases had re-appeared.

'It'll put us back in the spotlight.' Her voice was calm, steady, but I could read the tension behind her words. I didn't try and deny it.

'It's going to be unavoidable. Sooner or later the Renegades will figure out there's a co-ordinated action against them and they'll look to see where it's coming from. The Protectors too. If we're going to do this it's a risk we're going to have to handle. When we're with Sven we'll have the protection of his security shield. When we're away from him we'll have our own, but much enhanced. I've asked for Raisa to head a much bigger team. We'll have close protection as well as a shadow team from now on.'

Meg nodded, took a deep breath. 'OK.' She gathered herself, shook off whatever fears were threatening to weaken her resolve. 'So... What next?'

We had some work to do, to prepare. When it was done, I took Meg to meet Sven.

Chapter 37

As we travelled east, I sensed a change in us both. We'd left our refuge, the safety of an isolation that had allowed us both to grow and understand each other to a whole new level and were heading into the unknown.

'What kind of a man is he? Will I like Sven?' Meg asked thoughtfully. Not fearful, just trying to prepare herself.

I wondered how to describe him, thought for a few moments. 'He's unique. I think you'll find him challenging and charismatic.'

Meg frowned. 'Challenging?'

'Not like that,' I shook my head. 'I mean that he's intelligent, willing to argue a point. Challenging like a sparring match, not like a fight.'

'But you like him.'

I didn't have to think about that. 'Yes, but you'll have to judge for yourself whether you can as well.'

She thought some more. 'Will he like me?'

'What's not to like?' That earned me a sideways glance, a raised eyebrow. 'He's not a fool,' I said quietly, 'He'll like you. Maybe too much.'

'That's better.' She said, smiling to herself.

*   *   *

Sven had stuck with the plan we'd agreed and placed his own immediate ambitions on hold. Instead of manoeuvring to become President he stayed as Vice President, a role that would allow him far more freedom of action behind the scenes.

He'd sent us tickets to a White House Ball, to allow us a seemingly chance social encounter that would be witnessed by hundreds, and therefore seem innocuous to those who watched his every move and contact. But I knew him too well; it was also a chance for him to demonstrate to Meg the reality of his position, of his power and influence.

She took it in her stride, was outwardly totally unphased by the experience. In the Grand Ballroom, as we people-watched – waiting for Sven to break free from the shoal of well-wishers, lobbyists and hangers-on that followed his every move – Meg and I whispered to each other. We laughed at the need-to-see-and-be-seen insecurity of those who'd paid thousands of dollars to attend and be blessed by the presence of the richer and more famous, whose luck and good fortune they hoped would rub off on them.

'Quite an evening,' she smiled as I introduced her to Sven. 'Do you hold these often?' She gestured around at the lavishly dressed throng of politicians, business leaders and celebrities.

"Hail to the Chief" had long since sounded. The President had made an appearance and then left, leaving the real party to begin. Tables were beginning to fill with groups and cliques: some having a good time – their plates filled with a sumptuous selection from the buffet, their glasses filled and refilled by circling waiters – others eschewed the food, the wine, the dancing and were engaged in deep conversations. Political plotting and manoeuvring? Business deals? Rumour mongering, gossiping?

Sven's eyes were critical. They roamed over her face, her figure – Meg was dressed with an understated elegance that effortlessly outshone those she wasn't consciously competing with – and back again. She waited calmly. If she was unsettled by the inspection it didn't show.

'It would appear that Jay wasn't exaggerating.' Sven murmured. 'Thank you for coming. I look forward to working with you.'

Meg gave him a wintery smile. 'We'll work better if we start on the right foot. I know that Jay has told you very little about me, so no, he didn't exaggerate. And you'd do better not to patronise or to seek to flatter me.' She warmed her smile a little. 'At least not until you get to know me, and then only if you still think it wise.'

Sven's aides had watched and listened to the exchange, uncertain whether to intervene. They knew me, from my previous visits. Knew that I had some kind of special relationship with the Vice President that gave me some freedom with him that others were denied – did that extend to my partner? They relaxed now as Sven roared with laughter and waved them away. He led us to an empty table and the three of us sat as drinks were fetched.

'We should probably keep this reasonably short, tonight.' Sven said. 'It's enough for now that we're seen in public, socialising.' The time he spent with us would mark us as newcomers to his inner circle. That, of course, would excite comment. We planned that gradually, and with a little help and encouragement, we'd dampen down that interest until our subsequent meetings with Sven aroused neither comment nor speculation.

'I assume you've fixed your background stories, Jay?' he continued.

I nodded. We'd kept the Schoorl identities. 'There's a rock solid digital and paper trail behind both of us. I used the best, did some of the work myself and double checked the rest. Meg and I are – to all intents and purposes and as far as any checks will reveal – long married, reclusive, wealthy entrepreneurs who turned our focus from tech start-ups to charity work and eco-campaigning some years ago. The records will show that you and I were contemporaries at university and there's a photo of you with us at our wedding.' I slipped him a memory stick. 'There's a summary on this, you'll need to be familiar. No doubt you'll get some questions soon.'

'It helps that you've already been seen with me, in Vancouver and Colorado. It gives us some history we can embellish and build on.' He turned to Meg, regarded her carefully. There was a warmth, a compassion in his eyes that I hoped she couldn't read as a typical Rink attitude towards a Phem. It wasn't meant as condescension, it was more a wonderment. No Rink could understand what it might be like to live only one life, to have only one chance. 'And you, Meg. Are you really sure about this? It doesn't have to be your fight.'

'I shouldn't fight for my own kind? To create a better world?'

'You'll risk more than us.'

'And that way I'll gain more.' She held his gaze; resolute. He nodded, satisfied. Raising his glass, he toasted her and finished his drink, dropping the stick in his pocket as he stood and offered Meg his arm.

'Then, let's do this; together. But, now, perhaps you'd risk a dance with me?' His eyes twinkled. The barriers he'd raised when they'd first met were down. Meg's smile matched his.

'That would be my pleasure.'

*   *   *

We began to travel extensively. Where Sven went, Meg and I followed. Whenever his schedule allowed informal meetings with his counterparts and men of influence in other countries, we were invited too. Together Sven and I planted ideas and aspirations deep in their minds. In time Sven developed his image on the global stage. Becoming to the war on terrorism and crime what Al Gore had sought to become in the battle against global warming.

He spun a vision of a future, peaceful world that mesmerised and energised his targets – the voters, constituents, populations, societies who could empower the political leaders – using the full force of his charismatic leadership powers to enrol their support. Where there were individuals whose opposition was too strong, I used my skills to manipulate emotions and thoughts, to compel if necessary until they were receptive to Sven.

Meg's help was invaluable. We learned to listen to her when she cautioned us to be subtle; to take small steps when our enthusiasm urged us otherwise. It was her understanding of this need that allowed us to make progress without raising undue alarm at the change in political manoeuvring that began to transform the workings of the forces of law and order around the world.

Where corruption, or political self-interest, had caused obstructions – such as in the fight to defeat Boko Haram in Africa, and to release the thousands they'd enslaved or taken hostage – we battered them down. I sought out the corrupt and neutralised them. I was merciless, using my powers to change attitudes, behaviours. When they fought me, I left them damaged, mentally diminished. I cleared their banks accounts, unearthed their hidden treasures and redistributed their wealth to where it would do most good. "Robin Hood reborn", my other selves chortled as they applauded my actions. I quietened them down. Robin Hood had never existed, as far as I knew, and if he had I doubted that he'd have been as ruthless as I became. I waged war to destroy the venal and the corrupt – not to steal from the rich and give to the poor.

Meanwhile Sven inflamed populist outrage in the developed countries, raising demands that "something must be done" to overcome delays or reluctance in despatching foreign aid, security forces. In Africa, he influenced and motivated the more moderate countries who'd sought to isolate themselves from the conflict to become engaged, to collaborate, to unite and to invite help into their beleaguered continent. And when that help was delivered, we worked together to control the aid-givers worst inclinations to exploit the situation. We made them work exclusively for the good of those they were there to help, and not themselves.

Africa was, if you like, our testing ground. Slowly we developed tactics that supported our strategy. We learned what worked and what didn't and, in time, we began to see progress. Nothing showy or spectacular, just a hardening of resolve amongst those who could make a difference and an ever-strengthening containment of the worst excesses of the terrorist fundamentalist and the Renegades who were driving them on. But it was hard and often frustrating. Sven described it as like trying to juggle jelly. As we applied pressure in one area another would begin to bulge. As we suppressed crime or neutralised terrorists in one place there'd be a resurgence in another. But we persevered.

Throughout it all, Meg and I were ever watchful. We kept our security tight and ever present: Raisa and her teams maintained a discrete presence but there were no further attempts to threaten me or Meg. Though we'd been unable to avoid publicity, we'd been able to minimise it and no-one had questioned who we purported to be, or uncovered our real identities. I monitored the Rink web and though it was clear our activities were being observed and commented on, they were mostly curious rather than negative.

In time, our meetings with Sven became infrequent as, increasingly, Meg and I were drawn in one direction and he in another. Not least by the demands of his day job.

Then, after many months, we began to tire; our schedule since we'd started had been relentless. And something changed. Meg became increasingly distant.

She dismissed it when I asked her why and told me it was my imagination. I worried that she was again struggling to reconcile our activities with her own judgement of what was right and wrong. So, I accepted with some relief when Sven suggested we should get together for a short vacation, to catch up and regroup at his ranch in Colorado.

When we arrived, the snow was all gone and the thin Colorado air was warmed now by a summer sun that shone through cloudless blue skies. A welcome contrast to my previous visit to Sven's lodge.

The security checks were still the same but eventually we were let through. Sven met us as we parked to one side of the drive that circled the stand of pines that shadowed and sheltered his mountain retreat. He kissed Meg on the cheek and clapped me on the shoulder but as he led us inside I pulled back slightly, watching him carefully. Something was wrong.

Sensing my hesitation, Sven half turned, gave me a look that could have meant something or nothing, and waved me in. I followed, alert and not knowing why. I wasn't expecting physical danger – I knew that Sven's security was the best, and our own team was not far away – it wasn't that.

He led us to the cantilevered deck at the rear of the lodge. Chairs were arranged around low tables laden with drinks and snacks. The view swept out and across the valley where, before, he and I'd watched skiers swooping and racing but which, now, was a green haven of peace and solitude. I heard Meg murmur her delight, watched as she relaxed into one of the chairs and wished that I could do the same but Sven's body language was telling me that I shouldn't.

'Is everything alright, my friend?' I asked him quietly, lightly. He turned, with a nod and a shake, acknowledging ruefully that I'd been right to ask.

'Yes, and no.' He paused. 'It's so good to have you both here. I've been looking forward to this. I've needed it, as I suspect you both have too.'

I was really worried now. 'But?'

He hesitated, looked away. 'I'd hoped it would just be

the three of us, Jay. That we'd have a chance to let our hair down, to talk openly about those things that only the three of us can share and understand. But I'm sorry, that may not be possible.'

I studied him, reading him as carefully as I knew how but I still wasn't getting any danger signals. Then I saw it: if anything, I was reading sorrow.

'Late yesterday evening,' he continued, 'I had another visitor. Unexpected, very unexpected. It's someone you both need to meet.'

He looked past me refusing to catch my eye, as he waved a hand towards the French doors that opened into the lodge.

Meg, watching us and aware now that something was wrong, stood and, turning away from the view, moved beside me. Ready to confront whatever it was.

It was a young woman. A stranger. I stared at her as she stepped out through the doors and onto the deck. She attempted a poised assurance but it failed to mask a faint tremble in her shoulders. She stopped, as if unwilling to approach further unless invited to do so.

'Hello, Jay,' she said, simply.

I felt Meg flinch beside me as I tried, tried so hard to control the shock. But I couldn't. A shudder wracked my body. I didn't recognise her now-self, how could I? We'd never met, but I knew her in the most visceral way possible. I felt my face contort as her name was wrenched from deep within me. 'Lela...' I took a step. She moved. We took more steps. I couldn't stop myself. We held each other.

*　　　*　　　*

Meg left, almost immediately. I tried to stop her, asked her not to. Asked; I didn't beg or plead. I respected her too much for that.

But to no avail.

'No. You can't ask that of me, Jay. Not after everything we've been through.'

After the briefest of introductions Lela and Sven had retreated, giving us space. Meg and I talked but what was there to say?

'I didn't arrange this, Meg. This wasn't my doing.'

'I know, Jay. But that's not the point, is it?'

Neither of us could forget my reaction when Lela appeared. I had no words, yet, to try and deny it, or to ask forgiveness, or to explain.

Meg asked for some time alone with Lela and they spoke for a short time – I've no idea about what, exactly – me presumably – and then Meg asked for a car and driver to take her to the airport. I was devastated.

She wouldn't tell me where she was going. In a panic I called Raisa, double checked the security cover, gave her a garbled, brief explanation that Meg and I were taking some time apart for a while. Her confirmation was frosty, making it clear where her primary loyalty lay.

Meg's good-bye was brief. She hugged me but we didn't kiss. I was confused, miserable. She was stronger. As I held her, she reached up and stroked my face. 'Don't worry. I know how much I mean to you, and you to me. But you have to deal with this without me. And I have to be ready to deal with whatever comes next.'

She did kiss me then, a butterfly brush, and was gone. I was left, bereft, conflicted. Left with Lela.

*　　　*　　　*

Sven did his best. A gracious host, he arranged a room for Lela in the guest wing and gave instructions to his staff to provide whatever we needed but otherwise to leave us in peace. He apologised to me and then excused himself; stepped back and left us to it. Whatever *it* was to be.

Lela and I talked, what else was there to do? Whatever she might be feeling, whatever my body, my soul, might be feeling I couldn't just be with her as if nothing had happened. I couldn't ignore what had gone before, nor my thoughts about Meg. My other selves were full of helpful advice. I shut them down.

'Seven cycles, Lela: seven, and not a word. Now you're here. Why? What am I supposed to think, to say?'

Even during my worst shifts I'd never felt such conflict and confusion. I was flushed, my heart was racing but at the same time I was cold and my mind in turmoil. I wanted her with every fibre of my being – I'd missed her so much. And yet, I didn't want her. I felt such anger – that she'd been gone for so long and then re-appeared without warning – that I wanted to be anywhere but near her. And for every feeling of need I had for her I felt an equal disgust for the betrayal of my feelings for Meg.

I was a mess. Her next words didn't help.

'I'm here for you.' She made it sound so breathtakingly simple.

'For me? Why? Because of *us*?'

'Partly, but it's more complicated than that. If you come back with me , you'll understand. All of it.' She wasn't pleading but there was entreaty in her voice.

'Back? To what?'

'Back into the transition.'

'Why? Back to something I'll forget the next time I shift and then I'll spend more time tormented during another cycle in the here and now, searching for answers? Why would I do that?'

'Because I'm asking you to. Because the ones who sent you here are asking you, through me.' I looked at her blankly. 'You've done what you were sent here to do, Jay,' she continued. 'You don't know it but you have.'

Her words only deepened my confusion. 'Sent? To do what? By who? Why have you come here now? Did you know about Meg, about the pain you'd cause?' I didn't like what I saw in her eyes then – pity, compassion, tenderness – and there was something else; a superiority to it, a knowingness that I didn't share.

'I came here because I decided it would be easiest, safest to approach Sven and to arrange the meeting through him. And I'm sorry about Meg. But surely you can see that she'd have had to know that I'd returned.' She was willing me to forgive her, to understand. 'As for the rest?' She shook her head. 'I can't tell you that. Not here, not now. I've already told you more than I should. You're going to have to trust me.'

'Trust you! Why?' It was childish, churlish, but I couldn't help the bitterness in my voice. Dealing with my emotions – the misery and devastation of Meg's departure, the confusion caused by Lela's appearance – was exhausting me. I'd had too much to deal with in this here and now. I should have been elated. I was with Lela, the woman – the psyche – I'd searched for through seven long cycles and loved for countless more, but it didn't feel right. And it was too soon to know if it could ever feel right again.

'Because they'll give you some of what you've been searching for. They've told me that it's time, you've done enough, you've passed the test.'

I couldn't think straight. I heard her words, could make no sense of their meaning. 'What test? Who are they…?'

Her tenderness turned to sympathy as Lela said the words that she knew would only confound me more. 'I can't tell you that, Jay, not here, but I can tell that we've not synced in the last seven of your cycles because I haven't shifted. I've not been in your here and now.' She looked at me, beseeching me to trust her. 'But we've been together whenever you've been in transition, always, in the between times.'

My heart pounded as, stunned into silence, I fought to deny her words. Knowing in my heart that she somehow spoke the truth. 'Together?' She nodded. And I saw, then, the pain she was feeling too. I could see this was as hard for her as it was for me. It didn't help. 'But you can't tell me more. You're not allowed… *They* won't allow it.' I couldn't help the bitterness in my voice.

'Jay… Please–' But I waved her into silence.

'No. No more for now. I'm sorry.' Her face fell as I turned my back on her and left her in the guest wing as I walked out into the evening. It was the hardest thing I'd done: to walk away from her, the woman I'd searched for, for so long; to deny the feelings I'd long held at bay and which had come flooding back. But it was what I had to do.

I heard Sven's security team radio-in, reporting my movements as I hiked slowly down into the valley. All the time I was withdrawing further and further: communing with my other selves, considering her words, pondered their meaning, searching my memories for anything that would help me make sense of it. Hours later, I returned as dusk fell, went to my room and closed the door firmly. I didn't see, didn't *want* to see Lela.

Chapter 39

It was late, mid-morning, by the time I surfaced the next day. I'd slept fitfully, was no closer to understanding my feelings, nor what decision I should make. But when I went to find her, there was no sign of Lela in the guest wing. I made my way to the main house. Sven was in his study.

'Jay...' he started as I entered, half rising from his desk. I waved him back and perched on the arm of one of the matched sofas that flanked the open fireplace, filled now with vases of summer flowers. He tried again. 'I'm so sorry, Jay. I had no idea, really. And I didn't know what to do...'

I shrugged. What else could I do? What else could he have done? 'I know. Forget it. So...' I gave a deep sigh. 'Where is she now?' If it were possible, Sven looked even more miserable. He was silent for a moment, then:

'She's gone, Jay.'

It was numbing. Once again, she'd shocked, stunned me.

Eyes closed I rubbed a hand across my face. I should have guessed. 'Do you know where?' I was keeping it simple. It was all I could do for now; I was still having trouble processing it.

'She wouldn't say.' He took a deep breath. 'She gave me a message. She said if you want to find her it shouldn't be hard. She won't hide and that she'll stay in cycle – for a while. She said that what happens next is up to you.'

I slipped off the arm and onto the sofa, leant forward, my hands on my knees, fighting to control my pulse. 'Did she tell you what she told me?'

'She told me only that she'd come to find you. Not why, nor where she's been all this time.'

'She told me that we've been together whenever we're in transition; and that we can be again.' I couldn't help it, there was anguish in my voice. 'But I've no memory of that!' My elbows were on my knees now, my head bowed and cradled in my hands. 'What do I do, Sven? I've longed to be with her – but I long to be with Meg too. I want to stay in this cycle, to build on what you and I and Meg have started – but Lela wants me to leave. She tells me I've done what I was sent to do. What the hell does that mean? She won't tell me what that was or who sent me. Christ! What a mess! What do I do?'

*　　　*　　　*

I stayed with Sven for another week. My emotions swinging one way and then another as I couldn't help but compare Meg and Lela in my mind. I had a decision to make, but the decision wasn't just about them. Or was it? Sven didn't have the answers any more than I did. But he did what all good friends do, he listened. And he poured me into bed in the small hours when I'd finished looking for answers at the bottom of a glass. In the end he gave me one good piece of advice.

'Think like a Rink'.

It took me a while to figure out what he meant – and when I did the answers were obvious. I sobered up, traced her whereabouts and booked the flights.

*　　　*　　　*

She'd chosen to wait, to stay, in a wilderness. The drive from the airport took several hours and I spent the time trying to distract myself from composing and recomposing the words I'd need to say. Eventually the highways became roads and then a narrow track that climbed laboriously from valley to ridge. It was sound in places, treacherous in others where criss-crossing streams had left mud filled pits. As I approached the summit, thin wisps of smoke rose sluggishly then hung in the still air, coalescing in the leaden sky, signposting the cottage's location.

I made no secret of my approach but saw no signs it had been detected or that my arrival was anticipated. The door was ajar. Glowing embers in the open hearth illuminated the dim interior. I knocked: still no signs of life, no answer from within. I hesitated. To enter without invitation would be presumptuous no matter how much I hoped I'd be welcome. I decided to wait, took a seat on the logs stacked to one side – handy for the fire, sheltered from the rain that would return soon.

A lone buzzard soared over the ridge, its plaintive cry dying away unanswered. It was an hour before she emerged from the woods that surrounded, encroached on, the lonely habitation. I watched as she registered my presence with the most momentary of hesitations. At first there were no other signs. Was she in complete control or utterly indifferent? I did my best to match her demeanour. Until, finally, she spoke.

'Jay…' Her voice broke. My every instinct was to rush to her, to hold her. I told myself to stay seated – that it had to be her move, her invitation. I saw it break within her: whatever dam had held her feelings in check. The shotgun, slung across her shoulders, was suddenly more weight than she could bear. The brace of rabbits she'd been hunting dropped from her grasp as a shudder wracked her body. I was defeated by the changes I could see in her – the traces that spoke of pain, anguish, desolation – and the pulsing surge of emotions that, in turn, they evoked in me. I stood, took a step. She moved. We took more steps. We held each other. Together, as we were meant to be.

*   *   *

Later, much later, she asked questions.

'How did you find me?'

'Raisa,' I said.

Then she asked the question she really wanted answered.

'Do you still love her, Lela?'

It was the question I'd asked myself over and over.

'Probably'. It was the best I could do. 'But not in this here and now. No.'

I wasn't sure that it was enough. I turned away to stir

the stew beginning to simmer gently in the blackened old pot hanging over low flames she'd coaxed and fed from the embers. That we loved each other was not in question; nor was I in any doubt that it was Meg I wanted to be with. But was *she* sure? I wouldn't allow myself to read her: I needed to hear it.

We busied ourselves preparing plates, cutlery; trying for normality, as we both wrestled with our feelings. I gestured at the pot, the crude furniture, the cottage's earthen floor. 'What's this all about? Rustic self-sufficiency?' Meg nudged me out of the way as she served the stew.

'Back to basics. I needed a complete break from… From everything. It was Raisa's suggestion.'

I nudged back, still short of words; still suffused with relief that she seemed to have accepted me back. Her voice softened. 'I'm sorry this is so hard.'

Outside the light and temperature fell. I turned away to light some lamps as I thought about it.

'Hard?'

'Loving two people.'

I thought about it some more; my back still to her. 'Or maybe I'm blessed. There are some who never find any love at all.'

'So, this is it? You'll stay with us now?'

'Yes. Because it's you I want to be with. I'm sure of that..' I still couldn't look at her, scared at what I might see in her eyes. 'We have this one chance; I want to take it. I can't control what happens after, but I can control the now.' And that, I knew, was the truth. Whatever I felt about Lela, whatever she'd meant about a test I'd passed or said about *they* who wanted me back … None of it mattered in this here and now.

I felt Meg's hand on my shoulder, turning me back to face her as she wrapped her arms around me. I felt it then, what I should have felt before.

'When you said "us"…?'

She nodded into my chest.

Sometimes, some decisions are so right there's just nothing more to be said.

Epilogue

For most souls, time in the between place – the transition – was a time of testing; for passing or failing. A time for elation or reflection.

For those who failed, it was a place in which to contemplate, to reassess, to learn. For those who passed, it was a dwelling place where, with the elders, they communed and considered – not as individuals, a colony – before, later, moving on. Time was not the same as in the there and then.

'So, he refused to return with you?' The question was asked.

The one who had been Lela signalled it was so.

'And he still has no idea what he is? What he is to become.'

'No. He's matured but until he returns how could he know?'

'But…' The colony reflected, considered some more and then chose: to wait.

In the there and then, events occurred, were witnessed. Decisions were made. Actions were taken, or not. Sometimes the colony foresaw events… And so it was that, later, they once again saw the need to commune, to consider:

'Is it necessary?'

'Maybe not, but maybe wise…'

'To preserve the Phems?'

'Yes, and to preserve the nursery!' A forceful presence contributed now. 'And not just to preserve: to protect their development.'

A ripple ran through the colony as the wisdom, the truth of the words became clear. They reflected some more:

'His testing is complete…'

'He's failed more than any other…'

'...and yet is better equipped, now, than any of them...'
The wisest one spoke again. 'He has grown, matured. He will succeed.'
The colony considered, then calmed. It was settled.
'Then it must be so. When he returns, we must tell him everything. It's time to enlist the help of Jay – the Guardian.'

Acknowledgements

It's been a long journey, and I'd like to say thanks to everyone who helped me along the way. To my friends and family whose belief, doubts, encouragements and criticisms have all helped my writing in a multitude of ways. In particular I must mention Gail (aka Egan Hughes – author of great psychological thrillers). Without her guidance on how to navigate the ways of the publishing world and her critical analysis of my work, I doubt I'd have cleared the final hurdles to get to where I am. Many others have read and commented on early drafts but thanks especially to Pepi Sarvary, Mark Sarvary, Nick Tapp, Robin Lubbock, Chris Gibbon and Gerry Bell for their detailed comments and suggestions.

Finally, a special thanks to Peter and Alison Buck and all their colleagues: not just for accepting and improving *Rink*, but for creating Elsewhen Press – a publishing house that has built a community of authors and which values creativity above all else.

Elsewhen Press

delivering outstanding new talents in speculative fiction

Visit the Elsewhen Press website at elsewhen.press for the latest
information on all of our titles, authors and events; to read our blog;
find out where to buy our books and ebooks; or to place an order.

Sign up for the Elsewhen Press InFlight Newsletter at
elsewhen.press/newsletter

HER GILDED VOICE

K.C. AEGIS

**Lacey has a woman living inside her head
… or is it the other way around?**

Decades from now, technology has advanced, and everyone has a 'neuro-net' wired into their brain. This provides each person with a 'voyce' inside their head that offers advice that guides and ostensibly protects them; as teen Lacey Clarke puts it: "Voyces help us all make the right decisions. They give us reason, protect us from outside chaos. And in some cases, they protect us from ourselves."

In this republic, Lacey and her older sister, Yadira, barely make ends meet. Their lives are made worse when they discover they must pay off their late father's debt and that Lacey has been marked to become a Puzzler in a brainteaser competition in which losers are killed. Alina, Lacey's voyce, reassures her everything will be fine if only they follow the rules, but when an encounter with Ogden Oliver, a powerful Elite, ends with Alina being temporarily deactivated, Lacey is left alone with her own thoughts. For the first time in her life, she is able to perceive the world as it actually is – without augmented-reality illusions.

As Lacey navigates the competition, she realizes she may be a pawn but one that has hitherto unknown power.

ISBN: 9781915304544 (epub, kindle) / 9781915304445 (378pp paperback)

Visit bit.ly/HerGildedVoice

TERRY JACKMAN'S
WORLDS APART COLLECTIVE

HARPAN'S WORLDS: WORLDS APART

If Harp could wish, he'd be invisible.

Orphaned as a child, failed by a broken system and raised on a struggling colony world, Harp's isolated existence turns upside down when his rancher boss hands him into military service in lieu of the taxes he cannot pay. Since Harp has spent his whole life being regarded with suspicion, and treated as less, why would he expect his latest environment to be any different? Except it is, so is it any wonder he decides to hide the 'quirks' that set him even more apart?

Space opera with a paranormal twist, Terry Jackman's novel explores prejudice, corruption, and the value of true friendship.

ISBN: 9781915304179 (epub, kindle) / 9781915304170 (320pp paperback)

Visit bit.ly/HarpansWorldsWorldsApart

WORLDS ALIGNED: WORLDS APART 2

No longer invisible, Harp finds that fame, and family, might mean an even riskier future.

In *Harpan's Worlds* Harp faced his own personal history, and its repercussions. In *Worlds Aligned* he must deal with the results. Providing of course that he survives them.

So *Worlds Aligned* is a second glimpse of the humans who survive long after OldEarth is abandoned.

Note: *Harpan's Worlds* and *Worlds Aligned* form a duology, and can be read as two standalones; but together they connect some of the puzzle-pieces of a fractured humanity. And its evolution.

ISBN: 9781915304568 (epub, kindle) / 9781915304469 (380pp paperback)

Visit bit.ly/WorldsAligned

About Chris Matravers

Screwing up all his final school exams taught Chris that failure is an option – but not necessarily one to be feared. When he finally made it to university he stayed for 9 years, the last three as a post-doc research biologist. The experience revealed to him that while he loved the subject he was not cut out for academia, or poverty.

A move to join a major IT company surprised those around him but it seemed like a good idea at the time, and so it proved to be – enabling Chris and his wife to see more of the world, as they raised three daughters.

Things Chris thinks, or has even been heard to say about why he writes:

> *"One thing I know is that writing is good for the soul... if not for the wallet."*

> *"For me, writing is about sharing one's imagination – to give enjoyment, to challenge norms and preconceptions, to go in search of answers... If ever I achieve any or all of these, I'll be a happy man."*

> *"Writing keeps me sane when life threatens to pull me under. I consider myself lucky that a steadily increasing quality of rejection letters has raised me up until ... Well, here I am, now... "*

To find out more about Chris and his writing go to his website and blog at www.chrismatravers.com